THE SENDER OF THE DREAMS

CW01497751

OTHER MATADOR NOVELS BY BILL PAGE

The Moon on the Hills (2009)

The Sower of the Seeds of Dreams (2011)

One Summer in Arcadia (2015)

The Deceivers (2019)

www.billpageauthor.co.uk

The
SENDER
of the
DREAMS

BILL
PAGE

Copyright © 2022 Bill Page

The moral right of the author has been asserted.

Apart from any fair dealing for the purposes of research or private study, or criticism or review, as permitted under the Copyright, Designs and Patents Act 1988, this publication may only be reproduced, stored or transmitted, in any form or by any means, with the prior permission in writing of the publishers, or in the case of reprographic reproduction in accordance with the terms of licences issued by the Copyright Licensing Agency. Enquiries concerning reproduction outside those terms should be sent to the publishers.

Matador
Unit E2 Airfield Business Park,
Harrison Road, Market Harborough,
Leicestershire. LE16 7UL
Tel: 0116 2792299
Email: books@troubador.co.uk
Web: www.troubador.co.uk/matador
Twitter: @matadorbooks

ISBN 978 1803132 204

British Library Cataloguing in Publication Data.
A catalogue record for this book is available from the British Library.

Printed and bound in the UK by TJ Books Limited, Padstow, Cornwall
Typeset in 11pt StempelGaramond Roman by Troubador Publishing Ltd, Leicester, UK

Matador is an imprint of Troubador Publishing Ltd

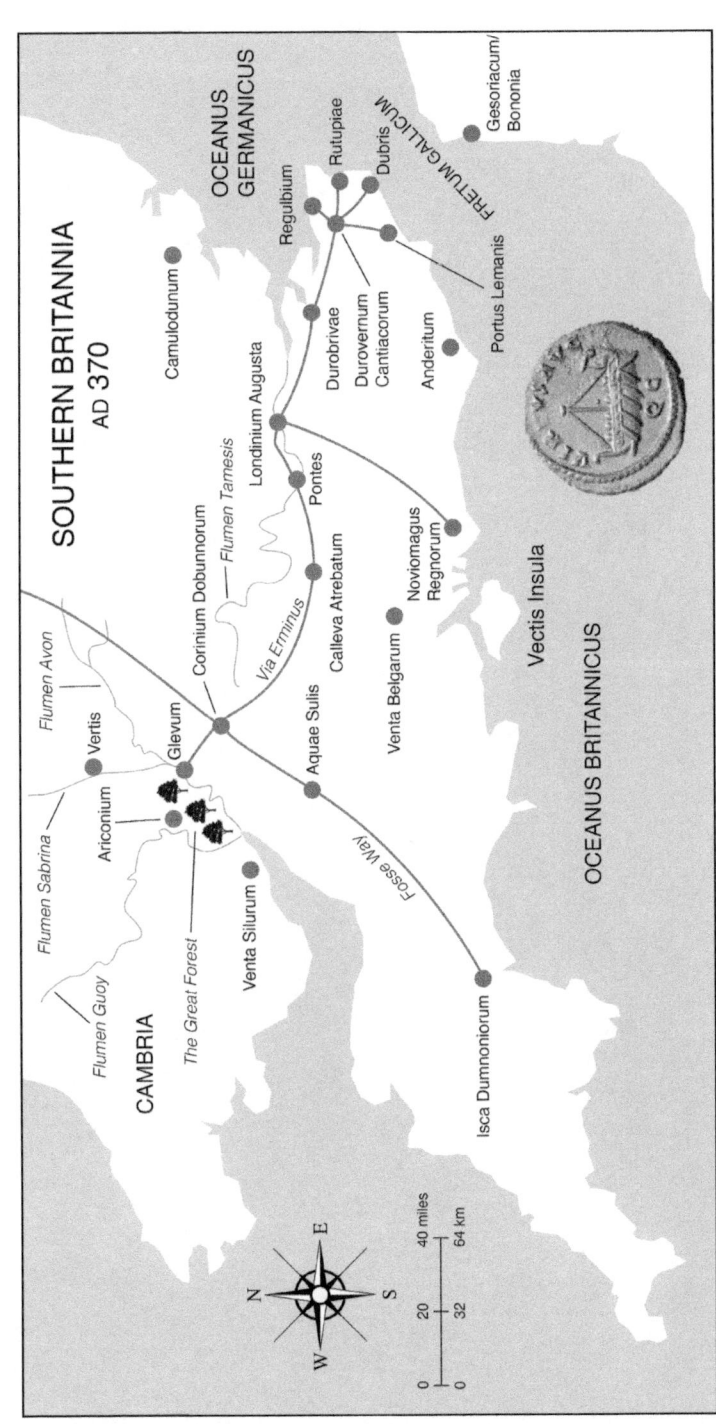

PART ONE

CHAPTER ONE

Night of 5th – 6th November AD 370

All three bodies had been taken away. Canio didn't know where to. He hadn't asked and didn't particularly care. Glancing down at the floor he noticed that, despite the best efforts of a frightened maidservant with rags and a bowl of reddening water, there were still several small splashes of blood and traces of a bloody footprint on the nearest of the eight pairs of satyrs and maenads radiating around the octagonal mosaic that lay between himself and the doorway of the triclinium.

Bacchus, standing in the central octagon, appeared quite unmoved by the bloodshed he had so recently witnessed. His cantharus wine cup was raised, as if he were about to propose a sardonic toast. Something like: *To the stupidity of mortals – and the amusement it affords we gods,* perhaps? Canio wondered. If so, it would have been quite appropriate.

His mind still racing, he stifled a yawn of sheer bodily weariness, then looked down at the blank sheets of parchment lying on the table in front of him. After muttering an obscenity (and ignoring the grunt of disapproval from the soldier standing woodenly behind him) he picked up the bronze pen, dipped it into the inkwell and began writing, murmuring the words under his breath as he wrote:

'I, Aulus Claudius Caninus, *honestior*, do solemnly swear that the following is a true and complete account of —'

Trifosa once told me that her God is supposed to have said that the truth shall make you free. That was, of course, before they arrested and crucified him. It seems he failed to realise what dangerous things some truths can be for those who are unwise enough to disclose them. And a wise man learns by the misfortunes of others.

'—account of everything I know of the events leading up to, and ending in, the tragic death of Caristanius Sabinus, *vir perfectissimus*, *praeses* of the province of Britannia Prima.'

Although, as far as I'm concerned, the only really tragic thing about that swine's death is that I wasn't miles away when it happened.

'I am writing this on the night of the nones of November, in the triclinium of Villa Censorini, while the events I am about to describe are still fresh and vivid in my mind.

'On or about the fourteenth day before the kalends of November, I was summoned to Villa Censorini by Julius Castor, *primicerius* of Caristanius Sabinus's bodyguard troops. There, in the presence of the said Julius Castor and a soldier called Peltrasius, the *vir perfectissimus* informed me of an allegation made by Peltrasius that I was the possessor of an *orichalcum* figurine of the pagan goddess Hecate.

'The background to this allegation was that, over two years ago, myself, Peltrasius and another soldier named Galenus, now said to be dead, captured a deserter calling himself Orgillus, who had in his possession the aforesaid figurine. Orgillus tried to escape, but Peltrasius chased after him and stabbed him to death.'

Because that's the sort of man he was – an evil bastard. As, indeed, were all three of the recently deceased.

'Upon examining the figurine, which he had imagined to be gold, Peltrasius found it to be merely *orichalcum*, and in apparent disgust he hurled it away into the surrounding undergrowth. This, as I say, was over two years ago, and after that day I never saw Peltrasius again until summoned by Caristanius Sabinus.'

4

I'm sure can still detect the smell of blood. Some smells you never forget. Curiously, it seems to be getting stronger as the air gets colder.

'Later that year, thanks to a substantial legacy bequeathed to me by a distant relative, I was able to leave the army and purchase a small villa estate some twenty miles north of Corinium. However, when we met in the presence of Caristanius Sabinus, Peltrasius made the extraordinary and unfounded allegation that I must owe my wealth to the Hecate figurine—'

Which is true, in a roundabout sort of way, but not in the way that fool imagined.

'—which he claimed, with no proof whatsoever, that I must have retrieved from somewhere in the undergrowth into which he had thrown it.

'But as I told the *vir perfectissimus*, the only time I had ever seen the figurine was in the moments before Peltrasius threw it away. Nevertheless, he and Julius Castor were insistent that I must have gone back and found it, and then, in some unlawful way – which I cannot even begin to imagine – invoked its supposed magical powers to enrich myself.

'This was, of course, complete nonsense, but with hindsight it is obvious to me now that Peltrasius had convinced Julius Castor that possession of that figurine would, by criminal means, bring them great wealth. I do not for one moment believe that the *vir perfectissimus* himself shared this delusion. I suspect that his intention was simply to acquire, and then destroy, a pagan idol around which rumours of black magic, something so rightly abhorred by our sacred emperor, Valentinianus, were apparently swirling.'

Actually, that turd Sabinus was in it up to his neck and beyond. There was nothing he wouldn't have done to acquire the riches he imagined that figurine would bring.

'In spite of my protestations, having doubtless been persuaded by Castor and Peltrasius, the *vir perfectissimus* insisted that the figurine must be in my possession and ordered me to surrender it to him. I swore I did not have it—'

Which happened to be true at the time, although I knew who did – something that I had no intention of ever telling Sabinus.

'—and suggested that it must still be in the place where Peltrasius had thrown it away. But Peltrasius and Castor were adamant they had already searched the spot, which was some five miles south of Corinium, close to the Fosse Way, and found nothing. The situation was ridiculous, but I realised I had no option other than to agree to attempt to find the figurine, although I had no idea where it could be. However, the *vir perfectissimus* generously gave me three weeks to find it.'

Grudgingly, more like. Obviously, I couldn't find what wasn't lost, so I paid a coppersmith in Vertis – a man by the name of Ivomandus – five gold solidi (five!) to make a remarkably good fake. I even got him to blacken it artificially to match the original, just as I remembered it.

'During those three weeks, I searched everywhere I could imagine that the figurine might possibly be, even riding as far south as the Niger Hills, where it was rumoured to have once been lodged in a temple of Apollo there. But I found that the temple had been sacked and burned during the *Conspiratio* and only its blackened shell remained.'

But the journey was worth it because an old, brain-sick priest who still lived in the ruins was convinced that my fake was the original, which made me certain that it would fool Peltrasius too. This priest also told me that, a year or two back, some soldiers had stolen the casket in which the figurine – the genuine one – had once been housed. How in the name of Hades himself could I have known that one of those thieving soldiers must have been Peltrasius?

'By then, the three weeks allowed me by the *vir perfectissimus* were almost gone. So I made my way back northwards until – at a point some five miles south of Corinium, on the Fosse Way –

I realised that I was near the place where we had encountered Orgillus over two years before.

'After enlisting the help of three passing foot travellers – mosaic workers, as I recall – we searched the area thoroughly, and after no more than a winter hour I was amazed when one of them found the figurine hidden in the middle of a large clump of brambles. It must have been lying there all that time.'

It was, of course, my fake Hecate that they found, and it had been there for less than a summer hour. Even as I write, I can feel the scratches on my hands and face that I got crawling into those accursed brambles to hide it under a layer of leaf mould.

'Carrying the figurine, I rode on to Corinium, where I was informed that the *vir perfectissimus* had returned here, to his Villa Censorini. On arriving after nightfall, I was escorted to the triclinium by Vibius Natalis, a young centurion—' *and prize jackass '*—on the *praeses'* staff. There, I found the *vir perfectissimus* himself, together with Julius Castor and Peltrasius.

'After dismissing Natalis, the *vir perfectissimus* demanded to see the Hecate figurine. I showed it to him; he examined it, then asked Peltrasius if it was all as he remembered it. Peltrasius said it was, but the *vir perfectissimus* said that there was one last test required and produced a small wooden casket, which I had never seen before. Lifting the lid, the *vir perfectissimus* attempted to fit the figurine into the hollowed-out recess inside the casket, which I afterwards surmised must have been specially made for it.'

Made for the real one, of course, not my fake.

'But on finding that the figurine would not fit, the *vir perfectissimus* was displeased and accused me of trying to deceive him. I was dumbfounded, but the only explanation I could think of – both then and now – was that the figurine I had been ordered to find, and indeed had found, was not the one for which the casket had been made.

'And so it proved. For as Julius Castor and Peltrasius were about to do violence to me, the door of the triclinium burst open and in strode a strange woman wearing a hooded *cucullus* over a long *stola*. She was followed by Vibius Natalis and several soldiers.'

Natalis squawking like a chicken with its tail feathers on fire.

'This woman held a figurine that appeared the exact twin of the one I had found, but which, upon being offered up, fitted perfectly into the casket. The *vir perfectissimus* asked the woman if it was I who had given her this second figurine, but she replied (and Vibius Natalis can confirm this) that she had never seen me before in her life.

'At that point the *vir perfectissimus*, still holding the second figurine, ordered myself, Natalis and the soldiers out of the triclinium and gave strict instructions that we were not to return unless summoned. And that was the last time I saw the poor *vir perfectissimus* alive.

'Waiting in the anteroom outside the triclinium, we could at first hear nothing behind the heavy door. But after a while we all became aware of raised voices, as if a quarrel had broken out, although we could not make out any words. Suddenly there came a terrible scream, and then another. We shouldered the door open and rushed back into the triclinium, where a horrible sight met our eyes.'

Best not to mention that vision I had of a vast pile of gold coins heaped on the table. It faded away in an instant, and in the confusion I don't think anyone else saw it. Perhaps it only ever existed in my imagination?

'The *vir perfectissimus* was slumped dead in his chair, and standing over him was Julius Castor, still holding the bloodied sword with which he had murdered him.'

Or as some – myself included – might say, he simply acted as the agent of Nemesis: one evil creature destroyed by another.

'Sprawled on the floor was Peltrasius, his throat slashed by the same sword. But before I could say a word, Julius Castor had rushed at Vibius Natalis and the other soldiers and begun attacking them like a madman.

'In the confusion, the strange woman picked up the figurine she had brought and darted out of the triclinium. I attempted to follow and detain her, but in the corridor I was obstructed by more soldiers hurrying to find the cause of the commotion, and when at last I reached the upper courtyard of the villa the woman had vanished. I searched for her in the short time before Vibius Natalis joined me, but I never saw her again. Natalis then informed me that the murderer, Julius Castor, was dead, killed by his own men in just retribution for the horrible crime he had committed.

'Even as I write, my mind is still reeling from the terrible events I have witnessed this night. Who that strange woman was, and where she and that second figurine came from, I have absolutely no idea.'

I owe you that, Bodicca, although little else.

'As to Julius Castor's motive for doing what he did, I can only speculate that he was unhinged by frustrated greed. It is my opinion that he and Peltrasius coveted that figurine in order to perform some abominable pagan rite – one they believed would bring them great wealth. So when the *vir perfectissimus*, good Christian that he was, insisted that it must be destroyed, Castor erupted with insane rage.

'And that is everything I know about this tragic affair. An affair into which I was most unwillingly dragged. In conclusion, I can only say that I am certain the *vir perfectissimus* himself was the blameless victim of the delusions and criminal conspiracies of those dogs Julius Castor and Peltrasius – as indeed was I.'

CHAPTER TWO

As the endless November night wore on, so the temperature in the triclinium continued to fall, and Canio assumed that the brushwood fire in the hypocaust stokehole must have smouldered out for want of fresh fuel.

He read over what he had just written, then read it over again, making a few scratchings out and the occasional insertion both times. He read it over for a third time, grunted in satisfaction or weariness or both, then half-turned in his chair and beckoned to the soldier standing behind him. It wasn't the original soldier; he had gone to relieve his bladder when Canio was only halfway through his testimony and had not returned.

'Well, that's it – finished. Is Vibius Natalis still here?'

The soldier shook his head. 'He left for Corinium some time ago, or so I heard. In the *vir perfectissimus's* carriage.'

'Well, he won't be needing it again, not where he's gone,' Canio murmured. Before the soldier could reply, he added, 'So who's in charge here now?'

'*Centenarius* Lucilius Pacatianus.'

'Right, then let's go find him.'

'He said you weren't to leave this room.'

Canio gave a growl of exasperation, but he was too weary to argue. 'Fine, then take it to Master Pacatianus yourself. But make damned sure you hand it straight to him and nobody else.'

The soldier left, clutching the parchment sheets, and Canio heard the grating of a slider key and the subdued thuds of the pins dropping into place as the man used the key to slide the bolt of the tumbler lock into its keep in the door frame.

'Bastards!' he muttered, but the nervous energy that had kept him alert and vigilant throughout the long day and these last traumatic hours of night was rapidly draining away. He pushed the pen and inkwell far across the table, rested his forearms on the polished fruitwood and pillowed his head on them. As he drifted into sleep he breathed in the faint perfume of spilled wine.

❖

And as he slept he dreamed of an old man. An old man he had almost forgotten in the twenty-five years that had passed since the time when he was living in Marcia's little house in that cold city beside the Rhenus. He had been five, or perhaps six, years old when he had listened to the stories the old man told as he lay in bed, a thin blanket pulled up to his chin, only his bearded face, his still-thick dirty-white hair and his large, gnarled hands visible. His voice had been weak and hoarse, but it still bore traces of the deep, resonant qualities it must have possessed when he was young.

On waking, his head still resting on his forearms, the memories of the dream came seeping back. He tried to remember the old man's name. He was fairly certain that it had begun with a "T", but the rest eluded him. Certainly, he had been very old, yet he still retained something of the bone structure of what had once been a tall, muscular body.

He had arrived – from where Canio never knew – only a few days before, and Marcia had let him stay because he was dying. Canio had been too young to realise that, but the old man must surely have known, although he must nevertheless have thought he had enough time and strength left to tell his story from the beginning.

And much later, thinking back, Canio was to realise how absolutely vital it must have seemed to the old man that he should tell the whole story, so that, when the child became a man, he would know the truth about those events that the old man had lived through so long ago, no matter what false versions he might subsequently hear.

Marcia, his late mother's half-sister, the woman who had cared for him since his mother had died a year before the old man arrived, often left him alone with the old man while she was out and about in the city. And in those long hours the old man had told stories of the things he had witnessed fifty and sixty years before. Stories of the time when a man named Carausius had made himself emperor in Northern Gaul and Britannia. Over the days that followed he had whispered them with the urgency of a man who realised his time left in this world was rapidly diminishing.

Back then, if he had thought about it at all, Canio might have assumed that the old man would have told anyone who happened to be there in that room. A quarter of a century was to pass before he realised that he alone was the one whom the old man so desperately needed to tell. It was why he had come.

Although growing weaker by the day, the old man had fought his mortality to the end. But about a week after he had arrived the old man died in the night – a chill early winter night, much like the present one. He had died only hours after finishing what Canio would eventually come to realise was not quite the last of his stories. In the wan morning light Canio had tried to wake him, wanting to hear more. But Marcia had pulled him gently away, saying that nothing would wake the old man now.

She had washed the old man's face and combed his hair and beard before leaving, saying that she had to arrange his funeral. In the afternoon two men that Canio had never seen before came to the house. They had swaddled the old man's body in rough sacking and carried it into the street, where a small cart drawn by an emaciated donkey was waiting. Then they had heaved the body into the cart, dumping it alongside a couple of spades and other tools.

With Marcia and Canio walking behind and the two men leading the donkey, the cart had trundled slowly through the uneven streets of the city. After passing under the gloomy portals of one of the gates in the high city wall they had continued on until they reached a sprawling cemetery. It was the place where the poor of the city were buried, mostly with nothing but weathered mounds to mark their long homes.

After wending their way along several muddy tracks, they had at last reached the far side of the cemetery and found there a freshly dug grave. It was no more than a spade's length deep – just a rough trench in the wet, dark earth. The two men had dragged the shrouded bundle off the cart, and with one at the feet end walking forwards and the other at the head end walking backwards, they had carried it over to the grave.

Canio had thought that they were about to swing the bundle sideways and toss it into the grave, like a sack of grain. It seemed that Marcia had thought so too, because he remembered her saying sharply, 'No!' She had said something else too, something that Canio did not understand, but that had caused the men to kneel reluctantly at either end of the grave and lower the old man's body into the ground.

Taking the spades from the cart, the two men had shovelled the dank earth back into the grave, trampling it down every few spadefuls and finally roughly profiling the mound with the backs of their spades. When they had finished they looked to Marcia, who had hesitated, then nodded. A few silver *siliquae* had changed hands, before the men had thrown the shovels onto the cart and begun leading the donkey back towards the city.

Marcia had waited until they were gone, standing silent and still, looking down at the old man's grave. Then, she had taken

Canio's hand and together they had walked back the way they had come, through the gathering dusk.

When they were still some way from the city walls, it occurred to Canio to ask Marcia why it was that she had taken in the old man, a stranger, and cared for him as best she could.

She had not replied immediately, but before they reached the city gate she had said quietly that the old man had not really been a stranger.

'Then who was he?' Canio had asked.

'He was your grandfather, your mother's father. You do know, don't you, that your mother and I had different fathers?'

Canio had been vaguely aware of that. But why, he had asked, had Marcia never mentioned his grandfather before?

'Because he was a bad man. I was told that he deserted your grandmother, the woman who became my mother, even before your own mother was born.'

Canio must have asked how long ago all this had happened, because he remembered Marcia saying, 'Oh, some twenty-five years ago at least. And he was quite old even then – well into his fifties, or so I heard – although still strong. But now that he's dead and buried let's not speak of him again.'

And she never did.

At the time, Canio had pretended that he had understood, and afterwards, as the days and weeks and months had passed, in the butterfly mind of a child his memories of the old man had receded to vanishing point. Although they must always have been there, stored in some long-unvisited archive of his brain.

That now, after a quarter of a century, those memories from the distant past should, for no apparent reason, suddenly return, as sharp and vivid as if it had all happened yesterday, struck him as very strange; ominous, even. But he tried not to believe in omens.

CHAPTER THREE

A sudden metallic rasp, which came as the tumbler key drew back the door bolt, disrupted his thoughts. Slowly, he lifted his head from the table and watched through half-closed eyes as two soldiers, one tall, one shorter but barrel-chested, pushed open the door and clumped into the triclinium. Grey morning light was filtering in through the high clerestory windows running down both long sides of the room.

'Rouse yourself, man; the *centenarius* wants to see you,' the shorter soldier said.

'And I want a piss,' said Canio, levering himself out of the throne-like wickerwork chair that Sabinus would never again sit in. He yawned and stretched, then followed the soldiers out into the corridor, which ran the length of the west wing. But when they turned left, he turned right.

'This way,' the tall soldier snapped. 'The *centenarius* —'

'Wants to see me.' Canio finished the man's sentence for him. 'You told me. And I told you I wanted a piss – unless you want me to do it all over your master's boots?' He did not look back, but after a few moments he heard the soldiers following him.

At the end of the corridor he went down a short flight of steps, pushed through the door into the large kitchen, and from there went through another door on the far side into the latrine.

Deciding that he might as well defecate while he was there, and ignoring the two soldiers, he unfastened the drawstring of his *bracae* trousers and dropped them, before settling himself over one of the holes in the wooden seat, which ran down the full length of one side of the room over the open sewer below.

To the undisguised irritation of the soldiers, he took his time, and when he had finished he carefully wiped his backside using one of the sponges on a stick, which he swished around several times in the water of the lead-lined gutter running through the centre of the latrine. The water flowing through the sewer and gutter was the same water which issued, limpid, from the sacred spring into the nymphaeum pool that lay beyond the north-west corner of the villa. He was vaguely aware of the incongruity.

'The *centenarius* is waiting,' the tall soldier reminded him.

Canio ignored him again: he needed time to think. Had he left anything significant out of his statement? More importantly, had he included anything that was best left out? He couldn't remember. That dream of the old man from twenty-five years ago was still at the forefront of his mind.

'Hades, that water's cold,' he muttered. After pulling his *bracae* trousers back up he swilled his hands and face in the corner basin, then looked around for a towel and found none. He grunted his displeasure. 'So where is he, your *Centenarius* Pacatianus?'

'Still waiting for you in the north wing.'

'Where you should damned well be now,' muttered the shorter soldier.

'Did you like him – Sabinus, I mean?' Canio asked casually.

'Why do you ask?' the man replied suspiciously.

For the pleasure of watching you lie, Canio thought, but said, 'I just wondered, that's all.'

The shorter soldier hesitated before replying, 'Of course I liked him – everybody did.'

'I never heard a bad word uttered against him.' The tall soldier's face betrayed absolutely nothing as he spoke, but Canio noted the curl of ironic amusement on the lips of the shorter soldier.

'Deafness has its uses,' Canio murmured.

They left the kitchen and started back up the long corridor of the west wing. They walked the full length of the corridor, then briefly went out into the upper courtyard, where the flower beds between the gravel paths were white with frost. Boots crunched on the gravel as they trudged the few yards to the entrance of the north-wing reception hall, which served as an anteroom to the two formal audience chambers beyond.

*

Once inside the reception hall, Canio saw that one leaf of the tall double doors of the first audience chamber stood open. It was in there, three weeks before, that Sabinus had demanded that he hand over the Hecate figurine. He hesitated, struck by a strange feeling that he was drifting helplessly on the boundless sea of time. Was it really only three weeks ago? It seemed so much longer. He became aware of voices from inside the audience chamber, voices that stopped abruptly as they were about to enter.

'Ah, Claudius Caninus – so good of you to spare us the time.' The speaker was a strongly built man in his mid-thirties wearing the uniform of a *centenarius*.

Lucilius Pacatianus, Canio assumed.

Canio gave him a smile calculated to irritate, but did not reply. His eyes shifted to the man who sat reading from one of several sheets of parchment scattered on the small table in front of him. A tall man, judging by the distance his legs stuck out from beneath the table, and strong too, if the thickness of his wrists was any indication. His black hair and beard were clipped short and neat, and his dark eyes kept looking restlessly down at the top sheet of parchment, then up at Canio, as if endlessly searching, hunting for weaknesses. The *orbiculi* roundels sewn

17

on to the chest of his tunic indicated that he was an *agens in rebus*, and quite a senior one too; a *biarchus*, if Canio's memory was correct.

'So you are Claudius Caninus?' the *agens* asked, his dark eyes now fixing Canio with a less-than-benevolent stare.

Canio nodded slightly in acknowledgement. 'I am; and you are?'

'Decanius Januarius, an *agens in rebus* of the third grade. Have you heard of me?'

As it happened, Canio had heard of him, and what he had heard was not reassuring. Like a hunting dog, once his teeth were gripping his targeted prey he was said to never let go until the prey was dead. 'No, I can't say that I have,' he lied.

If he was hoping to disconcert the man, he was disappointed. 'It's of no matter. This,' Januarius said, indicating the sheets in front of him with a long forefinger, 'is a copy of your statement.' And before Canio could ask, he added, 'The original has been sent to Corinium; I passed the rider on my way here. Leaving aside for the moment the appalling death of the *praeses*, there are several other things in your statement that particularly interest me.'

'And what are they?' Canio asked, trying to sound casual.

'Firstly, there is your reason for agreeing to assist Sabinus in locating that pagan idol.'

'That was because—' Canio began, before Januarius interrupted him.

'Why, if as you claimed, you had no knowledge of its whereabouts, did you agree to search for it? Surely it would have been a futile task? Unless, of course, you actually *did* know where it was.'

Canio contrived to look both surprised and affronted. 'I most certainly did not know. However, it soon became abundantly clear that Sabinus, having been fed a pack of infernal lies by Castor and Peltrasius, didn't believe me. So I felt that I had no choice other than to agree to search for the wretched thing. If I hadn't,' he added, 'I feared that I might not have left this place alive: Julius Castor was a violent man, as last night's terrible events demonstrated only too well.' *Which is a point that needs making,* he thought.

Januarius said nothing, but his expression indicated a certain lack of belief. 'Tell me, how did you acquire the money to buy your villa estate – Villa Canini you call it, don't you? – if not by means of the black magic which that man, Peltrasius, accused you of?'

Canio gave a weary sigh. 'As I say in my statement, I was bequeathed the money by a distant relative – a spinster aunt by the name of Peregrina. Her will is on record in the public notaries' office in Londinium Augusta. There's no mystery there.'

'And yet you still did as Sabinus asked, even though you don't appear to be a man who could be easily intimidated, not even by a creature like Julius Castor,' Januarius murmured, more to himself than Canio. But before Canio could object, he changed course yet again. 'This woman, who so obligingly stated that she had never seen you before – describe her to me.'

'She wore a—'

'Yes, I know what she wore; it's here in your statement,' Januarius said impatiently. 'But was she young or old, tall or short, dark-haired, blonde or redhead? Was her voice distinctive? Would you recognise it again if you heard it?'

'Her voice... perhaps, yes,' Canio replied hesitantly. 'Of course, the hood of her *cucullus* covered her hair and hid her face in shadow. And she was tall, quite tall – or perhaps the *cucullus* hood made her look taller than she really was? Her voice, though, was commanding, imperious even, almost like a man's. In fact—'

'In fact, what? You think it could have been a man in disguise?' Januarius interrupted again.

'I'm not certain, but now – thinking back – yes, it certainly could have been.' *Sowing confusion in the ranks of the enemy is always a useful tactic.* 'What does Vibius Natalis say?'

'I don't know. I haven't yet had the opportunity to question him in detail, but be assured I will.'

Januarius almost certainly had further questions, but from somewhere outside came the furious barking of one or more dogs. It brought Lucilius Pacatianus, who had been silently and sardonically watching the interrogation, back to life. 'Ah, the hunting dogs are back; let's see what they've caught!' He swung himself out of the big, throne-like chair in the apse, and with one hand on the hilt of his *spatha*, strode out of the audience chamber, leaving the double doors wide open for the other two to follow.

*

Outside, in the upper courtyard, a pair of Agassian hunting dogs, quite small spaniel-like creatures with shaggy coats and wickedly sharp teeth and claws, were yelping excitedly. Their handlers – two men in short, cape-like *cuculli* – and two soldiers, who Canio assumed had accompanied them on their search for Bodicca, were being berated by a junior officer, a man he did not recognise.

Pacatianus must immediately have realised the reason for the junior officer's wrath, and he probably realised too that their failure would reflect badly on himself. 'Am I to understand that you cretins haven't caught the bitch? You told me that those hounds could track anything, day or night, through rain, fog or snow – across rivers, even. So why, in the name of the Evil One, haven't you found her?'

'The dogs found a scent up there,' one of the handlers explained hurriedly, struggling to hold on to his yelping dog's leash, as with his free hand he pointed towards the gap between the north and west ranges and to the nymphaeum that lay beyond.

'And we followed it for miles,' said the other handler. 'Through thick woodland, up and down sheep pastures, and across a little stream – until it just vanished.'

'What? It couldn't just vanish; where was this?' Pacatianus demanded.

'Some three miles or so north of here, Master. We were following a small trackway – little more than a sheep path it was – as well as we could, for there was no moon. But then we came to a place where it was crossed by another path, a sort of little crossroads, and there the dogs lost the scent.'

'Well, she must have gone somewhere.' Januarius stated the obvious, studying his neatly trimmed nails. 'Did you search all three paths?'

'We did, Master, and the dogs found nothing.'

'Nothing? Well then, she must have doubled back the way she came; did you check?'

'That we did too, Master. We went back half a mile or more, one dog on each side of the path, but never picked up another scent.'

'Then go back and try again.'

'Now, Master?'

'Yes, of course now – before the frost kills the scent completely.' Turning, Pacatianus shouted, '*Biarchus!*'

'Sir!' responded one of several soldiers who had been listening in the background.

'Take every man here and go with these useless swine to the place where they claim they lost the scent. Then, fan out and question everyone you come across: men, women, children – everyone. Puncture a few hides if you have to, but find that damned woman. And don't come back until you've got her. Understood?'

'Yes, *Centenarius.*'

'Then move yourself!'

The *biarchus* scurried off and began barking orders to his men. Canio thought he looked distinctly unhappy, and guessed he feared that Pacatianus was looking for scapegoats – anyone and everyone the *centenarius* could use to divert attention from his own failure to send out more men to search during the night. Canio became aware that Januarius was speaking.

'"A sort of little crossroads,"' he mused. 'I seem to have heard somewhere, Caninus, that Hecate is worshipped at crossroads. Is that true?' the *agens* asked, as if the recollection had only just come to him.

'No idea. I try to keep away from such pagan nonsense,' Canio replied.

'Do you indeed? How very wise.'

'Have you seen the bodies?' Canio asked, seeking to change the subject.

'Yes, all three of them. They're quite dead, as I shall confirm to the relevant authorities in Corinium.'

'So can I go now?'

'Go? Go where?' Januarius seemed surprised.

'Home, of course.'

'Caninus, a *praeses* – a *vir perfectissimus* – has been brutally murdered, and you are, at the very least, a key witness to the crime. You will be coming back to Corinium with me, where there will doubtless be others who wish to question you.' He turned and called across to a pair of soldiers loitering in the near distance: 'You two, keep a close eye on this man while I have a few words with *Centenarius* Pacatianus.'

As Canio waited in the upper courtyard, stamping his feet irritably on the frosty gravel, which the slowly rising sun had yet to thaw, he became aware of raised voices. They seemed to be coming from the lower courtyard, beyond the roofed cross-gallery that separated the villa's two courtyards. Turning towards it, he saw two women emerge from the cross-gallery gatehouse and start running towards him. As they came closer, he realised that the trailing woman – the older of the two – was attempting to restrain the other, a handsome woman in her mid-twenties whose dark hair was arranged in an elaborate, waved coiffure.

'You killed him! You killed him!' the younger woman was screaming. 'If it hadn't been for you and that accursed figurine he'd still be alive, not lying stiff and cold like a butchered animal.'

A moment later Canio saw the knife, small but with a wicked-looking blade, and instinctively sprang back. Even so, the razor-sharp tip caught him on the chest, and he felt its sharp sting. Then the two soldiers were grabbing her, one arm apiece, and supporting her as she collapsed onto the gravel, sobbing uncontrollably. One of the soldiers stooped and wrenched the knife out of her unresisting hand.

'Who in Hades' name is that?' Canio gasped, beginning to feel a thin trickle of warm blood running down his stomach.

'Valeria Faustina,' said the older woman, who Canio vaguely recognised from a previous visit to Villa Censorini in happier times. 'She was a close friend of the *vir perfectissimus*.'

'So close there were times when you couldn't see daylight between them,' one of the soldiers muttered.

The other soldier sniggered.

Canio was about to attempt to explain to the still-sobbing woman (mostly for the benefit of his immediate audience) that it was Julius Castor and Peltrasius who had deceived Sabinus, and he had been little more than an innocent bystander. But at that moment Decanius Januarius emerged from the north wing and pointed to Canio and the two soldiers. He scarcely glanced at the two women.

'We – myself, Caninus, and you two – will be leaving for Corinium by the end of the second hour. Make sure that all four horses are saddled and ready by then,' he said crisply, before striding back into the north wing to have, Canio assumed, further words with Pacatianus.

CHAPTER FOUR

6th November

Riding Antares – with Januarius and one soldier ahead of him, and one soldier behind – the ten miles to Corinium, seven of them along the Fosse Way, passed quickly, and it was well before noon when Canio saw the weathered grey limestone of the city walls looming ahead of them.

They trotted under one of the main archways of the high, four-portalled Verulamium Gateway, and then carried straight on along the *decumanus maximus* before branching off onto the side street where the barracks' stables stood. There, all four men dismounted, and Januarius led them back to the *praetorium* at the northern end of the forum. As they passed through the streets, Canio noticed several people stopping and looking curiously at them as they went by, and realised that news of Sabinus's murder must already have spread though the little city.

And if he were uncertain before, from the remarks Januarius had made on the journey he was now convinced that the *agens* regarded him not just as a witness to the events of the previous night, but as someone who had played a significant part in them. It was an uncomfortable perception.

At the *praetorium*, Januarius left Canio in a small anteroom in the care of the two soldiers, saying that he would be back shortly. While he waited, Canio tried to engage the soldiers in conversation, but it soon became apparent that they were under orders not to fraternise.

Januarius eventually returned with the news that copies of both Canio's and Vibius Natalis's statements were on their way to Londinium, via the *cursus publicus,* to break the sad news to the *vicarius.*

'So why am I here?' Canio asked.

'To give your version of events to a small court of inquiry that has been assembled. Apparently, it interviewed Natalis earlier this morning. Come, they are waiting for us.'

❖

The *agens* led Canio up a flight of stairs and along a corridor, at the end of which was the *praeses'* audience chamber. Canio had been there several times before, in his previous military incarnation. The double doors stood open, and inside, seated in a semicircle, were half a dozen men. Canio recognised most of them: senior notaries, *rationales* and *quaestors*, drawn from the *praeses'* staff. On one side sat a notary behind a small desk, pen, inkwell and several sheets of parchment in front of him.

The only non-civilian – who was seated in the *praeses'* large, ornately carved chair on a low dais – was a big man, a soldier in his early forties. Canio recognised him, although they had never spoken: Flavius Vadomarus was – or so he claimed – the son of a king of the Alemanni, from the vast, dark forests beyond the Rhenus. He held the rank of *tribunus* and was said to have commanded a cohort of some five hundred *limitanei* frontier troops on The Wall during the *Barbarica Conspiratio.* How he had escaped the fate that befell the *Dux* Fullofaudes when the Picts invaded, and what he was now doing in Corinium, Canio had never met anyone who seemed quite sure.

He felt a slight draught of cold air as Januarius closed the doors. The *agens* then walked swiftly past him and sat in the one remaining unoccupied chair beside Vadomarus, who seemed to be frowning as he shuffled several sheets of parchment clutched in his massive fists.

Vadomarus suddenly looked up. 'So you are Claudius Caninus, *honestior*?'

'I am,' Canio replied, and smiled politely, although he didn't like the contemptuous way Vadomarus had said the word "*honestior*".

'So tell me all you know about what happened at Villa Censorini last night.'

'It's all there in my statement. That is what you're holding, isn't it?'

'But I want to hear it directly from you, so I can read your face while you speak,' Vadomarus said coldly.

So Canio repeated, as exactly as he could recall, the words he had written during the night.

When he had finished, Vadomarus said, 'These three so-called "mosaic workers" who helped you search for the pagan idol, what are their names?'

Canio paused to give the impression that he was trying hard to remember. 'As far as I can recall, one of them was called Olondus, and I think I heard him call another Glaucus. But if I ever heard the name of the third, I've forgotten it.'

Vadomarus turned to Januarius. 'Have you heard of either of them?'

'No, but they shouldn't be hard to find – if they actually exist, of course.' And the *agens* gave Canio a searching look.

And all the while the notary's pen was busily scratching away. Canio felt a stab of guilt at giving the mosaic workers' names, realising too late that Januarius would not hesitate to use torture on the men to verify whether or not they were telling the truth.

'This woman who brought the other pagan idol – you seem very anxious to tell us that she is supposed to have said that she had never seen you before. Perhaps too anxious?'

'I've only recorded what she said. Vibius Natalis heard her too.'

'Really? I don't recall reading that in his statement.' Vadomarus glanced at Januarius, who shook his head. 'And she still hasn't been found – or has she?'

'Not by the time we left Villa Censorini she hadn't,' Januarius confirmed.

'That isn't damned well good enough,' Vadomarus said irritably. 'It would appear that she's the only person left alive who really knows what happened in that triclinium, up to and including the moment that Sabinus was murdered. She's got to be found, and soon.'

'There are men with hunting dogs out scouring the countryside for her at this very moment. She'll be found,' Januarius assured him.

I wouldn't bet on that, thought Canio. *Remember, she disappeared at a crossroads – a place where two paths met.* And the implications of that scared him more than Vadomarus and Januarius ever could.

'She'd better be,' Vadomarus grunted. 'How soon will you hear from Londinium?'

'The dispatch rider should arrive there by noon tomorrow. Assuming a messenger leaves Londinium early the next day, he should be here by noon the day after. So, three days from now.'

'And in the meantime?'

'We make arrangements for the *praeses'* funeral,' Januarius replied. 'He didn't have any close relatives here in Britannia, did he?'

'Not that I'm aware of,' said Vadomarus. 'I know he kept a mistress at Villa Censorini, but the less said about her the better.'

Now that the focus seemed to be shifting away from himself, Canio thought that the worst was over. He was wrong.

Abruptly, Januarius asked, 'Tell me, Caninus, did you blame Sabinus for the death of your friend, Lucius Flavius Antoninus? You look surprised, though you really shouldn't be. After all, if Sabinus hadn't accused him of involvement in Valentinus's conspiracy, and Julius Castor hadn't then killed him – some might even say murdered him – Sabinus would never have come to enjoy the right to live at Villa Censorini, would he now?'

The question was unexpected, and Canio took several moments to reply. 'No, I didn't blame Sabinus; why should I? My understanding is that he discovered several incriminating letters written by Antoninus linking him to the conspiracy, and Castor only killed him in self-defence when he tried to escape after murdering your colleague Macrinius Lunaris.'

His answer seemed to amuse Januarius. 'Quite so. That is, of course, what happened. But say – and this is a purely hypothetical proposition – a man held a grudge, however unjustified, against certain others. And if, by some form of hellish black magic, that man found a way of driving his enemies insane, so that they destroyed each other in their murderous rage while he looked on, that would be a fine revenge, would it not?'

'If you say so,' Canio said cautiously, aware that Vadomarus was looking hard at him now. 'But surely you don't believe that this hypothesis has any relevance to the murder of Sabinus? In any case, I wasn't even present in the triclinium when the *vir perfectissimus* was killed.'

'No relevance? That, Caninus, is what I intend to discover,' Januarius replied.

Which worried Canio, but what worried him even more was then being escorted, under guard, to the barracks and locked into one of the guardroom cells. It was another stark confirmation that Januarius did not believe his version of events or, even worse, did not want to believe it. A *praeses* had been murdered, and Canio was beginning to fear that he was being set up as the sacrificial victim required to reflect the enormity of the crime.

It didn't help that the cell was the very same one in which, not three weeks before, he had been imprisoned by Julius Castor, and in which he had subsequently killed Crotilio – jailer and sadist – and escaped. A crime, if a crime it was, that had apparently been covered up by Sabinus and Castor – for their own devious purposes, of course. He fervently hoped that Januarius was unaware of that particular incident.

The cell was miserably dank and chill, and he hadn't eaten for over twenty-four hours. But nobody came with food or blankets, and when the November dusk fell he wrapped himself in his *cucullus* and eventually fell asleep on the cold stone flags.

CHAPTER FIVE

6th – 7th November

And as he slept, Canio dreamed that he heard the long-forgotten voice of the old man. It was telling the same story – as best he could remember it – that he had last heard as a child, a quarter of a century before.

*

'Carausius… Carausius… Carausius. For nearly fifty years I didn't dare to speak that name out loud. Too dangerous. Far, far too dangerous. Who was he, and where did he come from? His people were Menapians, or so I heard, and he was born on one of the islands of Batavia, in the delta formed by the Rhenus and Meuse rivers. So he must have grown up in the coastal lands of Gallia Belgica, where there is nothing but sea and sky and flat lands stretching to the horizon, and where the cold east wind can freeze the very marrow in your bones.

'He was a big man was Carausius, but not what you could call a handsome one. A neck like a bull, with a thick beard and hair, both kept trimmed short, as soldiers did in those days. And strong – so strong that in his younger days, before he joined the army, they say he could drag a small ship from one harbour berth to another, all by himself.

'I didn't know him in those early days, of course. He was well over ten years older than me, born around the time when Trajan Decius was emperor. His given name was Mausaeus Carausius – he only added the "Marcus Aurelius" in front when he made himself emperor.

'When he was little more than a boy, he followed his father onto the sea, learning the locations of the shifting sandbanks around the many mouths of the Rhenus, Meuse and Scaldis estuaries. So hardy and quick-witted was he that, by the time he was barely seventeen, he was helmsman of a cargo ship sailing between ports on the coast of Frisia and across the Oceanus Germanicus to Londinium.

'But it was a hard life, and not made any easier by the Franks and Alamanni raiding from across the Rhenus almost every year. And then, when Carausius was about twenty years old, a great storm – the ferocity of which had never before been seen – drove the sea inland, flooding all over the coastal plain, such that afterwards no man could live there for many a year. And that was why Carausius gave up the sea and joined the army. But they say he didn't stop worshipping Nehalennia: I don't think he ever did.

'Nehalennia? She was – is – a famous goddess. Her temples – and there were at least two before the great flood – stood on the island of Wallacra, between two arms of the estuary of the Scaldis River as it flowed out into the Oceanus Germanicus. Wallacra was where ships set sail for Britannia, and before they left, the sailors would leave little offerings for the goddess. And the captains or owners or both would sacrifice a chicken on one of her altars and pray that the goddess would send them a calm sea. A calm sea – that's what I sought for many a long year. A refuge from the storms of the world.

'Carausius, though… The first time I saw him, he must have been in his early thirties, already second in command of the army that Emperor Carinus himself had been leading, driving back the Picts – a tribe of painted savages that had invaded the wild north of Britannia. Awarded himself the title of Britannicus Maximus did Carinus, on the strength of his victories; although from what I heard, it was Carausius who led most of the fighting.

'Carausius had been in Britannia the previous year, and that was also because the Picts had been causing trouble – which, I suppose, was why Carinus chose him. It was on his way back south from those first skirmishes that Carausius chanced to meet Aelia Allecta. In the little city of Corinium it was, where the governor of what was then Britannia Superior happened to be staying for a few days while on his way back to Londinium, the capital of the province.

'Aelia Allecta was the daughter of a man called Gnaeus Aelius Quintus, who owned a small villa estate nestling in a sheltered valley in a countryside that, in the green late spring, was one of the loveliest in the whole world... or so it was said.

'Carausius became betrothed to Aelia Allecta. It was her father's doing. He knew only too well it was the army that ruled the empire, and he thought that having in the family a tribune who stood high in the favour of Emperor Carinus would protect them all. Particularly if the uncertain times that had ended only a dozen years before with the crushing of the Tetrici, the last of the rebel Gallic emperors, were ever to return. Protect them all – how the gods must have laughed at the irony of that.

'I don't think that Aelia Allecta wanted Carausius as a husband. She was barely eighteen, and he was the best part of fifteen years older. But she was an obedient daughter and understood that it was her duty to marry him. And so married they were, early one June morning in a ceremony at her father's villa. She wore a long white gown, an orange veil and orange shoes: her father believed in the old Roman traditions, although, in truth, his ancestors were no more Roman than Carausius's were. Afterwards, the couple sacrificed to the Lares who watched over the villa, which would continue to be her home while her husband was away with the army.

'As part of the wedding contract, it was agreed that Carausius would give her twin brother – a man called Aelius Allectus – a position in the army and take him under his wing, so to speak. Aelius Allectus, though, didn't really want to become a soldier. They say he would have been happy to continue living a quiet, private life, managing the estate that, in the fullness of time, would become his own. But it was not to be.

'Both twins were well educated. Aelius Quintus had arranged for both Aelia Allecta and her brother to be taught some of the classics of Roman literature, especially Virgil. It was said that she could recite whole passages of the Aeneid and the Georgics from memory, without so much as glancing at a scroll. But I'm getting ahead of myself. Carausius is the hero of this story... Or he was at first.'

✻

Waking sometime in the endless November night, Canio tried to remember the old man's name – the name he had last heard spoken twenty-five years before. And that was by Marcia, not by the old man himself. At first, he could not recollect it, but then – as sometimes happens – when he had given up and was trying to get back to sleep, it suddenly came to him. It was Tul... something. He was fairly sure of that. Tul... Tul... Tulius! That was it – Tulius. The more he repeated the name, the more certain of it he became. Which is often the way.

CHAPTER SIX

7th November

Canio woke again, shivering, just as the pallid dawn light was beginning to creep into his cell. From one of the other cells he heard a woman sobbing softly, an oddly disturbing sound. He decided against calling out to her: he had too many troubles of his own. Time passed, the light grew stronger, and then he heard voices from somewhere in the barracks. The voices grew louder and were accompanied by footsteps. A door opened, and through the bars of his cell Canio saw Januarius, resplendent in the quasi-military uniform of the corps of *agentes in rebus*, complete with elaborately decorated leather belt and scabbarded *spatha*. Two soldiers followed close behind him.

'Awake are you, Caninus? Ready for your journey?' Not waiting for Canio to reply, the *agens* nodded to one of the soldiers, who unlocked the cell door and swung it open.

'Journey to where?' Canio was so cold that the words came out ragged.

'Why, to Londinium, of course. To see the *vicarius*,'

'Civilis?'

'Just so. It has been decided that, since it is almost inevitable that the *vir spectabilis* will wish to question you himself, there is little point in waiting for the dispatch rider's return. So, we will be leaving at the end of the first hour. These two will show you where you can wash and make yourself ready for the journey.'

'Is my horse still in the stables here?'

'As far as I know. But you won't be needing it: we'll be using the late *praeses'* coach, seeing as Natalis can't ride with an injured wrist.'

*

There were still traces of frost on the lichen-stained red clay and split-stone roof tiles of Corinium when the coach carrying Canio, Januarius and a distinctly apprehensive-looking Vibius Natalis rattled through the streets of the city. After passing under the archway of the Calleva Gate in the south-east corner of the city they emerged onto the Via Erminus, the road that led to the town of Calleva Atrebatum, some fifty miles distant and halfway to Londinium.

Before they left, Canio had managed to bribe Bupitus, the head ostler at the barracks' stables, to send a lad to Villa Canini with instructions to Felix, his bailiff, to come and collect Antares. He was not about to let any of Bupitus's minions ride the horse.

The coach driver, whose name Canio eventually discovered was Mettus, sat huddled on the bench seat, swathed against the cold in a heavy *cucullus*. Two soldiers rode behind the coach. From the snatches of their occasionally overheard conversations, Canio picked up, among other things, the name and location of a brothel in Londinium that he had never himself patronised, but which they seemed to rate highly.

Watching Januarius's face when this house of ill repute was mentioned, Canio noticed the look of irritation it provoked. It seemed that the *agens* did not approve of such establishments. Canio was unsurprised.

After some fifteen miles, they stopped at the town of Durocornovium and changed horses at the *mansio* there.

The first thing Januarius did was to flourish his diploma of authorisation to use the *cursus publicus* under the nose of the surly *mansionarius,* and then command the man to hurry, stressing how important his business was. Having apparently breakfasted well himself back in Corinium he declined to allow Canio and Natalis time to eat.

With a fresh pair of horses, the coach started off again, its unsprung, iron-bound wheels jolting over the uneven stones of the Via Erminus. From time to time the coach lurched violently to one side when Mettus was unable (or unwilling) to avoid one of the many puddle-filled potholes that littered what was supposed to be one of the main highways of the province.

Natalis tried several times to discover what his current status was – witness or suspect – and each time Januarius smiled coldly and declined to give him a reassuring answer.

'Don't worry, young Natalis: I'm the one who's suspected of criminal activity; isn't that so, my fine *agens* of the third grade?' If Canio was trying to get Januarius to confirm what he strongly suspected, he did not succeed. All he got was the same cold smile.

It seemed that the *agens* was determined to say as little as possible to his two companions. Canio guessed that the man's aim was to let his and Natalis's imaginations frighten them into coughing up any information they had hitherto omitted. It was an old trick: Canio had used it several times himself.

They changed horses twice more at *stationes* along the way and, after crossing the High Downs, arrived in the late afternoon at the walled town of Calleva Atrebatum, clattering through the streets on their way to the large *mansio* on the south side.

Waving his diploma at the *mansionarius,* Januarius demanded accommodation for the night for himself and Canio, in separate rooms, and a fresh pair of horses for the morning. Natalis, he announced (to the latter's dismay), would have to share his own room. It seemed that he did not want the young centurion and Canio conferring during the night. He left the two soldiers and Mettus to fend for themselves, which turned out to be a mistake.

After eating a meal of lamb stew and vinegary wine, the suspect taste of the meat not wholly disguised by the copious use of *liquamen* fish sauce, Canio retired to his room and eased under the solitary blanket, the fragrance of which suggested that it had not been washed since the death of Emperor Constans some twenty years before. The *agens'* room was heated by a hypocaust. Canio's was not, so he spent another cold night wrapped in his *cucullus*.

Eventually he fell asleep, watching the dying flame of a solitary candle guttering in a lead candlestick on the washbasin table. And at some time during that long night he dreamed he heard Tulius speaking the words he thought he had forgotten a quarter of a century before.

CHAPTER SEVEN

'*Time is implacably cruel. It destroys everything, and it's unstoppable, always slipping through your fingers like dry sand; the tighter you try to grasp it, the faster it vanishes away. By September of that year – the year of Carausius and Allecta's wedding – Emperor Carinus was already in faraway Rome, celebrating his late father Emperor Carus's victories in Persia with games in the Coliseum. They say that dozens of gladiators and hundreds of rare wild beasts died on the blood-soaked sand. And for what? To honour the memory of a man who had been dead for almost a year?*

'*Carus was alleged to have been struck by lightning in his army's camp near the Persian capital of Ctesiphon. I don't think many people really believed that he did die that way, even when they first heard of it. And after his other son, Numerian, died in even more suspicious circumstances I'm sure even fewer did.*

'*It was while he was in Rome that Carinus heard that an officer – at least, I think he was an officer – called Sabinus Julianus had rebelled somewhere in one of the Pannonian provinces and was advancing westwards towards Italy. Carinus marched north, and then defeated and killed the rebel in a battle fought somewhere in Northern Italy. By my reckoning that must have been in the early spring of the following year.*

'*But that was only the beginning of his troubles, although he couldn't have known it at the time. Late in the previous year, Numerian, Carinus's younger brother, had been returning from* the East after his father's Persian campaign when he was found dead in his carriage. A man called Diocles, who led the protectores domestici (which was the elite cavalry unit answerable directly to the emperor himself), claimed that Arrius Aper, the Praetorian Prefect, had murdered him.

'But before Aper could protest his innocence, Diocles stabbed him to death, right in front of the whole army, then promptly proclaimed himself emperor – or as the official version has it, was proclaimed emperor by his army. So you can draw your own conclusions as to who really murdered Numerian.

'That proclamation took place at Nicomedia, twelve days before the kalends of December of that year, or so I heard later. And all our troubles can be traced back to that evil day and the days that followed, when Diocles started marching westwards through the Balkans.

'Now that he was an emperor of sorts, Diocles didn't think his name sounded Roman enough, or grand enough. So he took to calling himself – I almost said, "Christened himself," and how that would have irritated the bastard! – Gaius Aurelius Valerius Diocletianus, to be known henceforth to the world as Diocletian. But to me, he was always Diocles, the misbegotten murdering spawn of a Dalmatian ex-slave.

'Carinus marched eastwards, and in the middle of May the two armies met near the Margus River in Moesia, which is the Balkan province that lies to the south of the Danube.

'Some say that Carinus was killed in the battle. Others say that he won, but was murdered soon afterwards by one of his own officers whose wife he'd seduced. What the truth was I never knew. But I do know that it suited Diocles to paint Carinus as a debauched beast who couldn't be trusted with other men's wives, still less with the ruling of the empire.

'And I also know this: that if Carinus had won and survived that day at the Margus River, then the world today would be a very different place. No Diocles, no tetrarchy, and no Constantius or his son Constantine, who styled himself The Great and foisted the bizarre cult of Christus on the empire. And no Carausius Augustus, of course – or Allectus Augustus either. In short, a better world for everyone – perhaps.

'Carausius wasn't present at the great battle on the banks of the Margus. Before he left for Rome, Carinus had appointed him military legate in command of all the army units in Britannia and Northern Gaul, not that there were many left after he'd ordered several legions south to help crush Sabinus Julianus.

'Then, in Gaul, with Carinus gone, the Bagaudae rose in rebellion. They were a motley army of peasants, craftsmen, runaway slaves and deserters from the army – anybody and everybody who'd been driven to despair and destitution by the insatiable greed of the great landowners, the rapacious tax gatherers and the army those taxes paid for. The same army that took their sons to fight and die in the never-ending frontier wars, defending the borders of an empire they had come to see as an even worse enemy than the Germanic tribes from east of the Rhenus that were forever raiding into Gaul.

'The Bagaudae had two leaders, men who called themselves Amandus and Aelianus. Whether those were their real names I don't think anyone ever knew. Some say they were once minor landowners themselves, before they were forced off their land by crippling taxes they couldn't pay. Of course, if they'd been rich, they could have bribed the local rationales to get their tax quotas reduced, or perhaps not even demanded at all.

'At first, the Bagaudae only attacked and looted the villas of the great landowners, fighting pitched battles against their private militias of armed retainers who had tyrannised them for so long. But emboldened by their success, and as their numbers grew, they began besieging and storming towns, even walled towns. And when they'd breached the walls they robbed and killed every man who appeared rich, and they raped the women, rich and poor alike. Thus does cruelty beget cruelty.

'Carausius had been left with only a handful of legionary vexillationes, units seconded from the legions that Carinus had taken south with him. Each vexillatio was only a couple of centuries strong – no more than a hundred and sixty men at most – but he used them with great skill.

'By developing a network of spies, he discovered the locations of the various Bagaudae bands, and so could choose when and where to attack, and where he would have been outnumbered. And by concentrating his forces in one spot at any one time, he was able to appear much stronger than he really was. A couple of times he even intimidated a hundred or more Bagaudae into surrendering their weapons and slinking off home.

'In fact, the rebellion was already faltering when Maximianus arrived. That would have been in the August or September of the year before Carausius himself rebelled. Perhaps you've never heard of Maximianus? I certainly wish I never had; in fact, I wish the swine had never even been born.

'Marcus Aurelius Valerius Maximianus had been Diocles' second in command in the Persian War. He was about the same age as Carausius – about five or so years younger than Diocles – a big brute of a man, heavily built and bearded, looking every inch the military savage that he was. Merciless. Cruel. When Diocles chose to stay in the East, he raised Maximianus to the rank of Caesar in July of that year and sent him to Gaul to take charge of, and finish, the campaign against the Bagaudae.

'And finish it he did. He brought several whole legions with him and they fell on the Bagaudae like a pack of ravenous wolves. He killed every one of them he captured, crucifying hundreds. Carausius, although he could never have been called a soft-hearted man, urged Maximianus to be merciful, reminding him that these were the people who ploughed the fields and tended the herds that the army and everyone else depended on for food.

'But Maximianus wouldn't listen. Carausius had been appointed by Carinus, so his advice was inevitably suspect.

He probably wouldn't have listened anyway, whoever it was advising him to show mercy. Killing was his trade, and he was a master of his craft.

'Well before the end of the year the Bagaudae had been crushed – as far as you can ever crush men who have little or nothing to lose – but by then Carausius had effectively been demoted and put in charge of rebuilding the Classis Britannica.

'In decades past, that fleet had protected the seas between Gaul and Britannia from Saxon and Frankish pirates, but it had effectively ceased to exist some fifteen years before, neglected and starved of men and money during the years of the Gallic Empire.

'So when Maximianus learned that Carausius had been a sailor in his youth he must have thought it a good way of removing a commander who was more popular with his own men than he was. This came with the added advantage that, if Carausius failed, then all the blame could be heaped on him.

'But Carausius didn't fail. He went to the port of Gesoriacum (or Bononia, as it's called nowadays); conscripted shipwrights, timber, sailcloth and cordage from shipyards all along the coasts of Gaul and Frisia, and set to work.

'At first he concentrated on repairing those old warships that could be made seaworthy again. Then he began building new ones, and at the same time recruited men – soldiers and civilian seamen – to crew them.

'By the early spring of the following year, which was the year that he was driven to rebellion, Carausius had a small fleet of ten or so warships at sea, hunting the pirates. On several of those early patrols he commanded a warship himself, and as chance would have it, I was with him one fine April day when we encountered a Saxon war galley out on the Fretum Gallicum. And tomorrow, I will tell you what happened that day.'

CHAPTER EIGHT

8ᵗʰ November

Groping his way across the Calleva *mansio's* outer courtyard on his way to the latrine, just as light was beginning to filter reluctantly back into the world, Canio realised that there was fog in the air. And when he came out of that malodorous structure the fog had grown noticeably denser.

He made his way back to the communal dining area, where he found Januarius and Natalis eating breakfast, the former, between mouthfuls, shouting orders to the *mansionarius* to ensure that their coach was being readied.

'Ah, Caninus, be so good as to go and rouse our escorts and the driver. If we're to reach Londinium by nightfall we must be away from here without delay.'

'So where have they been lodging?' It was the obvious question.

'How should I know? Ask the *mansionarius*.'

Canio, after blowing out a long breath of exasperation, did just that and was told by the *mansionarius* – his name was Aurelius Verus – that he had recommended a *taberna* called the *Fighting Cock*, which was a couple of *insulae* blocks away on the west side of the town.

Pulling his *cucullus* tightly around him, Canio trudged through the Stygian streets of Calleva until he found what he assumed was the right *taberna*, identified as it was by a hanging

43

sign depicting what, in that poor light, could be taken for some species of fowl.

The door appeared to be locked, but repeated thumps at last brought an angry shout from somewhere in the depths beyond: 'Go away, damn you! We're closed.'

'Have you got two soldiers and a man called Mettus in there?' Canio shouted back.

'I might have; what's it to you?'

'Have you or haven't you?'

'I might have,' the voice repeated. 'Who are you anyway?'

At that point Canio's temper got the better of him. 'I'm the man who, if you don't open this damned door, is going to smash it to pieces and then ram what's left of it up your fool backside,' he roared. And to show he wasn't joking he took one pace back and gave the door an almighty kick, which made it shudder.

'All right, all right,' came the voice, sounding alarmed now. 'Give me a moment.'

There followed the sounds of several bolts being rasped back out of their sockets, and the door creaked open to reveal a woman of uncertain age with shoulder-length hair and what looked like a blackthorn cudgel in her right hand.

'Where are they?' Canio did not waste time with introductions. Nor was he intimidated by the cudgel, even though he was unarmed, being at least a head taller than the woman. He had been compelled to leave his *spatha* at Villa Censorini, something he increasingly regretted.

At the sight of the angry Canio the woman rapidly shuffled backwards and pointed to the dim interior of the room, where he could just make out three seated figures slumped over a table, their arm-cradled heads resting on the wood.

'Are those the ones you're looking for?' the woman asked, adding somewhat unnecessarily, 'They've had quite a lot to drink.'

'Rouse the bastards,' Canio commanded.

The woman took told of one of Mettus's arms and tugged it none too gently. 'Wake up… wake up! It's morning, and there's somebody come to see you.'

Mettus groaned and raised his head a few inches above the tabletop. 'What? Oh, it's you, Tertia; what do you want now?'

Pushing past Tertia, Canio grabbed Mettus by the neck of his tunic and hauled him to his feet. 'What I want, Hades take you, is for you to come and drive the coach. And you'd better sober up fast or Januarius will nail your private parts to the seat.'

Mettus still showed no sign of moving, so Canio propelled the unsteady driver towards the door, where he clung to the hinge post as though it were a long-lost friend.

The two soldiers were still unconscious, one of them snoring loudly, and no amount of shaking by Canio could produce anything but inarticulate and irritable grunts. A stink of cheap wine surrounded the two men like an invisible cloud.

Realising the hopelessness of getting them back to the *mansio*, and even less chance of getting them into their saddles, Canio cursed in exasperation and left them where they snored. Grabbing Mettus by the collar again, he frogmarched the driver though the foggy streets to the *mansio* and presented him to Januarius.

'So where are the other two?' Januarius demanded.

'They got into a fight with Bacchus. They put up a gallant struggle, but Bacchus won; he always does. It'll be at least noon before they're sober enough to sit on a horse without falling off. Do you want to try to find another couple of soldiers here in Calleva to take their place?'

'How long will that take?'

'No idea. You'll have to talk to the local garrison commander—'

'Who will almost certainly want to question me to discover whether the rumours already going around about the circumstances of Sabinus's death are true. No, we can't spare the time. We'll go without the bastards.'

'If you say so,' said Canio.

'I do, so get this wretch sober and on top of the coach, and let's be away as soon as possible. Londinium is fifty miles away, and I want to reach it before dark.'

Canio resented being ordered around by Januarius, but he decided it would be unwise to let his simmering irritation show. Instead, he found a bucket of water into which he thrust Mettus's head and held it there for a count of ten. Then he dragged him, spluttering, up onto the bench seat, and as the reluctant sun was slowly rising above the fog the coach rattled out of Calleva and onto the highway leading eastwards towards Londinium.

CHAPTER NINE

Out in the open countryside the fog came down thick again, closing in around the carriage and isolating them in a tiny world where the only sounds were the muffled clopping of the horses' hooves, the creaking of the axles and the occasional splatter on the roof as water that had condensed out of the fog cascaded off a wayside tree.

'What will happen to those two soldiers?' Natalis asked – probably, Canio suspected, just to break the oppressive near silence.

'Don't concern yourself with them; in due course they will be dealt with appropriately,' Januarius replied, 'I will see to that personally.'

I bet you will – and probably enjoy doing it, Canio thought.

They were perhaps three miles east of Calleva, or it could have been two or four – in the fog they had lost all sense of distance travelled – when Canio heard Mettus shout, 'Brigands!'

The coach came to a sudden halt. Canio felt it lurch, and a moment later caught a glimpse of the driver running past, back along the highway.

Januarius, on the other side of the coach, unlatched and swung open the door. Apparently seeing nothing, he leaned his upper body out to get a better view. There was a brief swish and the *agens* jerked back, just in time to avoid a blow from the quarterstaff wielded by somebody who was largely hidden by the body of the carriage.

The *agens* drew his *spatha* and leaped out of the carriage. Canio heard curses and the sounds of scuffing feet, but before he could do anything the door on his own side was wrenched open by a man with wild hair and beard and who was wielding a large axe two-handedly.

'Out – now! Quickly, quickly!' And to emphasise the point the man smashed the axe into the side of the coach, penetrating it and sending splinters flying across the seat. That was a mistake: before the man could wrench the axe free Canio had kicked him in the face, sending him sprawling backwards.

Scrambling to the other side of the carriage, Canio was just in time to see Januarius smash aside the quarterstaff brandished by a big man in an expensive-looking but ill-fitting tunic and stab him in the abdomen. The man screamed and dropped his quarterstaff, and as he doubled up in agony the *agens* slashed two-handedly at his neck with his *spatha*, half-severing his head. Blood sprayed everywhere and the man collapsed onto the road where he convulsed briefly and then lay still.

Breathing heavily, the *agens* muttered, 'That's the way to deal with scum like that.' Then, louder, he added, 'Now, let's be on our way; I've no more time to waste.' After clambering back into the carriage he slammed the door behind him and sheathed his *spatha*.

'The driver's gone; he ran away,' Natalis pointed out.

'What!? I'll have the bastard flogged!' Januarius twisted around, leaned out of the window, opened the carriage door again and was part way out when something hit him over the head. He collapsed with the upper part of his body hanging out of the coach, his legs and lower trunk remaining on the floor.

Canio pushed past Natalis, only to see a third brigand beginning to drag the *agens'* unconscious body out of the coach. Crouching down and grabbing Januarius's ankles, Canio tugged him back a foot or so, just far enough for him to grab the hilt of the *agens' spatha* and yank it from its scabbard. With

48

Canio no longer holding his ankles, Januarius's body was pulled completely out of the coach and disappeared from view.

Not knowing how many brigands were left, Canio turned and jumped, *spatha* in hand, out of the opposite door. He was just in time to whack the flat of the blade down on the head of axeman, who was attempting to stagger to his feet.

Racing around to the other side, Canio found the third brigand, dagger in hand, slashing through the strap that secured Januarius's purse to his belt. At the sight of Canio's *spatha* the man recoiled and held the point of the dagger against the *agens'* throat. 'One more step and he's dead,' he hissed.

Canio hesitated. To Natalis, now sheltering behind him, it probably appeared that concern for Januarius's safety was the cause of that hesitation. In reality, Canio was trying to decide what would best serve his interests. If he were "inadvertently" to cause the brigand to slit the *agens'* throat, it would remove a man who, even at this early stage of their acquaintance, was showing distinct signs of being a threat to his wellbeing.

On the other hand, if he were to appear to save the *agens'* life, witnessed by Natalis, he might earn the man's gratitude and perhaps turn an antagonist into, if not a friend, then at least into someone who treated him impartially. He decided that, on balance, the latter would be the more advantageous course of action. It was a mistake that anyone could have made.

He lowered the *spatha* slowly until it pointed at the ground, then stepped back a pace, almost bumping into Natalis as he did so.

Not taking his eyes off the sword, the brigand inched forwards, finished sawing through Januarius's purse strap, grabbed the purse with his free hand, sprang to his feet, turned and fled. In a moment the fog had swallowed him up; in another, even his footsteps had been silenced.

Canio considered running after him, but a groan from Januarius made him turn his attention to the *agens. In any case,* he reflected, *chasing a man with a knife, even if you are carrying a sword, is not a good idea in thick fog.* The fog would be a great leveller for a desperate man.

With Natalis's help, he lifted Januarius back into the coach and propped him up on the seat. Around the other side of the coach, he found that the first brigand, the axeman, the man he had hit with the flat of the *agens' spatha*, had disappeared. The blade of the *spatha* was too smeared with blood from where the *agens'* had slaughtered the second brigand for Canio to tell if his own whack had drawn blood. The axe was still embedded in the side of the coach. Canio twisted it free and tossed it onto the coach floor.

Hearing the faint sounds of footsteps approaching from along the stoned highway behind, Canio turned to face whoever it was, *spatha* gripped two-handedly and held out in front of him. A figure loomed out of the fog and his pulse rate quickened, but it was only a sheepish Mettus.

'Welcome back, my hero,' Canio grunted.

'I thought they were going to kill me,' Mettus said by way of explanation for his precipitate flight. 'One of them had a long spear.'

'It wasn't a spear, only a quarterstaff.'

'Could have done me in just the same.'

Canio couldn't be bothered to argue. 'Maybe. Now get back on top, and let's be away from here.'

As they drove off, Canio glimpsed the body of the second brigand sprawled at the side of the highway, his face a mask of blood. Moments later the fog had shrouded it.

Back inside the coach, Januarius slowly struggled back into full consciousness. He felt the back of his head where he'd been hit, and his fingers came away sticky with blood. However, after no more than a mile, he was complaining bitterly that Canio had failed to prevent the theft of his purse and contents.

'It was either your purse or your throat. Which would you have preferred?'

'Neither, Caninus – I don't believe you.'

'It's the truth, as Natalis can confirm; can't you, Natalis?'

Natalis looked distinctly uncomfortable, but after a few moments' hesitation and a glare from Canio, he said, 'That is what happened, Januarius. The brigand had his knife against your throat, and I thought he was about to kill you.'

'I might have known you'd back him up,' Januarius muttered, 'seeing as you're both in this affair together.'

Which, Canio thought, *has made Natalis look even more uncomfortable. Frightened, even.*

After fifteen miles they changed horses at a wayside *statio,* and after another fifteen miles reached the little town of Pontes. There, they rumbled across the massive timber bridge spanning the River Tamesis and then made their way to the town's *mansio.* With his precious diploma and the other contents of his purse in the hands of an exulting brigand somewhere to the east of Calleva, Januarius had a hard job convincing the *mansionarius* that they were entitled to use the *cursus publicus*. But eventually, by threatening various sanctions, including instructing a *rationalis* from the *vicarius's* office to audit his accounts, he got his way.

The horses were changed again, and the three men ate a meal of venison stew washed down with a fairly good Rhenish wine, which Natalis paid for, probably seeking to redeem himself in Januarius's eyes.

By the time they left Pontes to begin the last twenty miles to Londinium, the fog had gone and the weak late-autumn sun was breaking through the clouds, although it did little to improve Januarius's foul mood.

CHAPTER TEN

The low sun was still well above the south-western horizon when Canio, leaning out of one of the windows of the coach, saw in the distance the city walls of Londinium towering above the houses and other buildings of the extramural suburbs. Soon after, the carriage passed the surviving once-grand stone funerary monuments, which sporadically lined both sides of the highway there, before rattling over a bridge spanning a little river. A short distance further on, just before they reached those massive city walls, Canio saw an extensive cemetery away to the north and, on the other side of the road, a circular building that he recalled noticing before and suspected might once have been a temple. He doubted it still was.

The city walls were built largely of grey stone, interleaved with horizontal bands of red tile. From inside the carriage, Canio could see at least two of the semicircular bastions that projected at intervals from the walls, their flat tops supposed to be manned (but rarely were) by crews whose job was to operate the *ballistae*, as the oversized crossbows mounted on wooden frames were known.

The coach stopped just outside a monumental gateway in the walls, and Canio heard Mettus speaking to a guard who had emerged from one of the two square guardroom towers. The conversation ended before an increasingly angrily muttering Januarius could demand to know the cause of the hold-up, and the coach restarted and trundled under one of the twin archways of the gateway and into the city itself.

Londinium was the largest city in Britannia, at least twice the size of Corinium, and was the better part of a mile and a half wide, west to east, or so Canio remembered it from previous visits. They threaded their way through the streets, and from the direction Mettus was taking, Canio guessed that he was heading for the *praetorium*, which lay in the south-central area of the city, not far from the riverside wall, the river being the Tamesis.

Over the years, Canio had visited the city perhaps a dozen times, both for business and (increasingly) for pleasure, and thought he knew it fairly well. Drawing aside the curtain, he saw – away to the north and through a haze of smoke – the great circular amphitheatre, its high walls picked out by the wan late-afternoon sunlight. As they travelled past the timber-framed and stone-built houses, shops, workshops and stables, he breathed in the various odours of the city – of every city – the most predominant being woodsmoke, cooking odours (some appetising, others less so), and the distinctly unappetising perfumes of human excrement and urine.

After crossing over another small stream and then passing what had once been a temple of Mithras, they at last arrived at the *praetorium*. It was the headquarters of both the *consularis* of Maxima Caesariensis, the province in which Londinium lay, and his superior, Civilis, the *vicarius* of all five provinces of the diocese of Britannia.

There Januarius, after a few curt instructions to Mettus, ordered them to wait while he went inside, unchallenged by the guards who must have recognised him.

Time passed, and dusk – clammy and chill – was already falling when Januarius at last emerged from the terraced outer courtyard of the *praetorium*, then beckoned Canio and Natalis to follow him. Having both a fountain and a large ornamental pool, the courtyard must have been a pleasant place in summer, when the shaped beds around the edges would be full of bright flowers. Now, the beds were just sodden earth, and the pool was half-full of dark and slightly malodorous water. *And in November*, Canio mused, *spring is always so far away.*

As they walked through the echoing corridors of the strangely empty *praetorium*, Januarius explained that Civilis was at a dinner party at the villa of Statius Aelianus, the *consularis*. Aelianus's villa was situated some distance beyond the city walls, and the *vicarius* was not expected back until the next morning. There was, however, someone else who wanted to see them.

After leading them up a flight of stairs and along another dimly lit corridor, Januarius halted outside a door, rapped twice and entered, beckoning the other two to follow. The room was well lit by an array of oil lamps hanging from two ornamental stands.

There Canio saw, seated behind a large desk, a man who was perhaps nearer forty than thirty, with the sharp face and olive skin that suggested an origin in a land bordering the Mediterranean, possibly even on the North African shores of that sea. He did not stand up, but Canio could see that he wore a quasi-military uniform similar to Januarius's, but the *orbiculi* roundels sewn on his tunic were larger and more intricately patterned. Several neatly rolled scrolls lay on the desk in front of him.

'Sir,' Januarius said with studied formality, 'May I present Vibius Natalis and Claudius Caninus, the persons mentioned in my report?' As he spoke, he pointed to each in turn. 'I took the initiative of bringing them to Londinium, assuming that yourself and the *vicarius* would wish to question them personally, without unnecessary delay. Natalis, Caninus – I have the honour of introducing you to the *ducenarius* Antistius Adventus, *agens in rebus* of the fifth and highest grade.'

And perhaps an even bigger bastard than you are? Canio speculated.

Adventus inclined his head slightly in acknowledgement. 'Thank you, Januarius. Your assumption was correct.' He partially unrolled one of the scrolls and studied it, then looked up sharply. 'You say here, Caninus, that you found the idol of the pagan goddess Hecate in the place where that man Peltrasius, now dead and so beyond mortal justice, had thrown it over two years before. Yet the place had already been searched by others, and nothing had been found. How do you account for that?'

But before Canio could reply, Adventus went on, 'And you also claim that you had never before seen the woman who brought the second idol to the late Caristanius Sabinus – that being the idol that seems to have been pivotal in bringing about his appalling death... By the way, had they found this woman by the time you left Corinium?' This to Januarius.

'No, sir, they had not,' the *agens* confirmed.

Adventus noisily exhaled his displeasure. 'That is unfortunate, most unfortunate. From these' – and he waved a hand over the scrolls on his desk – 'it would appear that she is the only person still alive who really knows what happened in that triclinium. And yet you say she has not been found?'

'She may well have been caught by now, sir,' Januarius replied defensively. 'Before I left Corinium, I left strict instructions that no effort was to be spared to find her,'

'Perhaps... perhaps. Yet without her we will have to concentrate our efforts on your two witnesses – I was about to say, "prisoners" – to discover the truth, won't we? Especially on you, Caninus, who my instinct tells me knows more about this most heinous crime than you have so far seen fit to disclose.'

Was it really your instinct that did the telling, or was it friend Januarius? Canio wondered.

'Anyway, in the morning this interview will be continued in the presence of the *vicarius* himself. In the meantime, Januarius will find secure – and separate – accommodation for you both tonight. Sleep well.' And with a wave of his hand, Adventus indicated that they were all dismissed.

*

Down the wide staircase and along the shadowy, echoing corridors, Januarius once again led them, until they came at last to the barracks housing the soldiers who guarded the *praetorium*. They stopped opposite a small row of cells, and after a whispered conversation with a soldier in the adjacent guardroom, Januarius took a key, unlocked one of the cells and ushered Canio inside before locking it again.

'You're surely not going to lock me up here like a common criminal?' came Natalis's horrified voice. 'My father—'

'Yes, I know who your father is, Master Natalis,' Januarius said tersely. 'Don't worry, I'm sure we can find some more salubrious accommodation for you. Come.'

Canio listened to their retreating footsteps as they faded into a silence broken only by the occasional murmur of voices from the guardroom. He was hungry, cold and tired. And when the flame of the solitary oil lamp set in a niche in the corridor wall finally sank low and died, the cell was left in total darkness.

In that darkness, Canio rapidly lost all sense of passing time. He reflected that it was fortunate that he had emptied his bladder at the *mansio* at Pontes, since no one had offered him the opportunity to do so (or eat or wash) since arriving at Londinium. On the other hand, it was perhaps unfortunate, because it deprived him of the excuse to do so in the cell, which would have been one way of registering his displeasure at his treatment. Still, there was always the morning. And with that thought, he wrapped himself in his *cucullus* and eventually fell asleep on the stone-flagged floor.

And sometime during the night he dreamed that he heard the voice of Tulius again.

CHAPTER ELEVEN

'Even after all these years, I've never forgotten that day on the Andromeda. She was a fine ship, the first of the all-new liburnae, as warships were called – and still are, of course – which Carausius built at Gesoriacum. She had a crew of about thirty sailors and about half as many marines, plus the captain, helmsman and navigator.

'She had a single bank of thirteen or so oars on each side, and a large, square sail that was raised by ropes running over pulleys housed inside a big wooden box – or truck, as I think they called it – fixed to the top of the mast above the yardarm. The sail was almost new and dyed pale green to match the colour of the sea, so it couldn't be seen from a distance. That was the theory anyway, but the salt water soon washed the dye out. Some people will tell you that the crew all wore sea-green uniforms, but if they did, then I never saw them or even heard of them ever being worn.

'She was long and sleek was the Andromeda, with a wicked, copper-sheathed ram at the prow, and a high, curved stern to stop big waves from swamping her when she was running before a storm. The cabin, such as it was, was at the stern end, as was the big, broad-bladed steering oar that the helmsman clung to in all weathers.

'But on that April day the sun shone down out of a sky of cloudless blue, sparkling on the little wavelets whipped up by a warm breeze from the south-west.

'Carausius had received information from one of our scaphae – the fast skiffs that acted as scouts when the sea was calm enough *for them to be launched – that two Saxon galleys had been sighted heading westwards through the Fretum Gallicum, which is the name of the narrowest part of the Oceanus Britannicus, between Dubris and Gesoriacum.*

'*At the time, we were only ten miles or so west of Gesoriacum, so Carausius altered course slightly, and with the breeze behind us we headed north-east. With that breeze, there was no need to use the oars, so Carausius ordered some of the sailors to reinforce the marines and stand at the rails all around the deck, with instructions to shout out as soon as they spotted the enemy.*

'*And they weren't easy to spot, those galleys, because they had no masts or sails and they sat low in the water. Time passed, first one summer hour, then two, and I was beginning to fear that the Saxons had slipped past us, which they could well have done, because even at its narrowest the Fretum Gallicum is over twenty miles wide.*

'*Ah, that brings back another memory – one of standing on a headland a few miles north of Gesoriacum on a bright, clear summer day. From there, I could see the long line of white cliffs around Dubris, see them so clearly that it was difficult to believe they were twenty miles and more away. That headland was a mosaic of thousands upon thousands of little pink flowers, which rippled in the warm breeze. Thrifts, I think she called them, the woman I was with on that day so long ago. With the sun warm on her lightly tanned skin, she seemed extraordinarily beautiful, surrounded by that sea of flowers. That evening, army duties called me away. I went back, weeks later, but I never saw her again. I've often wondered what became of her.*

'*Two summer hours passed, and by then I was almost certain that we had missed the Saxons. Then, I heard one of the sailors up near the prow of the* Andromeda *shout excitedly and point towards the north-east. In a moment all eyes were staring in that direction, and I could just make out the long, sleek shape of a* single galley, and as I tracked it I could see tiny flashes of white spray as the oars struck the water.

'Carausius roared out orders, and moments later a dozen sailors were adjusting the fore and aft stays that held the sail in position – although the sail could only be turned a little to the right or left. Even so, the Andromeda began tacking northwards on a course that, I assumed, was to intercept the Saxons – although to my inexperienced eye it seemed that they would be past the intended intersection point before we reached it. But I hadn't reckoned on the south-westerly wind, which was steadily strengthening and against which the Saxons were rowing.

'With the Andromeda flying before the wind, the distance between the two craft closed rapidly, and soon I began to see the enemy galley clearly. It looked to be about the same size as one I saw later, one that had been captured and towed into the harbour at Gesoriacum, and that was some fifteen double paces long by three wide. The one we encountered on that April day had large, upwardly curved prow and stern posts, and a big, broad-bladed steering oar near the stern.

'Closer still, and I could see the rowers, fifteen at least on each side, their heavily bearded faces taut with strain as they tried to outrun the Andromeda. I realised then that if the Saxons could get to the west of us, they would escape, because the wind would then be against us, and we would have to furl the sail and rely on oar power alone, allowing that sleek, light galley to outrun us.

'But rowing against the headwind the Saxons couldn't get to the west of us. They tried all right, and almost made it. They kept bearing south-west until the last moment as the Andromeda bore down on them, so by the time they realised they were not going to get past us it was too late to change course.

'From the orders that Carausius was shouting to the helmsman, I think he was trying to ram the galley amidships, but as it was, the Andromeda's ram hit the galley nearer the stern than the prow. There was a tremendous crash of splintering timbers, and *the* Andromeda *stopped so suddenly that I was flung forwards and hit my head on the deck, momentarily stunning me.*

'From that moment onwards, everything was chaos. Carausius was bellowing orders and the sailors were scrambling to furl the sail and man the oars to row the Andromeda backwards to prevent her being dragged down by the stricken galley. Several marines wielding short-handled, double-headed axes were rushing towards the prow, and I stupidly wondered why, until I realised that two or three Saxons had jumped onto the ram before it disengaged, and were scrambling up onto the prow of the Andromeda.

'One marine raised his axe two-handedly and brought it down on the head of a Saxon the moment it appeared over the prow. It was a savage blow, and the man's face disappeared in a gush of blood and brains. He fell backwards, vanished into the boiling sea and was gone. But in my dreams for years afterwards, I sometimes saw his face, distorted with rage, caught in that last frozen moment before the axe came down

'By now, the galley was sinking fast, with most of the deck already under water, and the air alive with shouts and screams as the marines unleashed showers of arrows at the Saxons, both those still aboard the galley and others who were already in the water. And the strangest thing was that those men in the water were not trying to swim away from the Andromeda, but were actually trying to reach it. Not for safety, but driven by the need to die in the act of attacking their enemy and so keep their warrior status in whatever afterlife they believed in. So strange. And die they did, with the marines laughing and jeering as they shot them. I remember seeing the body of one man floating face down in the sea with at least three arrows sticking out of his back.

'A sinking ship is a terrible thing to watch as it slips below the surface of the sea. For several long moments it is still visible under the darkening water, then it fades like a ghost and is gone forever. And still the marines were shooting at every Saxon in *the water, living or dead. I spotted several who were now trying to swim away, but we were at least five miles from the nearest shore, so they had little hope of ever reaching it.*

'There was a time when it would have seemed to me a piteous thing that, on a fine spring day under a cloudless sky and with the air warm with the promise of summer, thirty men's lives should be ended so cruelly. But the things I had witnessed in the war against the Bagaudae had burned much of the ability to feel pity out of my soul, and at that moment I felt nothing but the savage joy of victory.

'The Saxons' galley had been on its outward voyage from their homelands beyond the River Albis, so it was carrying no plunder. If it had been, Carausius would have attempted to capture it and seize whatever the Saxons had looted. The galley I saw later at Gesoriacum was one such that had been captured at sea. The bloodstains still on the deck bore grim testimony to what had become of its crew.'

*

Waking only moments after Tulius had finished speaking (or so it seemed to him), Canio remembered something that he had long ago forgotten. The day before the old man died, he had given him a small copper coin. It had lettering on both sides, unremembered, since it had meant nothing to a child who had not yet learned to read. What he did remember was that it bore on one side the head of a bearded man wearing the radiate crown of the sun god, and on the other was a tiny warship with a central mast and rigging, but no sail. It had high, curved prow and stern posts; a row of oars; and above them little dots supposed to represent the heads of the crew, or so Tulius had told him. And below the ship were two letters, although for the life of him Canio could not remember what they were.

61

The old man had urged him to keep the little coin safe, because it was the last one he possessed, and not to show it to anyone or attempt to buy anything with it. And for the first few weeks after the old man's death, Canio had carried that coin with him wherever he went and looked at it whenever he was alone. But as the weeks turned into months, and other things of interest supplanted it in his grasshopper mind, he looked at it less frequently, until one day he realised that it had vanished. Mindful of the old man's words and feeling slightly guilty, he searched for it in every place he could think of, but he never saw it again. And after a few more weeks he had entirely forgotten it – until now.

CHAPTER TWELVE

9th November

Canio had long since drifted back to sleep again when he became irritably aware of one of the *praetorium* guards shaking him awake. It was not yet dawn, but the lamp in the corridor must have been refilled and relit, its wan light just sufficient to make the surrounding darkness visible. After an escorted trip to the latrine and a breakfast of bean soup and barley beer, he was locked in his cell again. His increasingly testy questions as to when Civilis would be sending for him were met with ignorance of the great man's intentions – perhaps feigned, perhaps real.

But around mid-morning he heard Januarius's voice. The key rattled in the lock, the cell door swung open, and the *agens* appeared in the doorway.

'Come with me, Caninus. The *vir spectabilis* is ready to see you.'

'Yes, I slept very well, thank you,' Canio muttered. 'If anything, the mattress in the cell was too soft for my liking. Perhaps you would be good enough to speak to the guards about it.' Januarius, however, was already walking away down the corridor. With a hissed expletive impugning the virtue of the *agens'* mother, Canio followed.

Up the same staircase as before, but along a different corridor this time, a corridor which led to what Canio came to realise was the main audience chamber of the *praetorium*. Januarius knocked once on the imposing double doors and walked in. As he did so, the murmur of voices that Canio had heard from outside ceased abruptly. Trailing behind Januarius, he found himself in a large, high-ceilinged room with natural light from glazed windows set in two of the walls, supplemented by several stands of oil lamps. The glowing charcoal in two openwork bronze brazier trays on tripod stands took away some of the November chill.

In the middle of the room was a large table behind which sat a number of men. Adventus was the only one Canio recognised. In the centre, sitting beside Adventus, was a man of forbidding appearance: mid-forties or perhaps older, receding grey hair and wearing the robes of a high-ranking official, decorated as they were with elaborate sewn-on *orbiculi* roundels and vertical *clavi* bands. This, it seemed, was Publius Ulpius Civilis, *vicarius* of all five of the provinces of Britannia and holder of the rank of *vir spectabilis.* As he approached the desk, Canio saw Civilis glance up briefly and then look down again at the scroll he had been reading. Several other scrolls lay on the table in front of him.

Januarius moved smoothly around the table and seated himself in the empty space beside Adventus. On the other side of Civilis sat two men, with sheets of parchment, pens and inkwells arranged neatly on the table in front of them. Canio assumed they were *exceptores* – secretaries – preparing to record whatever Civilis told them to.

For long moments no one spoke and an ominous silence pervaded the room. Then Civilis looked up again and stared at Canio. 'You are Aulus Claudius Caninus, *honestior*, owner of the Villa Canini in the province of Britannia Prima?'

The question was purely rhetorical, but Canio answered formally, 'I am, *Vir Spectabilis.*'

'Indeed. Well, I have read your statement, Caninus, but now I want to hear from your own mouth exactly what happened at

Villa Censorini on the night of the nones of this month, and also what were the events that led up to that fateful night. Begin.'

So Canio repeated everything that he had put in his statement. And all the while he watched Civilis's index finger moving slowly down each of the unrolled parchment scrolls in front of him, one after another.

'Almost word perfect. I congratulate you on your memory.' This in what Canio thought was a studiedly neutral tone. 'Now, tell me more about this mysterious woman. Was she young, old, tall or short? Was her hair dark or fair? What?'

'She was shorter than me—' Canio began.

'That is hardly surprising, seeing as you are, what? Six feet tall?' Civilis interrupted.

'She was perhaps half a head shorter than me.' Canio was conscious that he must not say anything that Natalis's unseen statement might contradict.

'And her face?' Civilis prompted.

'I never saw her face clearly; the hood of her *cucullus* was pulled right forwards so as to obscure it.'

Civilis sighed. 'Her voice then, was it distinctive? Would you recognise it if you heard it again?'

'It was quite low pitched, almost like a man's voice,' Canio replied, scenting the opportunity to sow confusion again, as he had with Januarius at Villa Canini. Even as he spoke, he noticed Januarius fidgeting, as if wanting to say something, but unwilling to interrupt Civilis.

'So it could have been a man in disguise?'

'Yes... I suppose that's possible.'

Civilis turned to Adventus. 'That won't make the task of finding him or her any easier, will it?' he enquired irritably.

'With great respect, *Vir Spectabilis*, Januarius has already investigated this possibility. It *was* a woman. Vibius Natalis, who apparently saw her for longer than Caninus did, was quite certain of that.'

Civilis gave Canio a sharp look, and he realised that his attempt to mislead may have been a mistake. 'And yet you ran after *her* when she left the triclinium, Caninus. Why was that? Was it to speak to her? Did you speak to her?'

'No, *Vir Spectabilis*. Outside the triclinium, I only once glimpsed her as she ran out of the far end of the corridor and into the night. After that, I never saw her again: it was the night of the new moon, and very dark.'

'Hecate's moon,' Civilis murmured, adding quickly, 'or so the pagans call it. And when you left Corinium, she still hadn't been found?' He said this to Januarius, leaning across Adventus as he did so.

'No, *Vir Spectabilis*, but that was two days ago, so I think it highly likely that she has been captured by now,' Januarius replied.

'And if she hasn't, what then? Without her, we'll never know for sure what happened in that triclinium... Well, will we?' Civilis demanded, frowning at Adventus and Januarius, the exasperation showing in his voice.

'We were – we are – doing everything in our power to find her, *Vir Spectabilis*. Believe me, she will be found,' Adventus assured him.

Civilis sighed. 'Very well. Let us move on. Caninus, these three mosaic workers who you say were present when you found the first figurine – your statement does not give their names.'

Adventus cleared his throat. 'We have the names of two of them now, *Vir Spectabilis*. I am confident they are being interrogated even as we speak.'

'Very good. You will inform me if their testimonies cast doubt on the accuracy of Caninus's statement?'

'Of course, *Vir Spectabilis*.'

'Are you a Christian, Caninus – or do you believe in the old gods?'

The tone was again so neutral that Canio couldn't tell where Civilis stood. Surely he was a Christian? And yet there were still men in high office who…

He decided to play it safe. 'Christian, of course, *Vir Spectabilis*. How could I not be when Christianity is the religion of our sacred emperors?'

Januarius gave a grunt of what, in another context, might have been taken for amusement.

Civilis nodded, his face inscrutable. 'And you believe that the only reason Sabinus wanted the pagan idol was to destroy it?'

'I do, *Vir Spectabilis*.' Canio had no intention of telling Civilis – or anyone else – that the reason Sabinus had given him for wanting the Hecate figurine was that the *vir spectabilis* himself had ordered him to find it. It had, of course, been a lie, but to repeat it would muddy the waters considerably.

'There are some people – pagans – who believe in the power of certain objects to induce their gods or goddesses to harm their enemies. It has been suggested to me that you may have wished to harm Caristanius Sabinus in revenge for the death of a friend of yours, one Lucius Flavius Antoninus, the previous owner of Villa Censorini. Is there any truth to that suggestion?'

Januarius poisoning the well, Canio thought bitterly. 'None whatsoever, *Vir Spectabilis*. It's absolute nonsense. I had only known Antoninus for little more than a month before he died, and during that time I only met him a few times.'

'And yet you went to Sabinus to plead his case when he was accused of treason. Why was that?' Adventus asked.

So Januarius knew about that too, damn him!

'Well, why did you?' Civilis demanded.

Canio hesitated, but at that critical moment no convincing lie would come, so he was forced to fall back on the truth. 'I did it, *Vir Spectabilis*, because a freedwoman of mine begged me to. Years before, when she was a child at Villa Censorini, she had been treated well by Antoninus and thought she owed him for his kindness. It's as simple as that.' He tried to sound casual.

'And her name, this freedwoman?' Adventus again.

'Does it matter? In any case, she left Villa Canini months ago, and I've no idea where she is now.'

'Why did she leave? Did Antoninus's death upset her?' Adventus persisted.

Canio could see where this road was leading, but he couldn't see a way back. 'It's possible – I really don't know. Is there a man on this earth who really understands why women do the things they do?'

The attempt at humour didn't work. It was Civilis himself who asked the killer question: 'Could she have been the woman who brought the second Hecate figurine to Sabinus?'

'No, I'm sure I would have recognised her.'

'And yet you say you never saw her face, hidden as it was by the hood of her *cucullus*.'

'But I would have recognised her voice.'

'Voices can be disguised,' Adventus mused unhelpfully.

'So, what was this freedwoman's name?' Civilis demanded.

Canio was trapped. He realised that it was inevitable that one of the *agentes* would now check at Villa Canini, and if he gave a false name it would make Civilis suspect that the other things he had said were also lies. 'Her name was Trifosa, but I'm certain she wasn't the woman who brought the second figurine. I would definitely have recognised her, even in that *cucullus*. And besides, she was a devout Christian who wouldn't so much as touch a pagan idol, particularly Hecate of all goddesses. '

Civilis ignored him. 'So now we at least have a name.'

'We do, *Vir Spectabilis*,' Adventus agreed. 'Although Trifosa is not an uncommon name among women of servile rank,' he added reflectively.

But Civilis was not to be deterred. 'Januarius, go back to

Corinium immediately and expedite the search for this woman. With both a name and a motive it should be that much easier.'

'Very good, *Vir Spectabilis*, if that is what you wish. I will leave at once… Shall I take Caninus with me?'

'Oh no. He stays here under lock and key. Who knows, given time to reflect he may remember other interesting things? So we don't want him vanishing like this Trifosa woman.'

Canio could feel anger welling up inside him. Anger that he had ever been dragged into this whole damned mess, and perhaps angrier still with himself for not being quick-witted enough to avoid giving these bastards Trifosa's name. 'With great respect, *Vir Spectabilis*, I am as much a victim of this foul business as Caristanius Sabinus himself was. It is completely unjust that I should be treated as a common criminal and locked in a tiny cell as I was last night. I would respectfully remind you that, as an *honestior*, I do have certain rights under the law.'

'As much a victim as Sabinus?' Civilis repeated incredulously. 'Yet you are still alive and he is dead.' But before Canio could reply, Civilis raised his hand to forestall him and continued, 'Nevertheless, in view of your status, Adventus will arrange more agreeable accommodation for you; although if you attempt to escape, you will indeed be treated like a common criminal. Is that understood?'

Canio managed to stifle his resentment sufficiently to reply, 'Yes, *Vir Spectabilis*. Completely'.

'Good. See to it, Adventus. And when you've done that, report back to me. There are one or two things I want your opinion on before I finalise my thoughts.' And with that, Civilis rose and strode briskly out of the audience chamber, the two secretaries scurrying behind him, clutching sheets of parchment, pens and inkwells.

✻

Accompanied by Januarius, Adventus escorted Canio through the labyrinthine passageways of the *praetorium* until they reached a room high up on the second floor. It had plastered walls and ceiling; the walls being painted with faded scenes from mythology, the ceiling decorated with a repetitive multicoloured geometric pattern.

A few of the mythological scenes appeared to have been partially overpainted in the recent past to conceal their more pagan or immodest aspects. In particular, Diana and her attendant nymphs around the pool had acquired rather elegant *stolas*, which, Canio reflected, must have somewhat hampered their attempts to bathe. Poor old Actaeon, though, was still being turned into a stag, and his hounds were advancing menacingly towards him.

However, the room was certainly an improvement on the cell in which he had spent the previous night, although he noticed that there was no brazier to lessen the November chill, or lamp or candle to keep the darkness of the endless nights at bay.

When he pointed out this deficiency, Adventus shrugged. 'You shouldn't be here for long.'

'Really? How long – a day, a week, a month?' Canio asked irritably.

'It depends on whether the *vir spectabilis* is allowed to handle the matter entirely himself, or whether Viventius wishes to become involved, Viventius being—'

'The Praetorian Prefect of Gaul,' Canio interrupted, annoyed that Adventus should think him so ignorant that he did not know who Viventius was. 'But he's in Treveri – hundreds of miles away across the Oceanus Britannicus – so involving him will take weeks.'

'It can't be helped,' Adventus said blandly.

'And I'm sure Viventius will indeed take a keen interest in this matter,' added Januarius, smiling humourlessly. 'Did you know that, some six years ago, when he was a *quaestor* in Rome, our sacred emperors Valentinianus and Valens both suffered near-fatal attacks of a strange fever? You didn't? Well, at the time, it was whispered that they were the victims of an assassination plot using the powers of black magic, and Viventius was the man appointed to investigate the allegation – which, I understand, he did most zealously. So I'm sure he'll insist on the circumstances surrounding Caristanius Sabinus's death being investigated in exhaustive detail. After all, there are obvious parallels between the sad fate that befell the *vir perfectissimus* at Villa Censorini and the events of six years ago.'

'Parallels? What parallels?' Canio objected. 'Sabinus was killed by Julius Castor's sword, not a fever or black magic.'

'Ah, but what possessed Castor to do such a thing? What madness – what induced madness – took control of his mind?' Januarius asked with the detached air of a rhetorician.

'Greed – disappointed greed. Greed for gold and all the things that it could buy, that's what possessed him. He deluded himself that a little brass idol would make him rich, and when Sabinus shattered that delusion his mind snapped and he went mad. You must have come across that sort of thing at least once in your illustrious career?'

'No doubt my colleague has,' said Adventus impatiently. 'We both have. But I'm sure Viventius will form his own views on the matter once he has studied the statements, plus Civilis's and our own recommendations.'

'So when will Civilis be sending them to Treveri?' Canio asked.

'Later today, probably. Anyway,' Adventus continued, 'you'll be let out once a day, under guard, for meals, et cetera. The meals will be at your own expense, of course.'

'Really? And there was me thinking that I was to be your honoured guest.' Canio didn't even try to keep the sarcasm out of his voice.

Januarius smiled coldly. 'Never that.' The two *agentes* left, the door thudded shut behind them, and as he heard the bolt rasp home into its keep Canio turned and scanned the contents of the room again. It did not take long. There was a single bed with two blankets, one chair and a little table. In one wall there was a small window, its tiny panes of translucent, greenish glass set in grids of rusty iron strips, with a four-pronged spike at the corner of each pane to hold the glass in place. One pane was missing, allowing Canio a clear glimpse of a tiny fraction of the Londinium skyline.

Shortly before dusk, a soldier brought him a bowl of mutton soup, which was already nearly cold. For a bribe of a *siliqua*, the man returned a little later with a pitcher of cheap wine.

Lying on the bed in the rapidly encroaching darkness, Canio asked himself why he put up with treatment that, only a few years before, would have earned his tormentors a good kicking at the very least. Of course, he already knew the answer: in Villa Canini he had too much to lose. He was not unaware of the irony of the situation. He look another swig of the vinegary wine and drifted slowly into an uneasy sleep. And in that sleep he heard the voice of Tulius again.

CHAPTER THIRTEEN

'After the last of the Bagaudae had been crushed – slaughtered by that Pannonian savage, Maximianus – the brute turned his attention to the Germanic tribes. Not for the first time the Alamanni, Burgundi, Heruli and Juthungi had crossed the Rhenus in their thousands and were pillaging eastern Gaul.

'In early April of the following year – thinking back, it must have been at around the same time that I was aboard the Andromeda with Carausius – Maximianus was raised to the rank of Augustus by Diocles. Which, in theory, made him the equal of Diocles, but Diocles was always that dog's master, and the dog knew it and never dared to disobey his owner's whistles and commands.

'Although he never said so, or not that I ever heard tell, after his successful handling of the early months of the Bagaudae rebellion, I think Carausius had hopes of being given a senior position under Maximianus: perhaps legatus legionis of a whole legion at the very least. That being so, it was inevitable that he would have seen the job of ridding the Oceanus Britannicus of Saxon pirates as something of an undeserved demotion.

'And when he was among men he thought he could trust, he said as much. Perhaps too much. He was also contemptuous of Maximianus's handling of the latter stages of the Bagaudae uprising, saying his actions had been those of a fool who only knew how to kill and destroy – which, incidentally, his subsequent conduct in the wars on the Rhenus frontier was to demonstrate only too well.

'However, there were informers everywhere. There always were and always will be. And so Carausius's unwise words got back to Maximianus, which further increased his distrust of a man who had owed his advancement to Carinus, a legitimate emperor whose very name was being chiselled out of inscriptions throughout the empire on the orders of that paranoid usurper Diocles. At first, though, Maximianus hesitated to strike, because Carausius remained popular with the soldiers. But in the summer of that year he saw his chance to destroy him legitimately.

'You remember I said that, under oar power alone, the Saxon and Frankish galleys could usually outrun our liburnae, particularly when the wind was in our faces and we couldn't use our sails? Well, that was when those galleys were carrying little but their crews. But when they were weighed down with loot from their plundering raids on the coastal towns of Britannia and Northern Gaul, or from the capture of a merchant ship at sea, then it was a very different matter. A good liburna, even rowing against a headwind, could catch any laden galley on the high seas, however hard its crew rowed.

'Realising this, Carausius decided his best tactic would be to wait until the Saxons were heading back north-eastwards and then pounce. And very successful it was too, because by midsummer our small fleet of liburnae was intercepting at least one galley a week, sometimes two. If their crews surrendered, we towed the galleys back to Gesoriacum and sold the crews as slaves. And if they didn't surrender, then our men showed no mercy, especially if the fighting had been hard and some of our own men had been wounded or killed. The flaw in this tactic was that we had to wait until the Saxons had raided before we went after them, which wasn't much consolation to their victims – those who survived.

'But that wasn't the worst of it. Maximianus kept Carausius starved of the money he needed to pay and equip his men, probably with a view to causing him fail and thus providing an excuse to dismiss him. So Carausius was forced to keep some of the loot he took from the Saxons – loot that, officially, he should have either given back to the people it was stolen from or handed over to the rationales from the imperial treasury.

'When Maximianus found out what was going on, he saw his chance to strike. I don't think he really gave a damn about the loot not being returned to its rightful owners or the treasury; given the chance, I'm sure he would have kept it for himself.

'No, what really alarmed him was the suspicion that Carausius might be planning a rebellion against him and was amassing a war chest for that purpose. This, given Carausius's popularity with the legionary vexillationes he had commanded during the Bagaudae rebellion, coupled with Maximianus's own unpopularity due to the harsh way he treated his own soldiers, was not an unreasonable suspicion.

'So, Carausius was summoned to Maximianus's headquarters to face trial. But he realised only too well that if he went to Treveri, he would almost certainly never return. He realised too that he now had three stark choices: rebel or flee or die. For a man like Carausius, that was no choice at all.

'He moved fast – so fast that, afterwards, people suspected that he really had been planning rebellion for some time. And perhaps he had, or perhaps it was simply that a confrontation with Maximianus was something he knew might well happen one day, and so he had made contingency plans. Plans that might otherwise never have been carried out if Maximianus hadn't tried to destroy him.

'That said, Carausius must previously have sounded out their commanders because, immediately his refusal to go to Treveri became known, many of the vexillationes he'd led during the Bagaudae rebellion pledged their loyalty to him. That loyalty was, as is always the way, increased by the prospect of substantial donatives, at least some of which were to be paid out of the plunder recovered from the Saxons. Most of those vexillationes were *only a couple of centuries strong, but the tribune commanding the major part of Legio XXX Ulpia Victrix, which was based at Castra Vetera on the Lower Rhenus, defected to our side, bringing nearly three thousand men with him.*

'And as well as soldiers from the regular legions, Carausius already had the use of several units of Frisian cavalry, whose original mission was to harry any Saxon pirates who might come ashore to raid the coastal towns of Gaul.

'Carausius also quickly recruited an irregular force of Frankish mercenaries from beyond the borders of Gallia Belgica. Those brave lads would have cut the throats of their own grandmothers if you'd paid them to do it – or maybe they'd have done it for free, just for the fun of it.

'So it was that Carausius, almost without bloodshed (there were a few junior officers who feared Maximianus more than him and tried to resist), declared himself emperor and took possession of the entire northern coastal region of the Gallic provinces – all the way from the many mouths of the Rhenus in the east to the furthest shores bordering the Oceanus Britannicus in the west. And because all Maximianus's forces were fully committed to fighting the Germanic tribes on the Rhenus frontier, there was nothing he could do immediately – except fly into such a terrible rage that, for days afterwards, nobody dared approach him for fear of their life.

'As is always the way with a new emperor, Carausius wanted to issue coins with his name and portrait on – tangible objects that would show the whole world who he was and that he was now the power in the land. So he set up a mint in the city of Rotomagus on the River Seine, and within a month it had started producing gold and copper coins.

'The gold coins were well made. They were intended to be given as donatives – bribes, some might call them – to the senior officers of Carausius's little army, to ensure their continued loyalty, and they were struck from dies cut by the only skilful*

die-cutter he could find. There were no silver ones: there must have been a reason for that, but if I ever knew what it was, I've long forgotten. And the copper coins were fairly crude because he had to use men who had never cut coin dies before in their lives, only seal stones for finger rings and the like. Carausius wasn't too happy with them, but they had to serve for the time being.

'Maximianus may have been temporarily tied down fighting on the Rhenus frontier, but Carausius knew that it was only a matter of time before he would march north and try to destroy him. Knew too that, when the time came, there was a very real danger of being trapped between the Oceanus Britannicus to the north and Maximianus's legions advancing from the south.

'However, if he were to add Britannia to his little empire, then with the control of the seas his fleet of liburnae gave him his position would be strengthened immensely. The great unknown was this: would the governors and legions of the two provinces – Britannia was only divided into two in those days – welcome him as a saviour or oppose him as a usurper? Carausius had to know. So, a hand-picked team of men, including myself, was sent across the Oceanus Britannicus on a dangerous diplomatic mission.'

✽

Canio was suddenly awake and staring into the darkness, the memory of Tulius's words so vivid that they might have been whispered in his ear moments before. And as he lay there, utterly still, the conviction grew that there *was* someone else in the room – someone whose presence had woken him.

He listened intently, but could detect nothing except the sound of his own breathing and rapid heartbeats and the cold breeze sighing through the missing window pane. Time passed, and his eyes adjusted gradually to the small amount of starlight that was filtering through the tiny window, until the room at last seemed to be in something close to twilight. Cautiously, he swung himself out of bed and searched, but there was nobody there. He tried the door. It was still bolted from the outside. If somebody really had been there, inside the room, they were now long gone.

CHAPTER FOURTEEN

10th – 16th November

The next seven days passed slowly, as all the while the city sank deeper into winter. From a guard, Canio learned that Januarius had, as ordered, set off for Corinium on the afternoon following his cross-examination by Civilis. The *agens* had taken Natalis with him; it seemed Civilis had concluded that the young man had nothing of relevance to add to his statement. He had also thought him a fool, an opinion with which Canio would not have been inclined to disagree.

Canio also learned that, at around the same time, a dispatch rider had been sent on the long journey to Treveri, carrying copies of his and Natalis's statements, together with covering letters from Civilis and Adventus. It was estimated that it would take the man at least seven and a half days to reach Treveri, using relays of horses from the *cursus publicus* to cover fifty miles and more each day. So, allowing for, say, two days spent at Treveri, the man would not return to Londinium until five days before the kalends of December at the earliest – seventeen long days away.

As for Praetorian Prefect Viventius, the great man who had apparently conducted a previous investigation into an attempt to kill the emperors using black magic, what would his reaction be? Particularly if Januarius's own opinions and prejudices had found their way into the covering letters. It was a disquieting thought. And the worst of it was that there was absolutely nothing Canio could do but wait.

Each day he was allowed out to wander around the city for a short time, although always in the company of two soldiers, different men every day, all seemingly under orders to say as little as possible to the prisoner, even when he bought them food and wine in one of the city's numerous *tabernae* so that he would not have to have to eat alone.

One particular *taberna* was a long, low building sited near the banks of a little river that flowed down from the north towards its confluence with the Tamesis, some two hundred yards further on. The interior was a sort of mini basilica, with a central nave separated from its side aisles by rows of rounded stone columns. On a previous visit to the city Canio had learned something of its history.

Once a Mithraeum, a temple of Mithras, it had been converted some fifty years ago into a temple to Bacchus, before the worship of that god too had been suppressed. Its present owner, however – either out of piety or ironic wit (probably, Canio guessed, the latter) – had managed to retain a small marble statuary group depicting Bacchus, old Silenus (on a donkey), a satyr, a maenad and a somewhat canine-looking panther.

This little group rested on a plinth in the apse at the far end of the *taberna*. The inscription carved into its base – '*HOMINIBUS BAGIS BITAM*' (*did the sculptor have some grudge against Vs?* Canio wondered) – had originally been intended to convey the message that it was Bacchus, as saviour of the dead, who gave life to wandering men. Canio was pretty sure, however, that most of its current onlookers interpreted the words to mean that it was the liquid product of the vine itself that had the same reviving effect on weary travellers.

And in Londinium, by far the most cosmopolitan of the cities of Britannia, there were many wandering men: visitors from distant parts of the empire, brought to the city by trade or imperial duties.

Then back out onto the cheerless streets. It had been late spring when Canio last visited Londinium, and what had been picturesque in May was squalid in November.

The basilica–forum complex itself was only a shadow of what had, in times past, been the beating heart of the civic and commercial life of the city. Once, it had been the largest of its kind north of the Alps, or so Canio had been told. And even now, despite its pervasive air of slow decay, it was an impressive place, with the vast paved (and puddled) forum surrounded on three sides by under-used offices and shops. On its fourth side stood the great basilica hall itself, where the city fathers still sat occasionally to bemoan their fate as unpaid and unloved tax collectors.

✽

On the last day before Januarius returned – by Canio's reckoning it was the sixteenth before the kalends of December – he was allowed to wander down to the waterfront. Once through the gateway in the high riverside wall, which had been built to complete the defensive circuit of the city, he sat on an upturned barrel and drank a beaker of red wine that, he was informed, had arrived only the previous day from faraway Burdigala. It was the best he had tasted since his arrival in Londinium, and the dockside *taberna* owner hinted that it was his contacts with the various ships' captains that enabled him to get a share of the best of everything, not just wine, before it was spirited away to various rich men's villas in the surrounding countryside and beyond.

As he sipped the wine – it was too good to swallow quickly – Canio watched the comings and goings of the various ships and the activities of the dockside labourers.

There was only one ship, moored out in the middle of the Tamesis, that looked anything like a proper seagoing vessel. All the others were smallish, wide-beamed, shallow-draught sailing boats, the sort that rarely ventured beyond river and estuary waters. The crews of two such vessels were engaged in transferring sacks of grain from the dockside to the large ship, which was swaying gently with the current, out in the deeper water of mid-river.

There was always something happening on the dockside, and Canio would have stayed longer, despite the cold east wind that came whistling up the river all the way from the Oceanus Germanicus. However, it seemed that his two guards of the day had other duties elsewhere – or perhaps they simply resented the fact that Canio, irritated by their unwillingness to converse, had not shared the good wine with them?

❖

In the evening Januarius returned from Corinium, and that night, for the first time since the *agens* had left, Canio heard the voice of Tulius again, this time telling the story of the delegation sent to Britannia to discover how much support existed in the island for Carausius's rebellion.

CHAPTER FIFTEEN

Night of 16th – 17th November

'*A party of about two dozen officers, including Allectus, all in civilian clothes, crossed the Oceanus Britannicus. They landed at the port of Noviomagus Regnorum, and from there travelled in small groups around Britannia. They talked to as many people as they could in the time available, discreetly gauging their reactions to Carausius's rebellion.*

'*Of course, the men who really mattered were the governors of the two provinces: Britannia Superior, whose capital was Londinium; and Britannia Inferior, whose provincial capital was the northern city of Eboracum. And perhaps even more important than the governors were the commanders – the* legati legionum *– of the two legions stationed in Britannia. Those legions were the Second Augusta, stationed at Isca in the south-east corner of Cambria, and the Twentieth Valeria Victrix, stationed at Deva. Deva was also on the borders of Cambria, but many miles to the north of Isca.*

'*Allectus and several other officers went to Isca. Because a strong south-westerly wind was preventing them from sailing further westwards, they decided to take the land route. They travelled northwards, passed through the cities of Calleva Atrebatum and Corinium, and continued on until they reached Glevum on the River Sabrina. At Glevum, they crossed the Sabrina, and then turned south and travelled down the highway*

83

that ran beside the ever-widening Sabrina estuary until they came to the city of Venta Silurum. From there, the highway ran west for another ten miles to the great legionary fortress of Isca, home of the Second Augusta.

'We had among us a tribune whose name, as best I can recall it, was Junius Marcellus. This Marcellus had been chosen by Carausius because he and the legatus legionis of the Second Augusta, whose name was Neratius Secundus, had once served together in the Twenty-Second Primigenia at Moguntiacum on the Upper Rhenus.

'Neratius Secundus, of course, knew of Carausius's rebellion, but he was understandably wary at first. Nevertheless, he had known Carinus and had liked the man – despite the lies put about after his death, as he was no seducer of other men's wives – and he owed his position as legatus legionis to him. And he certainly had no love for Diocles, who he regarded as the real usurper. And Carausius was Carinus's man: Secundus had met him several times during the wars against the Picts and had been impressed by his military skill.

'Also, Neratius Secundus was as aware as everyone else that only some thirteen years had passed since the Gallic Empire created by Postumus – which had ruled all of Britannia, Gaul and Hispania – had come to an end. This was the same Gallic Empire that would probably still have been in existence in Carausius's day, if Postumus hadn't been murdered by a bunch of malcontent soldiers after the siege of Moguntiacum, simply because he wouldn't let them sack that city. So what was to stop Carausius creating a similar empire – and rewarding those frontrunners who had come over to his side early? That decided Secundus: he took an oath to support Carausius.

'But the gods are ever capricious, and what man can ever be certain of what the future will bring? In those early days, after Carausius had seized the coastal lands of Northern Gaul, Diocles was just another rebel general who had killed the legitimate emperor – which Carinus certainly was – and then had himself declared emperor by his own troops.

'And the chronicles of the previous half-century were littered with such men – soldiers who had seized power and then, after a year or two, or sometimes much less, had perished violently, leaving little behind them but the corpses and chaos their reckless ambition had created.

'So why should anyone have believed that Diocles would fare differently? But it seems that the Parcae, or whoever or whatever it is that control these things, had decided he was to turn out more cunning – or ruthless or just plain lucky – than those who had gone before.

'When the other members of the group met up again they learned that the legatus legionis of the Twentieth Valeria Victrix had also pledged loyalty to Carausius. The governor of Britannia Superior, though, was a sly old bastard called Martiannius Quietus, whose grandfather had also been governor many years before. He wouldn't say yes or no, and it soon became obvious that he was waiting to see how things worked out on the other side of the Oceanus Britannicus before committing himself. However, it was thought that he wouldn't make trouble if Carausius invaded, but neither could he be trusted any further than the length of a gnat's private parts.

'As for the men who went north to Eboracum, they met a sad, sad fate. When they tried to persuade the governor of Britannia Inferior – a man whose name I have long forgotten – to swear loyalty to Carausius, he had them arrested, charged with treason and beheaded. I suppose the cur thought he was demonstrating his loyalty to Diocles, and he must have hoped to be rewarded for it.

'But not so very long afterwards, when he heard that Carausius had actually landed unopposed, he realised that he had backed the wrong chariot in the race. So, he burned all incriminating papers and fled south with his entire household, down to the port of Petuaria on the River Abus. There he commandeered a ship and sailed down the estuary and out into the Oceanus Germanicus. And as far as I know, he was never seen or heard of again in the land of the living.

'As we journeyed back from Isca, Allectus took the opportunity to visit his father's villa, the villa that he always believed would be his own one day. And no doubt it would have been, if the Furies hadn't turned their faces against him. Those cruel goddesses – who some call the Eumenides – the Kindly Ones – are the immortals who take vengeance upon those who they believe, rightly or wrongly, to be responsible for the deaths of their own kinsfolk.'

CHAPTER SIXTEEN

17th November

Next morning, two guards – always two different ones – came earlier than usual to Canio's room and escorted him to Adventus's office, where he found Januarius sitting alone behind the imposing desk. He did not invite Canio to sit down, but he did so anyway.

'So did you find Trifosa?' Canio asked, knowing what the answer would be.

It gave him a certain pleasure to read the ill-suppressed irritation on Januarius's face as he had to admit, 'No, they haven't located that woman yet, but be assured they will.'

'You're chasing smoke. I told you it wasn't Trifosa in the triclinium of Villa Censorini that night. I'm absolutely certain of that.'

'So you say, but then you would, wouldn't you? After all, she was your whore.'

'She was my woman. Nobody's whore,' Canio said quietly.

'Not even Flavius Antoninus's?'

'No, of course not. After seven years away in the army, Antoninus only returned home little more than a month before he... died.' Just in time, Canio stopped himself from saying, *'was murdered'*.

'And before that, at Villa Censorini? I'm told they were very close when they both lived there.'

'They were only children then. Childhood friends, nothing more.'

'That wasn't what I was told.'

'Who by?'

'By several people actually, both at Villa Censorini and, interestingly enough, at your so-called "Villa Canini". It seems that the Trifosa woman confided quite a few things to her maid, one Aniceta.'

'Really? So what exactly did Aniceta tell you?'

'Among other things, that your Trifosa claimed Caristanius Sabinus murdered Flavius Antoninus, just as surely as if he had stabbed the man himself. And furthermore, that although justice did not seem to exist in this world, divine retribution would surely pursue him into the next.'

'So? Trifosa is a Christian. Obviously, she meant that, after death, Sabinus would suffer the judgement and punishment of her God.' Too late, he forgot to say, '*our God*', although Januarius did not appear to notice.

'Ah, but who would bring about that death? You and she together, perhaps?'

'That's nonsense. Trifosa fled on the evening of Antoninus's funeral, way back in July, and neither I nor anyone else at Villa Canini has seen her since.'

'So you say. But to me, it all makes sense. You both hated Sabinus, so you conceived a fiendish plot to use the powers of that heathen idol to destroy him.'

'But as I told you, Trifosa is a fellow Christian. She wouldn't even believe in the existence of Hecate, let alone that a little lump of brass could possess magical powers.'

'Being a Christian wouldn't prevent her from believing in both. Plenty of others do.'

'Really – including yourself?' The suggestion was mischievous, but even as he spoke, Canio started wondering, *If—*

'Yes, as it happens.'

Canio feigned astonishment. 'And there was me thinking that you were a devout Christian.'

'I am; of course I am! But I also believe in the existence of the powers of darkness that stalk this earth – powers that only Our Saviour can guard and protect us against. Do you not understand that?' Januarius seemed genuinely puzzled that Canio should see a conflict between the two beliefs.

'So what else did you learn from Aniceta?'

'Among other things, that Trifosa told her you think Christianity is nonsense, and that should anyone wish to know if there is life after death, they should ask the worms... Did you really say that?'

'Certainly not. You must have misheard.'

'Oh, I don't think so. Between the screams, she was quite coherent.'

There was a long silence before Canio asked, 'You tortured her?' With an effort he kept his voice low and toneless.

'Of course. It was quite legal. In my position I have authorisation to extract the truth from persons of the *humiliores* class by whatever means I see fit. And I'm sure she'll recover in a few days: I don't think I broke any bones.'

'That was good of you. Did you torture anyone else at Villa Canini?'

'It wasn't necessary. After the Aniceta woman, everyone sang like larks.'

'But nobody knew where Trifosa was?'

'It seems not.'

'So what else did you learn?'

'That you hated Julius Castor, really hated the man, and that before you left on your search – your sham search, I should say – for that Hecate figurine, you left him a written message saying that if he harmed any of your servants, you would personally hack off his head and stick it on top of the longest pole you could find.'

'I don't recall doing anything of the kind.'

'Do you not? How strange.' And before Canio could reply, Januarius continued, 'In your villa, in one of the upper-floor rooms, I came across what appeared to be a Christian shrine, complete with an altar and a small hinged triptych. On the central panel of this triptych was the nimbussed head of Christus, flanked by two praying figures – *orantes* – a man and a woman. I assume the woman was Trifosa, but who was the man? Was it you or was it her lover, Flavius Antoninus?'

'How many times must I tell you? Antoninus was never her lover.'

'So the man must have been you then?'

'Of course it was. Who else?' It wasn't, but if Januarius wanted to think that…

'Who indeed?' Januarius stood, went to the door and called in the two guards who had been waiting outside. Turning back to Canio, he said, 'It so happens that I have other duties to perform today, but tomorrow there are a couple of places in this city that may be of interest to you.' And with a sweep of his right arm he signalled to the guards to take Canio away.

*

Back in his room, Canio didn't even bother to speculate what those "couple of places" might be. He couldn't get out of his mind the casual way in which Januarius had mentioned torturing Aniceta. He wondered what obscene things the bastard had done to the poor girl's body to make her break Trifosa's confidences and so burden her with a guilt that would probably haunt her long after the physical pain had gone. And he had been powerless to prevent it, even if he had known it was going to happen – which made it even worse.

The more he thought about it, the angrier he became, until

the rage, and perhaps the guilt too, boiled over at last. Snatching up the pottery water jug from the little table, he hurled it against the wall with such force that it shattered into innumerable tiny shards. The crash made the guards come running.

'Go away, Hades damn you!' he roared at them.

And taking one look at his furious face they hesitated, then went.

CHAPTER SEVENTEEN

Night of 17th – 18th November

Canio brooded all day, his animosity towards Januarius and his frustration at his own helplessness to protect the people – his people – at Villa Canini not lessening with the passing hours. Even after nightfall sleep was slow to come, but at last it did, and with it came the now-familiar voice of Tulius.

✻

'When Carausius was as assured – or as assured as a man could ever be in this uncertain world – of the acquiescence of most of the people who mattered, he crossed the Fretum Gallicum to Dubris and from there made straight for Londinium. There he confronted the governor, Martiannius Quietus, and demanded a public vow of loyalty. He didn't get it: Quietus wriggled and squirmed, but he had extensive estates in southern Gaul that he feared would be confiscated if he were to support Carausius.

'So Carausius, in a calculated display of generosity, let him and his household take ship for the continent. He even gave Quietus a letter of safe conduct through his territories in Northern Gaul. Then he appointed his own governor, a man called Junius Severus. In those early triumphant days perhaps he really did believe that he could catch more flies with honey than vinegar.

That merciful attitude didn't last; as men become accustomed to absolute power it rarely does.

'Now installed at Londinium, in what had been Martiannius Quietus's opulent townhouse, he set about consolidating his position. He had three main priorities.

Firstly, to ensure that the taxes from both provinces of Britannia all flowed into the imperial treasury – his imperial treasury – there in Londinium.

Secondly, to establish a mint to produce far more and far better coins than the temporary affair at Rotomagus had ever managed to do.

And thirdly – but perhaps most importantly – he wanted to establish a chain of forts around the south-east coast of Britannia, by both restoring existing ones and filling in the gaps between them with completely new ones. Officially, this was to protect the coastal towns against Saxon raiders, which it did. However, the real reason was to form a deterrent against any attempt by Maximianus to invade across the Fretum Gallicum.

'The machinery of government kept working as though hardly anything had changed, so the taxes kept rolling in. The only difference was that now they didn't have to be sent on to Treveri, which pleased everyone, except Maximianus and Diocles. And with that money, Carausius could afford donatives for the two legions at Isca and Deva – bribes that kept them sweet.

'I remember how impatient he was to see those thousands upon thousands of shiny new coins. Coins with his face and name on each and every one. Coins that would be sent to every corner of the land to show one and all that he was their emperor now. So, at the urging of his wife, Allecta, he put her brother in charge of setting up a mint in Londinium – the first in all Britannia.

'Allectus sent out agents to scour the cities and towns for skilled die-cutters, men who could engrave sealstones and the like, and he brought them to Londinium. Once there, he put them to work cutting the dies for Carausius's coins – coins which were the best that had been seen in Britannia for many a long year. There hadn't been any real silver coins around for decades before Carausius came to power; the closest to silver that most people had ever seen were silver-washed copper antoniniani, and precious few of those.

'The silver coins – denarii they were called in those days – were minted in their hundreds of thousands, and were of hundreds of different designs. One showed Carausius being welcomed by Britannia, and around their standing figures ran the legend "EXPECTATE VENI" – meaning "Come, long-awaited one." That's a quotation from Virgil's Aeneid; Allecta suggested it.

'On some of the coins, copper as well as silver, she had the die-cutters put the letters "RSR" where the mintmark usually is on today's coins. I don't suppose most people knew what that meant, but educated people in Britannia – the people who Carausius wanted to impress – they knew. It stood for "REDEUNT SATURNIA REGNA" – meaning "Saturn's kingdom has returned." And as they also knew, the reign of Saturn was supposed to have been a golden age long, long ago. It was another quotation from Virgil, taken from his fourth Eclogue, if I remember rightly, and it was another of Allecta's ideas. It seems that she was determined to portray the man she had married as someone more sophisticated than the rough brute of an uneducated soldier that the portraits on some of his early coins had made him appear to be.

'Nor did he forget the soldiers who had backed him. He struck a whole series of copper antoniniani in honour of the nine legions that, at least in part, had come over to his side. Each coin had the name of the legion and its emblem on the reverse: the Second Augusta and its capricorn, the Twentieth Valeria Victrix and its boar, and so on. They were handed out with the pay and went down well with the soldiers.

'Before Carausius's time there were already a few forts scattered along what was to become known as the "Saxon

Shore", forts such as Gariannonum, but they were mostly on the east coast, facing the Oceanus Germanicus. What Carausius really needed were fortifications on the south-east coast, ready to repulse any invasion by Maximianus from across the Fretum Gallicum or the Oceanus Britannicus. And if they happened to dissuade a few Saxon or Frankish pirates from trying their luck, then so much the better.

'Those Saxon Shore forts were built to last forever, with massive, towering stone walls that were ten feet thick at the base. Also, they had rounded projecting bastions, from the tops of which archers and ballistae men could shoot down any attacker.

'I actually saw some of them being built. That was over fifty years ago, but I can still see them in my mind's eye as if it were yesterday. Rutupiae, Dubris, Portus Lemanis, Anderitum and Portus Ardaoni – all places where Carausius thought Maximianus might try to land if he sailed from Gesoriacum or somewhere further west on the coast of Gaul.

'Of course, they weren't all finished when Carausius was... when Carausius died. But Allectus took over and finished most of them. I've heard that they're still standing to this day, just as we left them – still guarding the shores of Britannia. That's an achievement to be proud of, don't you think?'

CHAPTER EIGHTEEN

18th November

Next morning it was long after sunrise when Januarius again sent for Canio. With two guards following a short distance behind, the *agens* led him out through a door on the north side of the *praetorium* and into a street that ran eastwards, parallel with the Tamesis, which flowed some two hundred yards away, unseen behind the riverside wall.

For half a mile they walked along a wide street, bordered on both sides by substantial houses set behind high walls. From what he had gleaned from previous visits to the city, Canio was aware that some of those houses belonged to prosperous merchants, men with continental connections, while others were the town houses of wealthy men whose villas and estates were scattered for many miles across the surrounding countryside.

As they neared the rising ground on the eastern edge of the city, Canio saw a vast, basilica-like building, fully three hundred feet long by half as much wide. Although fairly newly built – Canio was certain that he had never noticed it before – much of the stonework and the once-red clay roof tiles had a weathered appearance.

Januarius stopped and turned to Canio. 'Behold the basilica church of Saint Paul! – an amazing sight, don't you think?' And before Canio could reply, the *agens* continued, 'It was built in only a year and a half by the labours of many willing hands, using materials salvaged from the demolition of a dozen or more pagan temples. Evil transmuted into good, you might say – a fitting symbol for this age of Christian emperors in which we are now living. Come, let me show you the interior. And don't look worried – there's nothing in there for a good Christian like yourself to fear.'

Remembering Aniceta, Canio found it easy not to laugh at the witticism.

The double doors – set in a great stone archway – stood wide open, and well before he reached them Canio became aware of the sound of chanting coming from the interior. The chanting swelled ever louder, until as he paused under the archway, he saw what must have been at least two hundred people, both men and women, inside the basilica. They stood in the cavernous nave, with their arms uplifted to chin height, hands outstretched and palms uppermost, as they chanted what even Canio recognised to be a Christian hymn.

These *orantes* were all facing the altar, which was set in an apse at the far end of the nave, below a stone canopy supported by four tall stone columns. In front of the altar, standing on a raised dais, was a small man dressed in what appeared from a distance to be a richly embroidered cloak that came down almost to his feet. In the dimness of the two side aisles, separated from the nave by two rows of massive stone columns, Canio could make out more *orantes*.

Shafts of weak winter sunlight were filtering in through the rows of clerestory windows set high up in the walls of the nave, allowing Canio to see that the inside walls were decorated with veneers of black and multi-coloured marble. He suddenly became aware that Januarius was speaking.

'Don't you wish to join the congregation, Caninus, devout Christian that you claim to be?'

'No, not just at the moment,' Canio replied.

'No? I am surprised. They follow the Nicene Creed here, of course, so you would be among friends… or do you perhaps follow the teachings of the heretic Arius and believe that the Son is inherently inferior to the Father?'

'I follow the Nicene Creed, of course. What is good enough for our sacred Emperor Valentinianus is certainly good enough for me,' Canio added, keeping his voice neutral while inwardly congratulating himself on actually remembered that it was his brother, Valens, the emperor in the East, who was supposed to favour Arianism.

Unfortunately, this did not appear to satisfy Januarius. 'You have been baptised into the church, haven't you?'

'Not yet. I intend to follow the example of the illustrious Constantinus Maximus, of blessed memory, and wait until my last day on earth is near before receiving the sacred rite of baptism. If it was good enough for him—'

'It's good enough for you,' the *agens* interrupted sarcastically. 'You can, of course, recite the Nicene Creed?'

'Of course – at the appropriate time.'

'But when could be more appropriate than now, in this most holy of places?'

Canio tried desperately to remember the words that Trifosa used to murmur when she thought he was asleep. 'I believe in one God...' he began hesitantly.

And then, by the weirdest of coincidences, at a signal from the small man standing before the altar, bathed in the yellow light from an array of oil lamps, the whole congregation began to chant: '*We believe in one God, the Father Almighty, Maker of all things visible and invisible...*'

Hardly able to believe his luck, Canio seized the moment and joined in loudly, word for word, '*And in one Lord Jesus Christ, the Son of God, begotten of the Father, the only-begotten; that is, of the essence of the father, God of God, Light of Light...*' And if he was fractionally behind most of the congregation the gap was inaudible because a substantial minority of the *orantes* also appeared to require a prompt.

The recital ended, and Januarius shook his head slowly in apparent disbelief. 'Even here, in this holy place, the Evil One looks after his own. Even here...' he murmured.

But Canio wasn't listening. Perhaps curious to discover the source of the (possibly remembered?) voice she had heard behind her, a young woman at the back of the congregation had turned around and was looking straight at him. She wore a long *cucullus* that left only her face and a fringe of hair visible, but he would have known those forget-me-not-blue eyes anywhere. It was Trifosa. If she was startled to see him there, of all places, nothing in her face betrayed it. But he saw her lips part slightly as if she were about to speak. Had Januarius noticed?

Realising the danger, Canio turned abruptly and walked back out of the doorway, around which a cold breeze was whistling, and started back along the way they had come. He blew noisily into his cupped hands.

'I'll grant you it's a very impressive piece of architecture, and I feel all the better for seeing it, but I'm freezing to death standing here,' he called back to Januarius. 'And didn't you say there was another place in this city that may be of interest to me?' He didn't wait for a reply, but kept walking briskly away, fearful that Trifosa might call out his name at any moment.

Fifteen yards, twenty yards – and then he heard the sound of hurrying feet; he glanced behind him to see Januarius and the two guards.

'What's the matter, Caninus? Afraid that a thunderbolt from heaven might strike you if you lingered too long in there?' Januarius mocked. Evidently he still did not believe Canio's claim to be a good Christian.

'I can't think of any reason why it should hit me, unless, my brave torturer of helpless women,' Canio mused as he stared across the rooftops of the city into the far distance, 'the thunderbolt might not have been aimed at me, but at someone standing close to me... Someone like yourself, perhaps?'

There was a dead silence, then a suppressed snigger came from one of the soldiers, and Canio turned to see the *agens'* face darkening with anger.

✻

In near silence they walked for over a mile, with Januarius leading, past the great houses and on through the bustling city streets, until they came at last to the old amphitheatre, which stood close to the spot where the fort had once dominated the north-west corner of the city. The fort was long gone, dismantled a century or more before – or so Canio had once been told – its north and west walls incorporated into the defensive perimeter walls of the city.

The amphitheatre's high, curved, rain-and-time-darkened outer walls were lichen blotched, and here and there a still-green fern grew out of a joint between the massive stones. Januarius paused outside the main eastern entrance and beckoned to Canio.

Puzzled, Canio followed the *agens* into the wide entrance passageway until the man halted opposite two side chambers, one on the right and one on the left, both dark, dank and smelling of urine. 'Did you know that these once held altars to your pagan gods?'

'*My* pagan gods? They're not my gods and never were.'

'That one,' continued Januarius, ignoring Canio's protest, 'was dedicated to Mercury, patron of thieves and other criminals, while the one over there contained an altar to Nemesis the avenger, punisher of sinners. Now tell me, Caninus, which one would you wish to sacrifice to? Whose protection would you seek on your last day on earth?'

'Neither. I believe in the existence of neither of them.'

'Hecate then?'

Canio gave an exaggerated sigh. 'Did you bring me here for a reason, or do you just enjoy asking stupid questions?'

'Oh yes, Caninus, I have a reason. Come.'

So Canio followed the *agens* past the side chambers and out onto the dirty sand of the large, oval arena. Turning through a full circle, he saw all around him – their continuity broken only by other entrances to the north, south and west – tier upon tier of wooden benches rising up to meet the encircling outer wall. Their wood was dark and sodden from the November rain, and in places was green with algae.

'So what is it that I'm supposed to see?' Canio asked, stretching out his arms as if to embrace the whole panorama.

'That's right, Caninus, take a good look. Because the next time you are in this place, or one much like it, you will have little time to do so.'

Canio half-guessed what was coming next, but said nothing.

'As you may know, gladiatorial contests and wild-beast hunts are rarely staged here now. A combination of rising Christian sentiment and – more particularly, I suspect – the sheer expense of such entertainments have seen to that. However, it is still used, and used quite regularly, for the execution of criminals. So when, Caninus, you are found guilty of bringing about the death of Caristanius Sabinus by black magic, it is here that you will be executed. Or possibly in Treveri,' the agens added, 'depending upon our sacred emperor Valentinianus's decision on the matter.

'It might be a beheading by the sword, but I strongly suspect that the heinousness of your crime will call for something more painful and prolonged. The blessed Constantinus Maximus forbade crucifixion, in deference to the memory of Our Lord's earthly torment, so I expect that burning at the stake will be considered appropriate in your case. The crowds always enjoy a good burning; they last so much longer than a mere beheading. Have you ever seen one, a burning at the stake?'

'I saw one once,' Canio confirmed quietly, so quietly that the two guards loitering beside the eastern entrance could not hear. 'A woman it was: my foster mother, my dead mother's half-sister. I was twelve years old at the time, and I did nothing to save her. But some years later, to try to rid myself of the guilt, I went back to the city where it happened – a city in a land far from here. There, I sought out the man who had tied her to the stake, got him drunk and lured him to a lonely place far beyond the city walls. I lured him with the promise that a wanton young woman called Marcia was waiting for him there. But there was no woman, only Nemesis.

'I tied him to a tree, took a sharp knife, slit open his belly and left him to die screaming in agony, just as my foster mother had screamed in the flames. Sometimes, in the dark of the night, I can still hear her screams. So to answer your original question, *agens* of the third grade, perhaps I would sacrifice to Nemesis. They say she wreaks her vengeance as she will, whether you believe in her or not.'

The story was a lie: he had never seen the face of Marcia's executioner, hidden as it was by a hood, and when he returned, years later, and made covert enquiries, he was told that the man it had probably been had since died. But he wanted to intimidate Januarius, to make him realise that he was a man who wouldn't hesitate to take vengeance upon anyone who harmed people he cared for. His usually docile conscience was still troubling him over Aniceta.

He had stared at Januarius as he spoke, and for a moment he saw what he thought was fear in the man's eyes. But the moment passed, as well it might with Canio being unarmed and the two guards only yards away.

Nevertheless, the *agens* stepped back several paces before asking, 'So what was the crime for which she was burned, that woman, your aunt? Witchcraft, sorcery… casting spells, perhaps?'

That's nearer the truth than you will ever know, thought Canio, but he had already said more than he had intended. 'No, nothing like that. She caught something nasty from one of her clients, so she cut off his private parts and he bled to death. Actually, now I come to think of it, he was an *agens* too.'

Januarius gave him a sour look. 'Next time you're standing here, Caninus, I can assure you that making offensive jokes will be the last thing on your mind. Before this year has ended you'll be nothing but ashes, blackened bones and a few greasy stains on the sand.'

While they had been talking, Canio had been slowly moving towards the western end of the arena, with Januarius following. Then, when he was confident that the guards were completely out of earshot, he said softly, 'But if, as you seem to suspect, I really do have the power to command Hecate to destroy a man as important as the *praeses* of a province, think how much easier it would be to use that power to make a mere nobody like an *agens* of the third grade vanish from the face of the earth.' And he gave Januarius his bleakest smile.

Januarius stared back at him, and in that stare Canio saw both astonishment and, again, a flicker of fear. But the *agens* recovered quickly; moments later the fear had gone, replaced by a look of triumph. 'So you admit it – you did invoke Hecate to kill Caristanius Sabinus!'

'I admit nothing. I've told both you and the whole world, in writing, how Sabinus came to die. Any other explanation comes solely from your fevered imagination, nowhere else.'

'Oh no, Caninus, it's too late for denial. Whatever faint doubts I may have harboured before have gone. I'm now certain that you are truly a creature of the Evil One – a creature that I have within my power to destroy, and destroy you I will. Guards!' Januarius shouted, startling the two men lounging in casual conversation beside the eastern entrance. 'Take this man back to his room and see that he's locked securely inside.'

'Aren't you coming with me?' Canio asked sarcastically. 'I've so enjoyed our little conversations today.'

Januarius shook his head. 'Don't worry, Caninus, we'll meet again soon enough. But just now I have enquiries to make elsewhere.'

CHAPTER NINETEEN

Night of 18th – 19th November

Once more alone in his room, Canio stretched out on the narrow bed and thought back over the events of the day. He reflected only briefly on Januarius and his threats. They did not bother him unduly: life had taught him that there is usually a back door through which one can escape from most problems, if only one is cunning enough to find it.

Trifosa though…

Seeing her had been a shock, but an exhilarating one. He wanted desperately to meet her again, although he was realistic enough to doubt that the wish was reciprocated. He was certain she had recognised him in Saint Paul's Basilica, which meant that she would now be on her guard, even if he could give his jailers the slip for long enough to find her again.

When at last he drifted into an uneasy sleep, he was still trying to devise a plan to not only find her, but also to talk with her alone. He was also struggling to decide exactly what he would say, if such a meeting were to happen.

And at some time during that long night, Tulius returned, continuing the story that he had seemed so desperate for the child Canio to know.

*

'As I said, for the first year of Carausius's imperium, Maximianus was tied down fighting the Alamanni and other Germanic barbarians on the Rhenus and Danube frontiers. It was around this time that he – with Diocles' approval, of course – appointed a man called Flavius Valerius Constantius as his Praetorian Prefect. This Constantius was a man of about Maximianus's own age – late thirties – and had been born, so I heard, in the province of Moesia Superior. So he was another Balkan bastard, but a cleverer man than Maximianus, though that in itself isn't saying a great deal. But – and this is what really mattered – with Constantius taking over day-to-day responsibility for the war on the Rhenus frontier, Maximianus was now free to turn his attention to Carausius.

'Over the next year, which was Carausius's second as emperor, Maximianus began to steadily drive our soldiers out of Northern Gaul, until at last, to quote the words of one of Maximianus's lickspittle panegyrists, as best I can remember them, "On the shores of Ocean the tides have swallowed the blood of your enemies slaughtered there." And the worst of it was that the miserable toad of a panegyrist was right: Carausius lost a lot of good men fighting that rearguard action. And all because he wouldn't admit what was evident to just about everybody else, which was that the northern seaboard of Gaul was inherently indefensible against Maximianus's superior numbers advancing from the south.

'Once he was back in control of what had once been Carausius's territory, Maximianus set about building a great fleet. One with which he intended to invade Britannia and put an end to the rebellion – as he saw it – once and for all.

'He conscripted shipwrights from all over Gaul and set them to work at ports on the Rhenus and Moselle rivers. He didn't dare use any of the yards on the northern seaboard itself, because Carausius's liburnae had complete control of the Oceanus Britannicus, and a lightning raid by them might have seen months of work destroyed.

'Under threats of floggings and worse, it took Maximianus's shipwrights only a year to build that fleet, and it was ready to sail in the early spring of the following year, which was nearer to three years than two after Carausius had first risen up against the tyrant. However, men who knew the treacherous waters of the Oceanus Germanicus advised him to wait until the time of the spring gales had passed.

'But Maximianus wouldn't listen. They say he was under orders from Diocles to crush Carausius without delay, and like the stupid dog he was, he seemed determined to obey his master, whatever the cost. And the cost turned out to be high. Very high.

'It was on a day towards the end of April that Maximianus sailed on the dawn tide out of the mouth of the great Rhenus estuary. Carausius's spies had reported that there were at least eighty ships in that invasion fleet, and it seems that each and every one had been grossly overloaded with far too many soldiers. With all those men, Maximianus must have thought he was making victory a certainty. And so it might have been, had they landed safe in Britannia. But they never did.

'His plan was to sail due west across the Oceanus Germanicus until he reached the estuary of the River Tamesis, and once there he would let the incoming tide sweep his ships all the way up to Londinium. And maybe – if the wind had been blowing from the east, the sea had been calm, and the ships weren't so overloaded as to be unmanageable in anything but the calmest of seas – the plan might have worked. But even as he set out, a gale from the south-west was rising, a gale that grew stronger with every passing hour.

'By the time the fleet was less than halfway across the ocean a terrible storm was raging, and it blew the ships inexorably northwards. With sails furled, their crews tried to maintain their westwards heading by oar power alone, but it was a hopeless struggle. Against that howling wind and the mountainous waves, which were striking them amidships, they had no choice but to run north-eastwards before the wind, heading ever deeper into the cruel wilderness of the Oceanus Germanicus. And it was there that most of those brave ships vanished, almost without trace.

'Over the following weeks, I heard stories of wreckage, even of nearly whole ships, being washed up all along the east coast of Britannia. Some bodies too, though not many, and nearly all were those of sailors, as far as they could tell from what was left after the sea and the fishes and the gulls had, in their different ways, eaten away at them. There were very few soldiers among the dead they found: it was reckoned that they must have been weighed down by their armour. And anyway, few of those poor bastards could swim, even if they had managed to tear off their breastplates or chain mail before the ships were overwhelmed by that merciless ocean.'

CHAPTER TWENTY

19th November

It was around noon on the following day when Canio saw Januarius again. After having been escorted to Adventus's office, he found both *agentes* there. Januarius did most of the talking, with Adventus seeming content to sit back and watch, his hooded eyes never leaving Canio's face.

'After I left you yesterday,' Januarius began, 'I started thinking about your Aunt Peregrina – the spinster lady you mentioned at Villa Censorini. The one who, allegedly, bequeathed you a considerable quantity of gold coins. Incidentally, didn't you tell me yesterday that your aunt was burned at the stake? The lady seems to have led an interesting life: instead of entering the kingdom of heaven, it would seem she chose to come back to this sinful world instead. Very odd.'

Canio gave the long sigh of a man assailed by an idiot. 'That was another aunt. Peregrina was my aunt on my father's side. As far as I know, the two ladies never met.'

'Is that so? Well, no matter. Tell Antistius Adventus here just how many gold coins this Peregrina is supposed to have left you.'

'It was nine thousand *solidi*.'

'Nine thousand!' Januarius echoed. 'And yet she appears to have lived in near poverty. ' Turning to Adventus he said, 'After an examination of her will, I went and saw for myself the house where she is recorded to have lived. It's in a narrow street in the north-east side of the city; not what you would call a fashionable neighbourhood. I talked to her neighbours too, those few that could remember her.' He returned his gaze to Canio. 'Now why, Caninus, would a woman with nine thousand *solidi* live in such a place when she could have lived in luxury?'

Canio had been asked the question several times over the past two years, and his answer was well rehearsed: 'Dear old Aunt Peregrina was a pious Christian—'

'As you yourself are, of course,' Januarius murmured, glancing at Adventus.

'Quite so,' concurred Canio, unruffled. 'And she was also somewhat eccentric. She believed poverty was holy, and consequently, ostentation and rich living were mortal sins. Camels passing through eyes of needles, and all that.' (He congratulated himself on remembering what he had once heard Trifosa say.) 'So she lived and died poor.'

'But where did she get nine thousand *solidi* from in the first place?'

'I never knew. It was a complete mystery to everyone,' Canio said blandly. *Give the bastards no trail to follow there.*

'From your father, perhaps?'

'It's possible, although he died many years ago.' *Don't ask me his name, because I never knew it, and from what Marcia once hinted to me, I suspect my mother didn't either.*

'She did exist, this Peregrina, didn't she?'

'Of course she did. Didn't you just say you'd spoken to people who had known her?'

'They could have been bribed to lie.'

'Where was she buried?' The question came from Adventus.

'In the Eastern Cemetery.'

'In an unmarked and untraceable grave, of course?' Januarius suggested.

Canio arranged his face into what he hoped was a look of shocked indignation. 'Certainly not. I commissioned a fine tombstone for her, which still stands to this day.' *At least, I hope it does.*

Adventus turned to Januarius. 'Well, that's something that can easily be checked. In fact, why don't you do it now? I have to see Civilis shortly about other matters.'

✻

So Canio, Januarius and yet another pair of taciturn soldiers trudged through the muddy streets until they came to the gateway in the north-east angle of the city walls, where the road leading towards Camulodunum emerged. Passing through the gateway, they turned right into the large, sprawling cemetery that stretched for several hundred yards to the east and south.

Here and there stood a few of the large masonry altar tombs that still remained from earlier centuries, although most had long since disappeared, their stones built into the city walls when they were first constructed a century and a half before.

The oldest graves lined a now largely vanished road, which had once led out of the city, but had been truncated when the city wall was built across it. There were some stone tombstones, even a few carved sarcophagi, but the majority of the graves were weathered mounds, the later ones with wooden markers in various states of dereliction.

There are, Canio thought as he stood in the cold drizzle, *few more depressing places than a November graveyard.* It brought back unwelcome memories of the other cemetery outside the walls of that cold city beside the Rhenus, where he had witnessed Tulius being buried a quarter of a century before.

As they had been walking through the city, he had been trying desperately to remember exactly where "Aunt" Peregrina's grave was located. For the truth was that he had only visited it once, and then solely to watch the stonemason setting up her tombstone. At the time he had debated with himself whether it was worth the trouble and expense. But whether it was instinctive caution or a twinge of superstitious conscience that had led him to commission the tombstone was a question he preferred not to waste time considering.

Near the edge of the graveyard he stopped and gazed eastwards towards the banks of grey cloud scudding in from the Tamesis Estuary, as if he were attempting to gauge whether the rain was going to become heavier. In reality, he was still trying to remember the exact location of Peregrina's grave.

Then, he spotted something he recognised: a weathered monumental tomb that, with the passing decades, had tilted to one side. Confident now, he strode eastwards between the graves for some fifty yards, his eyes covertly scanning from side to side as he went.

And there it was, almost as he remembered it, although beginning to look a little weathered as its third winter approached. The tall, brittle stems of the dead grasses that covered the entire area contributed to the general air of dereliction and neglect.

'Well, here we are,' he announced to Januarius. 'Dear old Aunt Peregrina's last resting place on this earth.' He crouched down and read the inscription aloud:

'"*Here lies Peregrina, a servant of Christ, who lived about forty-seven years and was laid to rest six days before the kalends of October in the year when Flavius Valentinianus Augustus and Flavius Julius Valens Augustus were consuls. A most noble soul. Live forever with Christ in eternal peace, bathed in the light of paradise.*"'

Above the inscription were two doves facing each other, each carrying an olive twig in its beak. The wording was suggested by the stonemason, based on several he had recently carved, but the two doves were Canio's own idea, copied from another tombstone he had chanced to notice while wandering through the cemetery. He had thought it a nice touch.

'I can read for myself, thank you,' Januarius murmured. 'So, Peregrina – Aunt Peregrina – died in late September two years ago.' Glancing around the immediate area of the grave he remarked, 'It doesn't look as if you've been back since.'

'Londinium's a hundred miles and more away from my villa, but I paid a man to keep the grave neat,' Canio lied indignantly. 'When I get the chance, I'll root out the cur and give him a good kicking.'

'Oh, I'm sure you will.' (Canio detected a certain disbelief in Januarius's voice.) 'It's not a very big or impressive stone for a woman who left you nine thousand *solidi*, is it?'

Canio had prepared for that observation. 'No, but it's what dear old Peregrina would have wanted. Simple, humble and declaring her faith to all who might pass by. It's the sort of stone I would want for myself, when the time comes,' he added shamelessly.

Januarius grunted his scepticism and began walking away.

Another river crossed, Canio thought. He straightened up, turned and looked across the sea of graves, many now only time-flattened, weed-covered, barely discernible mounds. He glanced at Peregrina's grave one last time, then began following Januarius out of the cemetery.

CHAPTER TWENTY-ONE

Night of 19th – 20th November

It was night, another endless November night, and Canio was sleeping uneasily in the narrow bed in that cold, locked room high up in the *praetorium*. As he slept, he again heard the voice of the old man, Tulius, speaking the words he thought he remembered from childhood.

✻

'*Carausius's spies had warned him that the invasion was imminent, so he had planned to intercept Maximianus's fleet out at sea, where he was confident that his superior seamanship and experienced crews would give him the advantage. But he'd also been a sailor long enough to recognise the signs of a massive storm brewing out in the vastness of the Western Ocean, which was why he decided to keep our* liburnae *safe in harbour at Dubris and Rutupiae and other ports around the south-east coast of Britannia.*

'*It was a wise decision. In the wake of the terrible storm that followed, the only ships of Maximianus's enormous fleet that ever reached Britannia were two commandeered merchantmen. They had set out from the mouth of the Rhenus a day later than the rest of his ships, and so they missed the worst of the storm. When*

they at last reached the mist-shrouded estuary of the Tamesis,
their crews probably assumed – or hoped – that the rest of the
fleet had already reached Londinium.

'*As chance would have it, Carausius had ridden north from*
Dubris to check if any of Maximianus's ships had actually made
it across the Oceanus Germanicus, unlikely though that seemed
after those ferocious winds from the south-west. He was at
Regulbium, a Saxon Shore fort overlooking the approaches to the
estuary of the Tamesis, when he received a report that a band of
Maximianus's soldiers had come ashore and were harrying the
countryside several miles to the west.

'*It must have been night when those two merchantmen*
slipped past Regulbium, but they had then become stranded on
a mudbank. Although the storm had passed, a dense mist was
blanketing the sea and coastline, so they had been forced to come
ashore in an attempt to discover exactly where they were.

'*With a hundred or so men from the Regulbium garrison,*
Carausius set off along the shoreline. It was a strange, eerie land
we walked through, with the mist swirling slowly around – almost
clearing one moment, but the next it had drifted back so thick that
you couldn't see anything more than ten feet away. Vapour was
condensing on the young leaves of the few trees we passed and was
pattering down like rain. That was almost the only sound we could
hear at first because the mist muffled our footsteps and settled on
our clothes until they looked like white fur.

'*It was pure chance that we stumbled across Maximianus's*
soldiers, because they hadn't heard us, nor we them. But in
moments we were in the middle of a savage fight. The shouts
and screams and the clashes of steel on steel acted like a lodestone,
drawing in both sides' soldiers from the shore and surrounding
countryside. But there were a hundred of us and only about
thirty of them, so the skirmish ended in a massacre.

'*Most of Maximianus's men were killed or wounded in the*
fighting, but half a dozen surrendered and were taken prisoner.

Carausius, desperate to know how many others had landed or were still on their way, lined up those who could still stand and interrogated them. One soldier, a brave man or a fool (sometimes the two are hard to distinguish), refused to tell him, and called him a traitor and a breaker of his military oath to Maximianus and Diocles.

'Carausius flew into a terrible rage, as he was increasingly prone to do in those days after the loss of his territories in Northern Gaul, and stabbed the man in the stomach. Ignoring the man's screams and without even looking back at him, Carausius went to the next prisoner and asked him the same question. The man told him – truthfully, as it turned out – that all Maximianus's liburnae had sailed a day before his ship, and he had no idea where the rest of the fleet was.

'Carausius, still enraged, swore at the man and declared that he didn't believe him. Thinking that he was about to stab him too, Allectus stepped forwards and said he suspected that the man was telling the truth.

'By then the dawn mist was clearing under a freshening breeze from the south-west. Carausius hesitated; then, without a word, he walked away and stood on the shore, staring out over the Oceanus Germanicus. He saw nothing: not a single ship in all that great sweep of grey water. Contemplating the vast emptiness seemed to calm him.

'So he gave orders that the prisoners were to be bound and taken back to Regulbium, together with all the wounded from our side and the remainder of Maximianus's men who could still walk. Those who could not had their throats slashed and were dragged, along with all the other enemy dead, down to the low-water mark on the beach and left for the tides to carry them out into the ocean.

'He remembered, as we all did, how savagely Maximianus had treated Carausius's own men who didn't manage to escape from Gaul. Even so, the man who had rebelled against

Maximianus three years before would never have slaughtered fellow soldiers like that or treated their bodies like dead dogs. But now he held a wolf by the ears and the strain of holding on was changing him – and not for the better.'

CHAPTER TWENTY-TWO

20th November

It was towards the middle of the following morning that Canio was once again escorted to Adventus's office, where he found Januarius alone and waiting for him.

He looked, Canio thought, distinctly pleased with himself.

'I've just some from a meeting with Civilis,' the *agens* announced. 'A meeting at which I managed to persuade the *vicarius* that, instead of waiting for the messenger to return from Treveri, it would hasten matters considerably if you and I were to cross the Fretum Gallicum and intercept the man at the port of Bononia. Then, when he confirms that Viventius does indeed wish to interrogate you personally, as I am confident he will, I can escort you to Treveri myself, thus shortening the time between now and your fate by at least five whole days.'

This was not good news: Treveri was definitely not where Canio wanted to be, not with Januarius pouring his poison into the ears of Praetorian Prefect Viventius or, even worse, those of Valentinianus himself. That emperor had a well-known horror of black magic, and an equally notorious savage temper and penchant for cruelty. Also, Canio had been contriving ways by which he could give his daily guards the slip and go looking for Trifosa.

However, he managed to sound casual as he replied, 'Well, anything's better than being stuck here doing nothing, and it must be nearly seven years since I last saw Treveri. So, when do we leave?'

'Noon today at the latest,' the *agens* said briskly, perhaps irritated by the absence of protestations of dismay from Canio. 'At this very moment the *praetorium* clerks are preparing the necessary authorisations and *cursus publicus* diplomas.'

'What route are we taking?'

'Horseback to Dubris, and then ship to Bononia.'

'Why not take a ship all the way?'

It seemed a logical question, but the *agens* was dismissive. 'You mean down the Tamesis Estuary? No, not at this time of year. The weather and the height of the tides are too unpredictable.' Januarius paused. 'Incidentally, what is the name of the person from whom you acquired your so-called "Villa Canini"? I think I'd like to confirm with him – or her – that you actually did purchase the estate and did not acquire it by other, possibly unlawful, means.'

Canio smiled. 'I thought you'd never ask. I bought it from a man called Aurelius Charax. It was all legal and proper, with the sale recorded by one of the notaries from the *praeses'* office in Corinium.'

'And how long had this Aurelius Charax owned the property?'

'I was told the estate had been in his family for at least sixty years – maybe more. Does it matter?'

'And before that?'

'I have no idea.'

'Really? Wasn't it recorded on the title deeds?'

'Not that I can recall.'

'How strange. Such documents usually set out a list of previous owners going back centuries.'

'I wouldn't know – and what does it matter anyway?' Canio repeated, beginning to be irritated by the *agens'* ceaseless probing.

Januarius shrugged. 'As you say, what does it matter, now that you are about to take a one-way journey to Treveri?'

*

But afterwards, when alone, Canio remembered himself thinking it odd that nobody seemed to know who had owned the estate before Charax's family. He had once mentioned this to Diovicus, the oldest person at Villa Canini.

And Diovicus had replied, in his usual gnomic fashion, 'I once heard someone say that every single one of them was killed, even the women and the children.'

But when Canio had asked who they were, those people who had been killed, all Diovicus would say was, 'That I don't rightly know. It all happened years before I was even born.'

Canio, by then familiar with Diovicus's tendency to give sometimes wildly inaccurate or exaggerated versions of past events, had let the matter drop.

*

Noon saw four men – Januarius, Canio and yet another two soldiers he had never seen before – clopping across the massive timber bridge that spanned the Tamesis, passing through the docks and suburbs on the south bank of the river, and taking the highway that led south-eastwards towards the port of Dubris, some seventy-five miles distant.

With one change of horses on the way, they managed to reach the town of Durobrivae, some thirty miles from Londinium, shortly before dusk. As they clattered over the planking of the long, flat bridge that spanned the Medway, Canio smelled the seawater that the incoming tide had carried up from the Tamesis Estuary.

Januarius took a room at the town *mansio*, but Canio, despite his indignant protests, was locked in a cell at the local army barracks. It was raw cold in the cell and pitch dark too after the last grey light had faded. He waited, but once again, neither food nor drink was provided. He thumped the cell door and shouted, but nobody came, and after a while he realised that the soldiers must have been under orders from Januarius to ignore him. Eventually, he managed to fall asleep, but it was nearly dawn before the now-familiar voice of Tulius came into his dreams again.

CHAPTER TWENTY-THREE

Night of 20ᵗʰ – 21ˢᵗ November

'Several months passed before those of us in Britannia realised the full extent of the catastrophic losses of men and ships that Maximianus must have suffered in that terrible storm. However, by the late summer of that year, Carausius's spies were reporting that Maximianus had only a few hundred soldiers left to garrison all of Northern Gaul.

'The Germanic tribes on the Rhenus and Danube frontiers – the Franks, Burgundi, Alamanni and the rest – had taken advantage of the disaster and renewed their incursions with even greater ferocity. So Maximianus and Constantius needed every soldier they had to drive them back and hold the line. To make matters worse, Diocles was so angry with what he saw as Maximianus's bungling of the invasion that he refused to send him any of the troops from his eastern legions, which Maximianus had been begging for to make up his losses.

'So Carausius should have been able to relax, confident that it would be a long time, or never, before anyone would try to invade Britannia again. But it seems that the gods had cursed him with a fatal weakness: he could never accept the loss of Northern Gaul or that, even if it were to be recaptured, it could ever be held for long. Not while Maximianus's army was a few dozen miles to the south, even though that army may not have been in a position to launch an immediate attack.

'But Northern Gaul was his homeland, and to possess it and be recognised as emperor there had become an obsession. In vain did Allectus and others attempt to persuade him to be satisfied with Britannia alone, defended as it was by the waters of the ocean, which no army, however large, could ever march across.

'But Carausius was deaf to reasoned argument; in that respect, and perhaps in others too, he was becoming ever more like Maximianus. So, in the summer of that year, which was the beginning of the fourth year of his reign, with a fleet of a dozen liburnae *from the Classis Britannica, he sailed across the Fretum Gallicum from Dubris and recaptured the port of Gesoriacum. From there, having encountered almost no resistance, his army spread out in both directions until, by late autumn, he was back in possession of the entire coastal region: all the way from Grannona at the mouth of the Seine in the west, to the rivers of the Rhenus Estuary and the border with the lands of his Frankish allies in the east.

'Fatally, with the recovery of Northern Gaul and the utter destruction of Maximianus's invasion fleet, came the delusion of invincibility. Carausius actually came to believe that the gods themselves were on his side. Like Aurelian before him, he thought his protective deity was Sol, the sun god, and that both Diocles and Maximianus would soon recognise that and realise the futility of continuing to oppose him. But the gods are on nobody's side but their own. I came to realise that when they appear to help you, it's only an unintended consequence of their desire to harm someone else.

'Carausius, though, basking in what he imagined was the favour of his god, believed that the imperial pair must surely now recognise him as their equal, as an Augustus. So he ordered Allectus to strike coins – some in his own name, and some in the names of Diocles and Maximianus – but with all of them including the letters "AVGGG", indicating that they were struck in the names of three Augusti; he, of course, being the third.

'He even ordered his Camulodunum mint to issue a coin showing the heads of all three men, side by side, under the legend "*CARAUSIVS ET FRATRES SUI*," meaning "*Carausius and his brothers*". I kept one of those coins for many years, as a reminder of what might once have been. Then one day, in a fit of despair, I threw it away – something I've always regretted.

'But you can never go back into the past and do things differently, no matter how much you may long to do so. The past is gone forever, and the people who lived there are gone – either dead or so altered by time as to no longer be the people you once knew. But in another world – the world of the mind – they still exist, just as you remember them, waiting for you to return.

'Of course, Diocles and Maximianus never struck coins in Carausius's name; why would they? Nevertheless, for a while there was a dialogue of sorts between the three men. Carausius offered, in exchange for formal recognition, to stay within the current boundaries of the territory he controlled and to protect the empire from the depredations of the Germanic tribes from beyond the Lower Rhenus. But since the main Germanic tribe in that area, the Franks, were allies of Carausius, I suspect that Maximianus was unimpressed by the offer. Yet he didn't altogether reject it, and the correspondence continued, with Carausius continuing to believe that he would be left in peace. And so the years passed.

'With hindsight, I have come to realise that Maximianus, with Diocles pulling his strings, was simply playing for time. Time in which his Praetorian Prefect, Constantius, was able to move north and begin attacking the Franks in their homelands, and so weaken Carausius. And when Constantius had at least partially subdued the Franks, he began recapturing Carausius's possessions in Northern Gaul, town by town, until all that was left was the port of Gesoriacum – or Bononia, as they now call it – and Carausius was almost back to where he had been before Maximianus's abortive invasion some three and a half years before.'

CHAPTER TWENTY-FOUR

21st November

It was about one winter hour after dawn when they rode out of Durobrivae, the heatless orange-red sun low in the south-eastern sky in front of them, dazzling off the frost-wet stones of the highway. Canio was in a foul mood, not having eaten since before noon on the previous day. When he tried to buy bread from a bakery just inside the town walls, Januarius stopped him, saying that there wasn't time, but that he could eat at the next town.

Canio stared at him, and for an infuriated moment he was seriously tempted to lean across in his saddle and punch the *agens'* head so hard that the man would probably have been sent flying off his horse. With a supreme effort he restrained the impulse, mindful that, however ill-disposed Januarius might feel towards him now, sending the man sprawling into the mud with a broken jaw or worse would do nothing to lessen his animosity.

That next town was actually a small city – Durovernum Cantiacorum – some thirty cold, wet miles and a change of horses further on along the highway. After crossing a bridge that spanned the small river flowing past the city walls, they rode in single file through the dripping streets until they reached the *mansio*. Canio had never been to Durovernum before, but he was in no mood for sightseeing. The only building that caught his eye was the large, old, semicircular theatre, which dominated the skyline near the centre of the city.

Less than a winter hour later they were off again, heading south-eastwards on the highway that ran mostly along the edges of valleys through the North Downs, heading towards Portus Dubris, some fifteen miles distant. They approached the town along the valley of the Dubris, a rapidly widening chalk stream that had bubbled up from springs about four miles north of the town but which, by the time it reached the town, had become a small tidal estuary with many seagoing ships anchored along its banks.

Dominating the centre of the town was the Saxon Shore fort. It stood on the west side of the estuary, its massive stone walls buttressed with the now-ubiquitous projecting semicircular bastions. Standing up on the high ground on each side of the estuary, silhouetted black against the darkening sky, was a *pharos* lighthouse. Both were tall, stone towers, their circumferences decreasing in stages from base to top.

The Dubris *mansio* was located some fifty yards north of the fort. It was a two-storey stone building, and after Januarius had waved his authorising diploma in the face of the *mansionarius*, they ate a meal of mutton broth washed down with a fairly decent wine made from locally grown grapes. Tired though he was, as he looked around in the lamplight, Canio could not help noticing that the plastered walls of the communal dining room were painted with a design of pilasters and plinths so skilfully done that, from certain angles, they appeared three-dimensional, as if actually projecting into the room.

When he remarked on this to the *mansionarius* the man shook his head disconsolately and said that they were nothing, not compared to the magnificent ones in the previous *mansio*, which had been pulled down to make way for the Saxon Shore fort. 'Eighty rooms that *mansio* had – eighty rooms! This place is a dog kennel by comparison.'

Puzzled by this, since he'd noticed that the fort's stone walls had a hoary, time-weathered appearance, Canio asked when it was that the previous *mansio* had been demolished?

'Oh, a hundred years or so ago,' sighed the *mansionarius*, 'but when he was a boy, my grandfather talked to old men who remembered those frescoes well.'

'They must have been quite a sight,' Canio sympathised, not entirely sincerely.

'Oh, they were; they most certainly were,' the *mansionarius* agreed sadly, before wandering off towards the kitchen.

*

As he had expected, Canio learned that he was to be locked in a cell in the fort overnight, while Januarius slept in a warm bed in the *mansio*. By the time he was escorted through the massive gate of the fort it was well after sunset, and glancing over to the east, he saw a great orange flame rising from the beacon fire on top of the eastern *pharos*. It swayed silently in the frosty but almost windless air.

Free of Januarius's presence, Canio thought he might be able to fraternise with the two guards, soldier to soldiers, but it soon became apparent that they, like all their predecessors, were under orders to say as little as possible to him. They would not even give their names.

The cell into which Canio was thrust was below ground level, and the roughly squared masonry blocks of the walls and the uneven stone-flagged floor were both dank to the touch. Once again, Canio wrapped himself in his *cucullus* and tried to sleep in the chill darkness. And in that darkness he dreamed that he heard Tulius's voice again, speaking the words that, on waking, he thought he remembered from a quarter of a century before.

CHAPTER TWENTY-FIVE

Night of 21st – 22nd November

'So it had come to this: nearly seven years after Carausius had first seized Northern Gaul, then lost it and then seized it again, Constantius had driven Carausius's forces out once more, so that the only toehold he now had left was the port of Gesoriacum.

'To reward Constantius for this achievement, Maximianus – with his master Diocles' permission, of course – raised him to the rank of Caesar. That was in early March, with the anointing ceremony taking place in Mediolanum, or so I later heard. And at the same time a man called Asclepiodotus – remember well that accursed name – was raised to Constantius's old rank of Praetorian Prefect.

'Up until then, in spite of all the reverses of the previous two years, Carausius still clung to the illusion that, one day, Diocles would grant him official recognition as a fellow Augustus and leave him in peace. But after Constantius was confirmed as Maximianus's heir apparent, and with his position being further strengthened by marriage to Maximianus's daughter, Theodora, even Carausius must have realised that it was never going to happen.

'But rather than accept the inevitable, he gave orders that, whatever the cost in lives, Gesoriacum was to be held. In his mind he saw it as the cornerstone of his resurgence, the place where his second reconquest of all he had lost would begin.

'It was insane. Utterly, utterly insane. His most senior officers pleaded with him to accept that Gesoriacum could never be held for long against Constantius's besieging forces, and that he should be content with retaining Britannia, an island encircled by seas that were ruled by his own fleet of liburnae.

'But Carausius wouldn't listen. Holding Gesoriacum and recovering Northern Gaul had become an obsession, and he was determined to achieve it, whatever the cost. Looking back, I think it was then that the steelyard finally tipped and self-preservation began to outweigh blind loyalty in men's minds. Soldiers will risk their lives for an audacious general if they can see a realistic prospect of victories and rich rewards. But not for a deranged one they fear will squander their lives by driving them down a road that leads to nowhere but defeat and death.'

CHAPTER TWENTY-SIX

22nd November

Canio woke to the sounds of his guards' voices in the corridor outside his cell in the Dubris Saxon Shore fort. After unlocking the door they escorted him to the estuary quayside, where they found Januarius in the middle of an ill-tempered exchange with the captain of one of the two *liburnae* warships moored there.

'I'm sorry,' the tough-looking man whose uniform bore the insignia of a *centenarius* was saying, 'but my orders are clear: any report of Saxon or Frankish pirates is to be investigated immediately.'

Canio thought that he didn't sound at all sorry.

'But didn't you say that the sighting was to the south-west of here, way out on the Oceanus Britannicus?' Januarius pointed out. 'So it would only require a slight diversion to carry us to Bononia.'

'Any diversion would take time, and I have no time to waste,' the *centenarius* replied briskly.

'You have read my diploma, haven't you?' the *agens* asked coldly. 'I am travelling on imperial business, and this diploma clearly instructs whomsoever I may request to give me all necessary assistance on my journey. And I am instructing you to carry us to Bononia, without delay.'

'It instructs all *civilians* to assist you, and I, as you may have noticed, am a soldier – a real one – although my uniform may not be as fancy as yours.'

The insult must have stung, and the two men glared at each other before Januarius hissed, 'So what about that one?' And he pointed to the other *liburna*.

'It's awaiting caulking; it sprang a leak between the starboard strakes yesterday.' And before Januarius could reply, the captain added, 'Look, if I were you I'd wave that diploma under the nose of the captain of that merchant ship over there. I heard he's sailing for Bononia today.' And with that he turned, clumped up the gangplank and started bellowing orders to his crew.

The merchant ship in question was moored about fifty yards downstream of the two *liburnae*, and with a muttered expletive Januarius began striding towards it.

In other circumstances, Canio might have found the confrontation amusing, but he was cold, stiff and hungry, and he had slept only fitfully on the damp cell floor. He blew out a long breath of annoyance. 'Well, I don't know about you,' he said to the two soldiers, 'but I'm going to the *mansio* to get some breakfast.'

'We've already eaten,' one of them replied comfortably.

'Well then, you can damned well have the pleasure of watching me,' Canio snarled. And before either of them could object, he began walking away.

The guards did not try to stop him, and given the state of his temper at that moment, it was probably a wise decision.

He was finishing the last of what the *mansionarius* had sworn was venison stew when Januarius strode into the communal dining room looking pleased with himself.

'Right, stop eating and come with me. The merchantman, which that unhelpful bastard of a *centenarius* pointed out, *is* going to Bononia, and we are going to be on it. The tide's about to turn, so hurry! I've instructed its captain not to sail without us, but if he does, I'll have his skin stretched out on a drying rack. And yours too,' he added, pointing at the two guards, who each promptly grabbed one of Canio's arms and attempted to drag him out of the *mansio*, before his enraged roar persuaded them to desist.

*

The captain of the merchantman, whose name Canio subsequently learned was Frontinus, was waiting for them at the top of his gangplank when they arrived at the quay, and by the expression on his face he was not a happy man.

'Mercury's balls, will you damned well hurry! If we miss this tide we won't get away before tomorrow.' And apparently to save Januarius asking, Frontinus added, 'I wouldn't set off at nightfall onto a winter sea, not even if Emperor Valentinianus himself went down on his knees and begged me.'

'We're here, aren't we?' Januarius growled. 'So be so good as to stop whining and cast off immediately.'

As he stood on the planking of the deck, watching the sailors unfurling the sail and poling the ship away from the quayside, Canio relaxed and began looking around. The name of the ship, which he'd noticed painted on the bows before he embarked, was *Capricornus*. It was, he judged, some thirty-five single paces long by eight wide, with a cabin towards the stern and, just forward of the mast step, a cargo hatch through which two sailors were hurriedly lowering the last of the sacks of wheat that had been piled on the deck.

Once free of her mooring ropes the ship began to swing slowly with the current. The helmsman hauled on the twin steering oars at the stern, and the ship turned sluggishly until its prow was facing downstream and a cold breeze from the north-east began to fill the sail.

The *Capricornus* passed beyond the harbour mouth, and then they were out on the open sea, heading southwards towards

Bononia, the Gallic port over thirty miles distant as the gulls flew. Looking back as he stood on the gently swaying deck, Canio watched the high, white cliffs on either side of Dubris harbour gradually receding. And as he stared at them, he found himself wondering if he would ever see them again.

The intended course, or so Canio had been told by the sailors, was to head south-east for some twenty to twenty-five miles until they sighted the headland known as Promunturium Itium, and then follow the Gallic coast due south for another ten miles until they reached Bononia. This, they said, was the usual route, minimising as it did the time spent out on the open waters of the Fretum Gallicum.

*

They were perhaps halfway across the Fretum Gallicum – certainty was impossible in the misting rain that had descended, swirling around them and reducing visibility to a couple of hundred yards at best – when Canio heard one of the sailors give a hoarse shout of alarm. Peering into the rain, he saw what he realised was a Saxon or Frankish galley approaching rapidly from the west and heading straight towards them.

He heard Frontinus bawl something at the helmsman, and then saw the latter throw all his weight against the tiller arm of the steering oars, as if trying desperately to make the ship alter course, although in those few frantic moments there was no discernible deviation either to port or starboard.

By then the galley was only some fifty yards away – so close that Canio could see the shaggy, rain-drenched heads of the rowers straining at their oars. He cursed Januarius for leaving him defenceless, without a *spatha* or even a dagger, and began hunting around for something to use as a weapon, finding nothing useful on the sodden planking of the deck.

The galley was within a few dozen yards of them now, and everything was happening so fast that it was several moments before Canio realised that the Saxons were not attempting to intercept them. They shot past the *Capricornus's* stern, and Canio had a momentary glimpse of the entire galley side-on: the high, curved prow and stern posts; a near-score of rowers on the visible side; and the helmsman, seemingly preternaturally tall and clutching the shaft of the single big steering oar as he stared forwards into the curtain of rain. And then it was past them, and a few pounding heartbeats later it was gone, unchecked on its wild flight eastwards.

Hardly had the galley disappeared when, out of the drizzling rain, no more than a hundred yards astern of where Canio stood, there appeared a *liburna* warship – almost certainly the *liburna* from Dubris – in grim pursuit of the barbarians' galley. Squinting into the rain, Canio saw its hazy outline, its now-useless sail furled, and the heads and shoulders of the marines pulling on their oars to the sound of a drum's harsh, rhythmic beat. Only that, and then it too was past and fading rapidly into the murk before vanishing completely.

It was the stuff of dreams – weird dreams. Like something out of mythology or folklore. As if one spectral crew had been condemned to pursue another for all eternity across an endless, rain-swept sea. Uneasily, he remembered similar tales he had heard as a boy, and also the story Tulius had told about the fatal encounter he himself had witnessed between a *liburna* and a Saxon galley over eighty years before. He reflected that all those men who sailed on the *Andromeda* on that April day over eighty years gone, even the youngest and strongest, must be long dead by now. Themselves just ghosts.

✻

The *Capricornus* sailed steadily on, its drenched sail sluggishly filling out and snapping weakly in the north-easterly breeze until, early in the afternoon, the sailor on lookout shouted that the coastline to the east of Promunturium Itium was visible. Peering into the murk Frontinus confirmed the sighting, then ordered the helmsman to steer towards the south-west, which soon brought the *Capricornus* into sight of the headland itself.

Always keeping in sight of the land off their port bow, they now headed due south until, in the late afternoon of that winter day, under a clearing sky, they sailed into an estuary and reached the port of Bononia.

It was built on the east bank, below the point where a little river, flowing from the south-east, widened out to form the tidal estuary. On the headland where the estuary met the sea, Canio had noticed a *pharos* lighthouse, similar to the ones at Dubris. He had scanned across the estuary to see if there was another on the opposite shore, but if there was, he failed to spot it.

The incoming tide had recently turned, pushing the *Capricornus* up the winding channel between mudflats on both sides. The port of Bononia was situated on rising ground between two little streams that flowed down from the east into the estuary. The harbour itself was in a sheltered bay into which the second of these streams entered.

Up on the higher ground, beyond the huddle of buildings near the shore, Canio saw, in the failing light, the grim outline of the fortified town itself. Semicircular bastions – like those at Dubris, Londinium and a host of other towns and cities – projected from its encircling stone walls at regular intervals.

Well before they docked, Januarius emerged from the cabin in which he had spent most of the voyage and ordered the two guards to make absolutely certain that Canio was given no chance to escape. And the moment that the *Capricornus* had been tied up securely at the harbour side, Januarius had Canio marched through the huddle of warehouses and timber dwellings behind the quay, uphill to the walled town itself, and then into the fortress that stood within its walls. There, after much flourishing of his diploma and other documents of authorisation, he watched as his prisoner was taken and locked inside a cell at first-floor level. A cell whose tiny, barred window gave Canio a panoramic view over the cemetery that lay beyond the walls.

Staring out through that window in the early part of the night, before the sky had completely clouded over, he saw that the rising moon, already several days past full, was shining fitfully down onto the cemetery. By its wan light, he saw a cloaked woman standing motionless beside what appeared to be a recent grave. Then clouds hid the moon, and when it reappeared she had gone. Canio tried not to believe in omens, but he was still thinking about her as he fell asleep.

CHAPTER TWENTY-SEVEN

Night of 22nd – 23rd November

'There wasn't the remotest chance that Gesoriacum could hold out for long against Constantius's besieging army, even if the garrison were to be reinforced by sea. But Carausius wouldn't listen to those who tried to convince him of that unalterable fact. Only Allecta was said to have supported him; why, I never knew. She must have realised the folly of trying to retake Northern Gaul just as clearly as the rest of us did. But over the ten or so years they had been married a mysterious bond had formed between them, something that I don't think anybody – not even her own brother – really understood.

'In the beginning their marriage had been little more than a contractual arrangement on both sides, but in those final years I believe he confided his innermost thoughts and hopes and fears to her, as he did to no other mortal creature. They had no children – I sometimes wondered if that was why they became so close, just the two of them against the world. And who can even guess what they whispered to each other in the stillness of the night, and what plans they made? Did she share his dreams – were they her dreams too? Did she encourage him to believe that all things were possible, if only he would never accept defeat?

'Whatever the reasoning, or lack of it, Carausius ordered Allectus to take a fleet of some twenty liburnae, loaded with as many soldiers as they would hold, then sail across the Fretum

Gallicum to Gesoriacum and lift the siege. And Allectus, despite his misgivings, obeyed that order.

'But Constantius was no fool. He knew that the most likely way Carausius would attempt to relieve the town was by a seaborne attack. So he had ordered a barrier, a sort of mole or breakwater, to be constructed across the full width of the estuary by driving a row of stakes into the sea bed and buttressing them with shiploads of dumped rocks.

'Allectus and his captains tried everything they could think of to break through, even repeatedly smashing into the breakwater at the fastest speed the rowers could reach – it was hopeless trying to use sail power to ram the accursed thing, because the wind was forever shifting and blowing from the wrong direction.

'Even using the oars, the foul weather and the unpredictable, swirling tides made it almost impossible to hit the same spot twice, and the hails of arrows and ballistae bolts fired from the shore and the screams of the poor bastards they hit, all served to unnerve our men.

'There was no point in trying to disembark the soldiers on the muddy shores of the estuary: they would have been cut down before they could reach firm ground. Only a massed attack on the besiegers from the harbour itself might have had any chance of success.

'In the end, the captains told Allectus bluntly that further attempts would be madness and only result in the pointless deaths of more men. And so, reluctantly, Allectus gave the order to sail back to Dubris. And shortly afterwards, realising that their position was now hopeless, the garrison of Gesoriacum surrendered to Constantius. Thus it was that the tyrant Diocles regained complete possession of Northern Gaul – a possession he never again relinquished.

'Carausius, standing on top of one of the twin pharos at Dubris harbour, awaited Allectus's return, and when he learned that the mission had failed he raged like a wild beast. He called

Allectus a useless, incompetent coward and shouted that he would have every single one of the captains chained to the oars of one liburna and sent back to Gesoriacum, where they would stay until either the barrier was smashed or they all drowned like rats when the ship sank under them.

'One of the captains protested that even he, Carausius, could have done no better than they had, and furthermore, that he would not be speaking to them so harshly if he had any understanding of the appalling conditions they had faced.

Though they were no more than the truth, the words so enraged Carausius that he drew his sword and, before anyone could stop him, hacked the man to death in front of Allectus and the other captains.

'In the immediate shocked aftermath, not a voice was raised in protest, but I noticed the men present looking from one to the other, and I saw in their eyes something I had never seen before. At the time I was unsure what it was, but now I know: it was uncertainty mutating into certainty – the certainty that, if they were to survive, Carausius had to die.'

CHAPTER TWENTY-EIGHT

23rd November

There was a muffled thud as the door of Canio's cell was unbolted and Januarius strode in. The weak, wintry sun was already high enough to be shining through the barred window, casting the elongated shadows of the bars onto the stone floor.

'Good news, Caninus! I've just been talking to an imperial messenger who arrived from Treveri yesterday evening. He tells me that he's fairly sure – almost certain, in fact – that the man Civilis sent to inform the Praetorian Prefect of *Praeses* Sabinus's tragic death was due to leave the city the day after he himself had left it, which was five days ago. That being so, our man should be here by this evening. His name, by the way, is Atropos – or at least that's apparently what he calls himself. I can't believe it's the name his father gave him, but in the circumstances it is rather appropriate, don't you think?'

Canio said nothing, so Januarius continued, 'After all, isn't Atropos one of the Fates, the *Parcae*? The one who cuts the thread of life? At least, she is according to your pagan mythology. And our Atropos will be bringing the summons for us to proceed to Treveri, where the order will be given for the thread of your life to be cut for the abominable crime of conjuring up the powers of darkness. A crime of which you, and that Trifosa woman, are unquestionably guilty, as I shall prove before Viventius himself.'

'Really? And is that something for which you expect to receive a splendid reward in your Christian heaven – assuming, of course, that the miserable place actually exists?' Canio had not slept well. He was cold, hungry and in no mood to appease the man.

'Oh, it exists, I assure you. And I shall be there when your soul, or what is left of it, is a blackened cinder in the bottomless depths of hell.' There was a fervour and conviction in the man's voice that was chilling, but it suddenly occurred to Canio that it was perhaps the fervour of a man more desperate to convince himself than others.

Canio stared at him, then said softly, 'That's what really drives you, isn't it? The fear of the Christian hell and the things that will await you there if you don't persecute your way into heaven.' He hesitated, but he was now fatalistically past caring, realising that nothing he could say would alter the *agens'* obsessive determination to see him executed. So he added, 'And the really amusing thing is, that your hell and your heaven are both mythical. They don't exist, just like all the old gods and goddesses don't exist.'

He knew that he had already said too much, but the urge to wound was too strong for him to stop now. 'Except, of course, for Hecate – oh yes, she exists all right. And if you harm me or the Trifosa woman, then one dark night she will rise up out of the earth and destroy you, just as she destroyed Sabinus and Castor and Peltrasius.' And he gave Januarius a savage, mirthless grin.

He was well aware that it was unwise to goad the man and to feed his fears, and well aware too that he himself did not really believe – or perhaps, more accurately, did not want to believe – in the truth of what he was threatening. But by now he was beyond caring; he had found a gap in the man's armour and was determined to stab his dagger in as far as it would go.

And by the look of stunned terror that momentarily crossed the *agens'* face he knew he had succeeded. A small crumb of revenge perhaps, but welcome all the same.

'So you admit it! You admit your dealings with the handmaiden of the Evil One?' Januarius's voice was little more than a whisper, but as well as fear, Canio fancied he heard both astonishment and triumph in it.

'I admit nothing, but with every short day that passes the nights are getting longer and darker. Think on that, *agens* of the third grade. Think on that, in the depths of every one of those endless nights.'

'Oh, I will, Caninus, because every one of those nights will bring you closer to the stake. Enjoy you time here because, tomorrow, we'll be setting out on the road to Treveri – a road along which you will never return.'

It was brave talk, but Canio could still detect fear in both the man's voice and the way he seemed to press himself against the cell wall as he edged towards the door, as if trying to maximise the distance between them.

*

The daylight hours dragged past interminably, as all the while the dank chill seemed to seep out of the very stones of the cell walls. It was already dark when the two guards came for Canio. 'Is he here yet, the messenger from Treveri?' he asked.

'No, not yet,' was all the information he could extract from them. He had already guessed that they were, as usual, under orders to say as little as possible to him.

They escorted him to the *mansio*, where he found Januarius in one of the private rooms. It was warm and well lit, in marked contrast to the cell where he had spent the last night and day.

'Help yourself to the food,' the *agens* said, indicating several small loaves and the remains of what appeared to have been a substantial joint of mutton on the table. 'We can't have you fainting with hunger on the road to Treveri, can we now?'

The temptation to tell the man to stuff the food into a bodily orifice other than his mouth was great, but Canio's hunger was greater. He was still gnawing the last of the flesh off the white bone when one of the guards came back into the room and held a whispered conversation with Januarius.

'Yes, I'm sure the man is tired and hungry, but his needs can wait. Bring him here immediately,' Januarius demanded.

The guard left and returned moments later with a tall, wiry man in a soaking-wet *cucullus*, which dripped a trail of water as he walked into the room.

'Ah, welcome back to Bononia, Master Atropos,' the *agens* said. 'I gather you are carrying a dispatch for *Vicarius* Civilis?'

'My name is Atepaccius – as I'm sure you well know,' the man said impatiently. 'And yes, I carry a dispatch for Civilis. What's it to you?'

'Atepaccius?' queried Januarius in mock astonishment. 'I'm sure somebody told me your name was Atropos.' This was said looking at Canio. 'No matter. This,' he said, flourishing a small scroll, 'is my authorisation from *Vicarius* Civilis to open, read and act upon the contents of the message you have brought from Treveri.'

Atepaccius looked surprised and held his hand out, palm upwards. It seemed he was not prepared to accept Januarius's unverified word. The *agens* handed over the scroll, and Atepaccius took it over to the nearest lamp before unrolling and studying it carefully. Then he grunted, shook his head and handed the scroll back to Januarius before unbuckling the large purse hanging from his belt, taking out a scroll encased in a protective leather cylinder and giving it to the *agens*.

'Why, thank you,' said Januarius, accepting the cylinder with a faint, sarcastic bow. 'And never fear, by the time you've changed out of those wet clothes and had something to eat I will return this to you – along with a short message of my own for Civilis. Something to let him know that, by the time he reads it, we will be already halfway to Treveri – won't we, Caninus?'

Canio said nothing.

Atepaccius hesitated, as if tempted to ask questions; then, perhaps deciding that he simply did not want to know, he stalked out of the room.

Even before the door had closed behind Atepaccius, Januarius had extracted the scroll from its leather cylinder, broken its wax seal and begun unrolling it. Eagerly he read the first few lines, but as he read on, Canio noticed the expression on his face slowly change, first to bewilderment, and then to anger. Finally, he dropped the scroll onto the table, turned to the two guards and said coldly, 'It seems, my brave lads, that we won't be going to Treveri after all. In the morning we'll all be returning to Londinium.' He paused, then added, 'Be so good as to wait downstairs until I call for you; Caninus and I have matters to discuss.'

After the guards had gone, Januarius wordlessly tossed the scroll over to Canio. Skimming past the short, formal opening paragraph, he read:

From Lucius Flavius Viventius, vir illustris, Praefectus Praetorio Galliarum, to Publius Ulpius Civilis, vir spectabilis, vicarius of the five provinces of Britannia – greetings!

Having given the matter our most careful thought and consideration, it is the opinion of both Valentinianus Augustus and I that the testimony of Aulus Claudius Caninus should be accepted as true. By which we mean that the late, cruelly slain Caristanius Sabinus, praeses of the province of Britannia Prima, should indeed be seen as the innocent victim of the deluded greed and criminal conspiracies of two members of his personal bodyguard troops. And furthermore, that the actions of the late Caristanius Sabinus in attempting to acquire and subsequently destroy the figurine of a pagan goddess should be regarded as wholly commendable and consistent with his duties as a Christian appointee of the state.

With the guilty pair now dead and beyond further earthly punishment, we consider the matter closed. We therefore order that the inquiry should be taken no further, in order to avoid arousing morbid curiosity in the minds of those still unconvinced of the truth of the Christian revelation.

Canio thought that final sentence to be somewhat curious, although the substance of the letter was most welcome to him, of course. He also thought it odd that no mention had been made of the mysterious woman who had brought the second Hecate figurine, until he realised it was probably because she, and the second figurine, did not fit in neatly with the narrative that Viventius evidently wished to be the authorised version of events. He could not stop himself smiling, knowing that he was now free from Januarius's power. Or so he thought.

Januarius must have seen that smile. 'No, don't grin, Caninus. For one thing, I'm still certain that you contrived Sabinus's death – you and that Trifosa woman, who, incidentally, I'm still determined to find and bring to justice.'

Canio slowly shook his head in mock disbelief at the man's obduracy. 'No, the game's over – finished. Viventius himself says so, and you can't argue with a Praetorian Prefect. And if I've told you once, I've told you a dozen times – the woman who brought the second Hecate figurine wasn't Trifosa.'

'And every time you've told me has made me more certain that it really was her. But there's something else, something much closer to home – your home, actually.' And Januarius chuckled at the uncertainty he must have seen on Canio's face.

The *agens* waited for a few moments, letting the uncertainty fester, then asked, 'Tell me, does the name Bruscius mean anything to you?'

It did, but Canio decided to look baffled and shook his head wearily. 'Bruscius? No, I don't think so.'

'Well, that is surprising. He's a notary in the office of the master of records in Londinium. He's the man who authenticated your Aunt Peregrina's will. I met him when I was making enquiries about that will.'

'Ah, him. I remember now.'

'And so you should, because by authenticating that will he did you a great service. A valuable service too, one might say.'

'It was no more than his duty,' Canio replied, uneasy now as to where all this was leading.

'Oh, indeed. And sometimes doing one's duty can be its own reward, but at other times... What about the name Vepogenus?'

'Never heard of him.' For once, Canio was able to tell the truth.

'No more had I, until that morning three days ago when we getting ready to leave Londinium. But shortly before we left, Vepogenus came to see me. He too is a notary, a colleague of the helpful Bruscius, and he'd heard that I'd been asking about your Aunt Peregrina's will. And do you know what he told me?'

'No idea whatsoever.' Actually, Canio had a horrible suspicion what was coming, but he shook his head in feigned impatient indifference.

'He told me that, a little over two years ago, which must have been around the time that Bruscius was authenticating Peregrina's will, he – Bruscius – seems to have come into a nice little legacy of his own. Of course, Vepogenus didn't know this at the time. It only emerged a month or two ago when the wine at one of the best *taberna* in the city had been flowing somewhat freely. I gather Vepogenus then asked Bruscius to share a little of his good fortune, but he declined to do so, which left Vepogenus somewhat aggrieved... You do see where this is leading, don't you, Caninus?'

'Not really.'

'Not really?' the agens repeated. 'Then let me explain. You acquired the gold, with which you went on to buy your villa, by some unlawful means – quite possibly involving black magic and that accursed Hecate figurine. But you were then faced with a problem: how to explain your new-found wealth to a suspicious and envious world? The answer: a forged will, or some similar document. Something to prove to the world that you were indeed the rightful owner.'

Canio gave a sigh of impatience. 'So are you really going to allege that I bribed this Bruscius character to authenticate my aunt's will? Even if that were true – which it most certainly is not – you could never prove it. Among other things, Civilis would never allow you to torture a member of his own staff, not even a humble notary.'

'Oh, but he would, Caninus. Only three months ago, according to my master, Adventus, he allowed the torture of a *rationalis* accused of embezzlement. The way Civilis sees it, any member of his staff who commits a crime and goes unpunished impugns his own integrity. A very upright man is Civilis. And one with a terrible temper too. He'll certainly allow Master Bruscius to feel the red-hot iron, and I wonder what secrets will then come tumbling from his lips?'

'Or what lies? To end the agony men will say whatever they think their torturer wants to hear, whether it's true or not – as I'm sure you know as well, or better, than any man alive.' Canio tried to sound unconcerned, but inwardly he was seething: he still could not forget Januarius's casual admission of having tortured Trifosa's maid, Aniceta.

'We shall see; we shall see. In less than three days from now we'll all be back in Londinium, and the helpful Bruscius will be singing like a lark. I can't wait to hear that song, although it might not be to your liking. But sleep well tonight, Caninus. It seems that you still may not have many more chances to do so.' Grinning at his own humour, Januarius crossed the room, opened the door and summoned the guards to escort Canio back to his cell.

✳

Unable to sleep, Canio stood beside the tiny, barred window of the cell, gazing up at the waning moon as scudding clouds, only fractionally lighter than the ink-black sky, alternately revealed and hid its enigmatic face.

Bruscius would talk under torture; he had no doubt of that, and there was absolutely nothing he could do to prevent it happening. Of course, he would deny bribing the man, but he suspected he would not be believed, not with Januarius so determined to see him dead.

It was well into the endless November night when bodily weariness at last overcame his churning thoughts. Wrapping his *cucullus* tightly around him, he slid down into one corner of the cell, and after a while fell into an uneasy sleep. And in that sleep he heard Tulius's voice once again.

CHAPTER TWENTY-NINE

Night of 23rd – 24th November

'It was five days later that the last act in Carausius's tragedy began. We were in Londinium when news came that the barrier across the Gesoriacum estuary, the accursed row of stakes that had resisted all our attempts to batter them down, had been breached by the first high tide that swept in after we had sailed away. The power of the sea will always be greater than anything we feeble mortals can produce, but even so, we cursed the gods for their mocking cruelty. Perhaps what was happening was all in accordance with a plan devised by the gods long, long ago? Or perhaps there was no plan – and no gods either? Nothing but random chance.

'Whether again by chance, or something more sinister, no sooner had news reached us of the breaching of the mole, than there came the discovery of several letters, apparently sent by Constantius, that were addressed to Allectus and several other high-ranking officers in Carausius's forces. They had been intercepted before they reached the men to whom they were addressed.

'These letters offered a free pardon and promotion to the equivalent, or even higher rank in Constantius's army to anyone who would assassinate Carausius. Of course, Constantius had almost certainly intended them to be intercepted, because their effect was to cast a net of suspicion over everyone in Carausius's immediate circle. For who could say that there were no other letters that had reached their intended targets, but had never been reported to Carausius?

'In vain did their purported recipients protest that those letters were entirely unsolicited, and would, if received, have been treated with utter contempt. However, to Carausius's increasingly paranoid mind they were the final proof of what he had already come to suspect: that the loss of Northern Gaul in general, and Gesoriacum in particular, was the result of systematic betrayal by men he had previously trusted.

'Oblivious to reason and deaf to rational argument, he gave orders for the immediate arrest of all those men to whom the letters were addressed, including Allectus. They were to be loaded with chains, like the meanest criminals, and then executed in a manner befitting traitors. With hindsight, I can see the terrible irony of that order, because it led not to their deaths but his own.

'I believe Allecta must have suspected that those letters were indeed a plot devised by Constantius to destabilise Carausius's regime, because afterwards I heard it was she who persuaded him to let the accused speak and not to have them executed unheard.

'So, Carausius had them brought before him in chains, but when Allectus attempted to indignantly protest the innocence of them all, Carausius began raging at him like a maddened wild beast in the amphitheatre. Grabbing a heavy brass inkwell, he hurled it at Allectus, striking him on the forehead and knocking him down.

'"Traitor, traitor, traitor!" he hissed, and then, drawing his sword, he advanced towards Allectus, as if about to stab him as he lay helpless on the floor, blood streaming down his face.

'But at that point, the others suddenly dropped the chains that had seemed to bind them, but were, in reality, only draped about their waists and arms, and not secured by padlocks. The guards made no attempt to restrain them, and when commanded to do so, handed them their swords.

'With memories of Carausius's savage treatment of that captain at Dubris fresh in their minds, and the sight of Allectus writhing in *agony, I think those men realised that the gods were forcing them to make a stark choice: either they killed Carausius or he would kill them. And not just them, but all the other men who would perish as a result of his insane determination to retake Northern Gaul.*

'They say that, in those last moments of his life, an odd, puzzled expression came over Carausius's face, like that on the face of a man awaking from a strange dream and trying to make sense of it before the memory fades.

'It was over quickly, or as quickly as it can ever be when four or five swords are stabbed into the body of a strong man. And when Carausius's body had given a last convulsive twitch, there was an eerie silence while, still clutching their bloodstained swords, the men who had killed him stared down at his lifeless corpse in complete silence, as if the enormity of what they had just done had struck them dumb.

'But whatever guilt they may have felt, then or later, was tempered by the utter certainty that, if they had not destroyed Carausius, then he would have destroyed them. Either kill or be killed – sometimes the Parcae present you with a choice as stark as that. Always remember that, Canio. Always remember that.'

*

Suddenly awake, Canio stared into the Stygian gloom of the cell and listened intently, convinced that, this time, Tulius's voice had definitely not been inside his head but had come from somewhere out of the darkness only a few feet away. And that if he were to reach out a hand, he could touch the source of that voice. But Tulius was a quarter-century dead, so who or what…?

He waited, but the voice did not come again, and after a while he clambered stiffly to his feet and groped his way warily around the cell, encountering nothing but the dank stone of the walls.

CHAPTER THIRTY

24th – 25th November

It was shortly after daybreak, frosty and with a clear sky, that the two guards came again to collect Canio from his cell. They hurried him down to the harbour, where he found Januarius engaged in another heated argument with Frontinus, the captain of the *Capricornus*.

Looking around and listening, it rapidly became apparent to Canio that, during the previous day, Frontinus had loaded a sizeable cargo of wine. The barrels were not only piled high down in the hold, but there were also quite a few lashed together in various places on the deck.

'There's no room for any damned passengers – surely even you can see that?' an exasperated Frontinus was saying.

'Well, unload some of those barrels then.'

'Why in Hades' name should I?' Frontinus replied angrily.

'Because this gives me the right to demand your assistance at all times, that's why,' Januarius snarled, waving his *cursus publicus* diploma under the captain's nose.

'Whatever you imagine your rights to be, it took half a day to load those barrels. So, by the time I've unloaded even half of them, the tide will have turned, and I won't get away today – and neither will you. Look, do you see those ships over there?' Frontinus pointed to a row of vessels tied up against the wharf and rocking slowly in the current. 'I know for a fact that at least two of them are due to sail for Dubris tomorrow, and both are bigger than the *Capricornus*. They could carry all five of you.'

Five? Looking around, Canio saw the previously unnoticed messenger, Atepaccius, sitting on a mooring bollard and watching the argument with ill-concealed amusement.

Januarius, however, was not amused. 'I'm not waiting here another damned day,' he said tersely. 'I have important business in Londinium – business that will not wait.'

Frontinus said nothing, but he looked away across at the estuary, as if gauging the amount of time left before the turning of the tide.

The *agens* muttered something under his breath, but he must have realised that even a diploma signed by the *vicarius* of the five provinces of Britannia could not stop the tide from turning. 'All right, all right! Just take myself and Caninus here. And don't try to tell me that you haven't room for even two passengers,' he growled, wagging an angry finger inches away from Frontinus's face.

'Three!' Atepaccius slid off the bollard and began walking towards the *Capricornus's* gangplank. 'I'm carrying imperial dispatches from the Praetorian Prefect himself, so even if you only have room for one, that one should be me.'

Which Canio took as confirmation that Januarius had indeed returned those dispatches to Atepaccius, either that morning or the previous evening.

Frontinus threw up his hands.

In... what? Anger, resignation...what? Canio wondered.

Whatever it was, Januarius took it as a sign of victory. He had a few hurried words with the two guards who, Canio thought, did not look at all unhappy at the prospect of being left behind to spend a few days off the leash in Bononia. Then he marched up the gangplank, pushing Canio in front of him. Atepaccius followed, a few steps behind them both.

✤

The tide carried the *Capricornus* out of the estuary of the Liane – Canio had at last remembered the name of the river that became the estuary on which Bononia stood. Watching as the crew unfurled the sail, he became aware of another reason why Frontinus was so keen to leave harbour: the breeze had changed direction from the north-easterly it had been two days before, and was now blowing from the south, roughly in the direction of Dubris.

As they slipped down the estuary, Canio suddenly realised that he must be passing over the very spot where, nearly eighty years before, Allectus – and presumably Tulius too – had tried unsuccessfully to break through the barrier of stakes and rocks that Constantius had constructed to prevent them reaching the besieged town of Gesoriacum, as it was then called. There was no sign of that barrier now: stakes and rocks had both vanished.

The *Capricornus* made good progress northwards up the Gallic coast until they reached the headland of Promunturium Itium, where they turned slightly towards the north-west, intending to head across the Fretum Gallicum. But then, slowly but remorselessly, the wind changed, slipping round to the south-west and strengthening rapidly.

By the time they were only a quarter of the way across the Fretum, the wind was blowing them ever further north-eastwards. Frontinus tried to tack to the north, but, as Tulius had apparently noticed all those years before, the sail could only be moved a few degrees to port or starboard. When it became obvious that they were being swept ever further towards the Oceanus Germanicus, Frontinus ordered the sail to be furled, and the *Capricornus's* progress north-eastwards was slowed, but not halted, before the now gale-force south-westerly wind.

With the strengthening wind came the rain – a cold rain that soaked everyone on board who had not already been drenched by the salt spray, and from which neither cabin nor hold offered complete shelter. Canio's *cucullus* became saturated and as heavy as lead, providing no warmth, but rather sucking the heat out of his body.

Squinting through the rain, he watched as the helmsman lashed the tillers of the twin steering oars together, such that the blades presented the least possible resistance to the water. Canio did not need to ask why: he realised that any attempt to turn would have risked the raging sea striking the *Capricornus* amidships and capsizing it.

That terrible day, which became almost as dark as night, passed slowly in an unremitting welter of rain, spray, roaring wind and the disquieting creaking of timbers as the ship rode the heaving sea.

Nightfall found them out in the wilderness of the Oceanus Germanicus, still running before the wind. Wet, cold, and drained mentally and physically, there was nothing anyone aboard could do but huddle down, soaked and shivering, and try to sleep – the crew in the hold among the barrels, and Frontinus, Januarius, Atepaccius and Canio in the cramped aft cabin.

Once, even above the howling of the gale, Canio heard a tremendous crash as some of the barrels that had been lashed together broke loose, thundered across the deck and smashed through the guardrail before disappearing over the side.

It woke Atepaccius. 'Old Neptune likes his drink,' he commented wryly to Frontinus. 'Perhaps we should throw him a few more barrels? – make the old bastard really happy, so he'll command the sea to turn as calm as a woodland pool.'

'Neptune doesn't rule these seas!' Seemingly angered by the joke, and perhaps fearful that his saviour goddess might have been offended, Frontinus had to shout to make himself heard. 'It's the Lady Nehalennia who holds our lives in her hands now. Pray to her, imperial messenger; pray to her!'

Nehalennia? Still feigning sleep, Canio tried to remember where he had heard that name before. And then it came to him: she was the goddess who, according to Tulius, Carausius had worshipped in his youth – the goddess whose temples had stood on the island of Wallacra, between two arms of the estuary of the Scaldis River. He also remembered where it was that Tulius had told him of Nehalennia: it was in the cell in Corinium where Januarius had first imprisoned him.

Which led on to him recalling the previous night's dream – the dream where Tulius had told of how Allectus, and others, had been faced with the stark realisation that, if they did not kill the tyrant that Carausius had become, they themselves would inevitably die.

He knew now – or perhaps he had known from the moment of waking last night? – that there was a message for him in that dream. It was as though Tulius was showing him what must be done, and now it seemed as though the *Parcae* were gifting him the opportunity to do it. And if he were to refuse their gift...

He continued to feign sleep, his ears straining and brain racing, waiting for the chance he was now certain would come.

Time passed. Frontinus and Atepaccius seemed to be sleeping, theirs the sleep of utter exhaustion, but Januarius was beginning to stir. During the day, the *agens* had been violently sick over the side of the ship several times. Now, in the darkness, Canio heard and felt the man clamber to his feet and stagger out of the cabin, smothering his retching as he groped his way outside, while the *Capricornus* pitched and rolled, completely at the mercy of the sea and the roaring wind. He waited until he was as sure as he could be that the *agens* was outside the cabin and that the other two were asleep, then he eased himself upright and crept silently after Januarius.

On the heaving deck the darkness was almost absolute, and he could see nothing and hear nothing above the moaning of the wind. Suddenly, the clouds momentarily cleared the waning moon and he glimpsed Januarius clutching the rail with both hands, his head and upper body bent forwards. The moon disappeared again as abruptly as it had emerged, but the image of the *agens* was fixed in Canio's brain. He edged forwards until he was so close he could actually smell the vomit on the sodden wool of the man's cloak. He paused for an instant, absolutely still, conscious that he had not quite reached the point of no return. If he chose, he could...

But there could be no turning back. He readied himself; then, in one fluid movement, he crouched, grabbed an ankle with each hand, and with an almost superhuman burst of nervous energy, he straightened up, lifting Januarius bodily and pivoting him over the rail. The *agens* cried out and twisted around frantically, and in that eternal moment, before the man's own weight overbalanced him and sent him tumbling into the abyss of the raging sea, the moon again slid out from behind the clouds, so that, for an instant, the two men stared into each other's faces.

And what Canio saw was not fury or hatred – the emotions that, in hindsight, he would much preferred to have seen – but something more akin to the terror of death seen in the pleading eyes of a frightened child. In that frozen moment, while his hands still grasped the man's ankles, it was possible – just possible – that, had he chosen to do so, he could have dragged the man back onto the deck. But seemingly possessed of a will of their own (or so he told himself afterwards), his hands released their grip, and Januarius was gone.

Atropos, the Inevitable, had cut the *agens'* thread, and Canio was alone on the pitching deck, his chest heaving with effort and choking as his lungs sucked in the almost-liquid salt-laden air. Through stinging eyes he stared out into the infinite blackness.

He was struck by the unwelcome thought that, perhaps, the endless night of eternity, something he had once heard someone – possibly a Christian, but almost certainly not Trifosa – say awaits the irredeemably wicked, would be like this? He shook his head violently, as if to dislodge the disquieting idea.

He was certain – or more accurately, wanted to be certain – that there was nothing beyond death: that the concept of eternal punishment was a fiction, invented to frighten the sheep of the world into acceptance of their undeserved miseries. Alone in the Stygian darkness and amid the howling of the wind, that was something which, more than ever now, he needed to believe. But absolute belief would not come.

Creeping back into the cabin, he listened intently until he was as certain as he could be that both Frontinus and Atepaccius had not woken. He lay down and tried to sleep, but in his mind's eye he kept seeing that final image of terror on Januarius's face, and with it came the certainty that the *agens* had recognised his murderer. It was several hours before he eventually drifted into sleep, a brief escape into oblivion.

CHAPTER THIRTY-ONE

25th – 26th November

When Canio awoke, the interior of the cabin was bathed in a wan light. Peering out through the doorway from where he lay, he realised that the longed-for dawn had come at last. And with it's coming the wind had dropped and the sea had calmed to a gentle swell. He stood and walked slightly unsteadily out onto the deck, and moments later Frontinus emerged and proceeded to bang on the hatch cover with his open palm.

'Look alive, you vermin,' he bawled. 'The storm's passed, and now there's work to be done.'

While the sailors were clambering out of the hatchway, several of them kissing the small wooden idols that he guessed they had been clutching throughout the storm, Canio gazed all around. From horizon to horizon there was nothing but the sullen, grey waters of the Oceanus Germanicus, relieved only by a few dirty-cream smudges of waves breaking in the far distance.

'Have you any idea where we are now?' he asked Frontinus, all the while wondering how long it would be before someone noticed that Januarius was missing.

'No damned idea at all,' Frontinus replied brusquely. 'All I know is that the sun is over there, so that must be the south-east.' And he pointed to a faint glow that was visible through the low clouds off the starboard bow.

'Where's *agens* Januarius?' Canio turned towards the voice and saw Atepaccius standing a few feet outside the cabin, looking all around the deck.

'Where he's been all night, I expect – puking in the corner of my cabin!' Frontinus called back impatiently.

'No, he's not there – come and see for yourself.'

Frontinus muttered something under his breath and stomped over to Atepaccius. Canio followed, waiting for the inevitable.

It took only moments to establish that Januarius was no longer aboard the *Capricornus,* and only a few more to establish that nobody had seen him fall overboard, or knew how or when it had happened. Canio certainly didn't.

Then, since nobody else appeared to be about to do so, he pointed to the gap in the port rail where the barrels had smashed through it at the height of the storm. Obligingly, Frontinus speculated that the most likely way it had happened was that Januarius, feeling his way in the dark to puke or piss, had leaned on or fell against the rail that wasn't there. Canio got the distinct impression that it was the loss of the barrels, rather than the tragic death of the *agens,* that the captain regretted most. If, indeed, he regretted it at all.

But although Atepaccius did not actually dissent from Frontinus's theory, Canio wondered if it was just his imagination that made him see scepticism in the sideways glance the courier gave him.

✳

Although uncertain as to their position, Frontinus was at least sure that they were a considerable way to the east of Dubris and moving slowly further eastwards all the time, blown by the south-westerly wind. However, by mid-morning the capricious wind had swung around again and was blowing from the south-east.

'Damned thing's fickle as a woman,' Frontinus muttered irritably. 'It'll probably change back again soon.' Nevertheless, he ordered his men to unfurl the sail, and with the helmsman hauling on the tiller that controlled the twin steering oars, the *Capricornus* turned slowly and began heading north-westwards.

Throughout the remainder of that short day, Canio spent most of his time right up in the prow of the ship, partly in an attempt to let the wind dry his sodden clothes, partly to escape the stench of the cabin, and partly to avoid the risk of being asked potentially awkward questions by Atepaccius or Frontinus about Januarius's untimely departure from the world.

At sunset there was still no sight of land, but there was enough starlight faintly shimmering on the sea from a now almost-cloudless sky to encourage Frontinus to carry on.

Later in the night the moon, which was nearing its last quarter, rose in the north-eastern sky, making the night less Stygian.

Towards dawn, Canio was woken by the helmsman on his high platform behind the cabin, shouting that he could see two pinpoints of light on the horizon, that could be the twin *pharos* at Dubris. After altering course slightly, the *Capricornus* headed towards those lights, which steadily increased in size until Canio could make out the swaying beacon flames themselves. And so at last the little ship sailed into Dubris harbour, just as the sullen dawn was breaking.

*

After the ship had berthed, they all stumbled ashore onto land that felt strangely static after the constant motion of the *Capricornus's* deck. Canio and Atepaccius thanked Frontinus, but the man seemed interested only in getting his cargo of wine barrels unloaded, while bemoaning those lost overboard in the storm. As to the disappearance of Januarius, it was agreed that Atepaccius would report his sad fate to the *agens'* superior, Antistius Adventus, as soon as he reached Londinium.

In other circumstances, Canio would have chosen to spend the day resting at Dubris, but Atepaccius was intent on delivering his dispatches to Londinium without further delay and offered to take Canio with him. Canio hesitated, but realised that if he declined the offer he would be left wondering uneasily what the courier was going to tell Adventus (and possibly Civilis too) regarding Januarius's death?

In his slightly paranoid mind's eye, he could imagine Atepaccius wanting him present, in a place from which he could not escape, after denouncing him as a murderer. Were that to happen, then he would at least be there to deny the charge immediately, and even perhaps muddy the water by claiming that he had seen the courier himself tip Januarius over the side. So he decided to travel with Atepaccius.

After a meal at the town *mansio*, Atepaccius used his diploma to get horses for himself and Canio, and they set off together for Durovernum Cantiacorum, some fifteen miles away to the north-west. In doing so, they retraced the route that both had followed, respectively some five and fifteen days earlier. Pausing only to change horses in that small city, they then took the highway that led westwards towards Durolevum and Durobrivae.

It was a dreary, wet day; a day when the drippings from the black branches of the now mostly leafless wayside trees sometimes splashed into their faces as gusts of wind caught them. The only trees with any leaves remaining seemed to be the oaks, and those leaves were brown and yellow and shrivelled. Only the young wands of coppiced hazels they occasionally passed still retained large, bright-green leaves, evoking memories of a summer now utterly gone.

On the road they spoke little at first, but as the lonely miles passed they began to exchange reminiscences of the places they had visited over the years. The conversation then moved on to how they came to be where they were on that drizzly late-November day.

Atepaccius explained he had been a soldier in a cohort of Legio II Augusta, stationed at the Saxon Shore fort of Rutupiae. Being a good horse rider, which few of his fellow soldiers were, he had frequently been chosen to carry dispatches between there and Londinium, and when a vacancy arose he was seconded to the *vicarius's* staff in Londinium to carry messages and other official documents to the other provincial capitals of Britannia and even as far afield as Treveri.

Having been sent to Treveri the day after Canio arrived in Londinium, it seemed that Atepaccius knew nothing of the circumstances surrounding Sabinus's death; it was normally more than his life was worth to hand over any dispatches with their seals broken. That being so, Canio felt free to give him an edited version of the events of the last five or so weeks, including why Januarius had been about to escort him to Treveri.

'Did you know him well, that *agens*, Januarius?' the courier asked.

'I scarcely knew the poor man,' Canio replied carefully. 'He was just a soldier, of sorts, doing his duty.'

'As am I,' Atepaccius replied. 'But, from our brief acquaintance, I got the impression that escorting you to the butcher's shop in Treveri was a duty he was rather enjoying.'

'I'm sure it was nothing personal; just a man obeying orders,' Canio replied, scenting a possible trap and realising that the courier had probably read the message from Treveri, after Januarius had broken the seal. 'In any case, I became a free man from the moment in Bononia that Januarius read the dispatch you're carrying – as Civilis will no doubt confirm in due course.' *So you can see I had no reason to hate or fear the man, still less feed him to the fishes*, he did not say, but hoped Atepaccius would come to that conclusion all by himself.

*

They arrived at Durobrivae shortly after dusk and took rooms at the *mansio* there. Both men, being bone weary as the events of the last days caught up with them, ate in near silence and then took to their beds. Canio was indeed very tired, although even if he hadn't been he would have feigned drowsiness to escape any further questions that Atepaccius might have asked concerning the late Januarius.

Canio dreamed again that night, but not of Tulius. It was the face of Januarius that he saw, superimposed on a huge full moon that rose on the horizon out of a dark sea and sent its eerie light shimmering across the water, sparkling on the silent wavelets. The eyes, those terror-stricken eyes, were staring directly at Canio, saying that they knew he was the one who had tipped him into the icy waters of the Oceanus Germanicus. They knew, despite Canio's futile attempts to convince himself that Januarius could not have recognised him in the moment before he sent the *agens* tumbling to his death. And even in sleep, Canio was only too well aware that the *agens* did not need to have seen him: for who else had a motive for doing what he had done?

Still asleep, he twisted and turned, trying to look away from that unnaturally vast moon. But whichever way he looked – east, west, north or south – it was always there on the horizon, growing ever larger until it seemed about to fill the entire sky. And if there were some shadowy afterlife, which Canio had always fervently hoped there was not, would the *agens* pursue him forever through the perpetual twilight of eternity, as had happened in the whispered stories he remembered from childhood?

He woke in darkness, with the dream still vivid. In the morning, in daylight, he would tell himself that such superstitious fears were nonsense, but in the chill of an endless winter night, disbelief in there being an existence in a twilight eternity beyond death was harder to achieve.

*

Early the next morning, as they ate breakfast together, casually exchanging anecdotes about their soldiering days, Atepaccius mentioned that he had a wife in Londinium.

'And another in Treveri?' Canio suggested drily.

Atepaccius smiled. 'No, just the one. She's all I want.'

'She must be a rare woman then,' said Canio, half sardonically, but thinking of Trifosa, now only some thirty miles distant.

'Oh, she is that. She was a widow when we married. I knew her first husband – we joined the Second Augusta on the same day.'

'What happened to him?' Canio felt obliged to ask.

'He was killed.'

'In the *Conspiratio*?' It seemed a logical guess.

'No.' There was a long pause while Atepaccius seemed to study the pattern of knots on the surface of the oak table. 'Sometimes these things look like faces – strange faces; have you ever noticed that?'

As it happened, Canio had noticed, but before he could reply, Atepaccius said, 'Actually, "killed" isn't the correct word. He was executed.'

'For what?'

Atepaccius glanced behind him, as if to make sure that there was nobody within earshot. 'In a *taberna* outside the fort where he was stationed, after he'd drunk perhaps one too many cups of barley beer, he was overheard – or alleged to have been overheard – saying that Emperor Valens was a fool, and that he would have been lucky to have made the rank of *biarchus* in a frontier unit if he hadn't enjoyed the good fortune to have Emperor Valentinianus as a brother.'

'But everybody knows that.'

'Perhaps, but not everybody is unwise enough to say it – not in public anyway. Certainly not in a place where there was an informer on the prowl.'

'And?'

'And this dog of an informer went to his master, an *agens in rebus*, and... I'm sure you can guess the rest. Everybody who could have saved my friend didn't, either through fear or self-interest or both. Nobody wanted to be seen to defend a man who had insulted Valentinianus's brother. So, they tied his hands behind his back, forced him to kneel down and then chopped off his head.'

Canio had witnessed only one military execution, and that was one too many. There was a long pause, and then he asked, 'This *agens*, his name wasn't Januarius by any chance, was it?'

Atepaccius gave a faint smile. 'No. Nor Adventus. My only reason for telling you this is to make it clear that I have no love for *agentes in rebus*. Understood?'

'Understood,' Canio replied, but in truth, he did not – not wholly. He was now fairly certain that the courier suspected that he was responsible for Januarius's death.

But is the man trying to say that I have nothing to fear from him, because he too has reason to hate agentes in rebus? Or is he trying to lull me into a false sense of security out of fear that I might attempt to silence him before he can lay an accusation before Civilis?

Perhaps the man was genuinely empathising with what he had done to Januarius? But the depressing fact was that there was now nobody in the whole world whom Canio felt he could trust absolutely. Nobody. Not Trifosa, and perhaps not even Vilbia. It was a melancholy thought.

Admit nothing; behave as if you are completely innocent of any complicity in Januarius's death.

So he said blandly, 'Well, I can certainly understand why you would hate that swine of an informer, but the *agens*? I mean, once the accusation had been made, what choice did he have but to investigate it? If he didn't, for all he knew it might have been a trap laid by one of his enemies who wanted to accuse him of disloyalty to the emperors.'

There was a silence – only lasting moments, really – but it seemed so much longer.

Then Atepaccius said quietly, 'You may well be right. Anyway, we'd better be going if we're to reach Londinium by noon. I'll go and see if our horses are ready.'

When he had gone, Canio was left with the feeling that he had been put to some kind of test. A test, perhaps, of his ability to recognise and accept genuine friendship when offered. A test that, only a few years before, he would have passed with ease, but now had failed utterly.

CHAPTER THIRTY-TWO

27th November

Despite the muddy and often potholed state of the highway, with one change of horses at Noviomagus they covered the remaining thirty-odd miles fairly rapidly and reached Londinium not long after noon.

After leaving their horses at the stables that served official travellers journeying to and from the Saxon Shore forts and Durovernum, Canio and Atepaccius walked together through the streets, past the old forum complex, until they reached the *praetorium*. They had spoken little since leaving Durobrivae, with Canio at first still puzzling as to whether Atepaccius was friend or foe, before fatalistically concluding that he would find out soon enough.

Following a brief interrogation by the sentries guarding the main entrance to the *praetorium*, the two men were escorted to an anteroom and a notary was sent to inform Civilis of their arrival. Canio barely had time to look around the room before Atepaccius, clutching the packet of dispatches he had extracted from the large purse at his belt, was summoned by the notary.

The notary was accompanied by a pair of soldiers from Civilis's bodyguard; Canio had seen them before. These two remained after the courier had gone, standing one on either side of Canio. Their presence made him uneasy: he suspected that the notary must have informed Civilis that he was not being escorted by Januarius or anyone else. If so, then these two soldiers must be under orders to thwart any attempt to escape.

Time seemed to pass infinitely slowly, but Canio's mind raced, trying futilely to guess what Atepaccius was saying to Civilis about Januarius's disappearance during the storm. Was the courier saying that he had actually seen him tipping the *agens* over the rail, or was he simply voicing a suspicion? In his imagination Canio could almost hear the accusing words. In spite of the November chill in the unheated anteroom, he became aware that a trail of icy perspiration was trickling down from his armpits and over his ribs. His right hand moved reflexively to rub the itch on his left side.

Suddenly, he realised that the notary was standing in the doorway and beckoning him to follow. Escorted by the two soldiers, he followed the man along a corridor, up a wide stairway and along another corridor, which ended in the remembered pair of high double doors guarded by a further pair of soldiers. The notary rapped on the door once, opened one leaf and walked into the room beyond, signalling Canio to follow him.

So Canio followed, and found himself once again in the main audience chamber of the *praetorium*. The large, high-ceilinged chamber was well lit by numerous polished-bronze oil lamps hanging from four ornamental stands placed around the room. The lamps swung gently on their chains in the draught from the opened door. As before, the room was heated by a pair of bronze braziers, their glowing charcoal visible through the high fretwork rims. The lamps and the braziers combined to cast strange moving shapes of light and shadow on the frescoed walls.

Seated behind the large table of polished hardwood were two men. One was the *vicarius* himself, Publius Ulpius Civilis. The other was the *agens* Antistius Adventus, the late Januarius's superior. The notary slipped silently around to the other side of the desk and took a seat at a respectful distance from Civilis, leaving Canio and the two soldiers standing. There was no sign of Atepaccius.

Without any preliminaries, Civilis said, 'So, you stand before me again, Aulus Claudius Caninus.'

'Yes, *Vir Spectabilis*.'

'I believe you are acquainted with the contents of this dispatch from Treveri?'

'Yes, *Vir Spectabilis*. Decanius Januarius showed it to me, before—'

'Then you are aware that the Praetorian Prefect of the Gauls has decided that no further action is to be taken regarding the unfortunate death of Caristanius Sabinus.'

'So I understand.'

'I wonder if you really do,' Civilis murmured, stony-faced. 'But we will discuss that later. At the moment our focus is on the loss of Decanius Januarius on the voyage back from Bononia to Dubris. We have heard from our courier, Atepaccius, that it is assumed the man fell overboard at the height of a storm, although, unfortunately, he says he saw and heard nothing. Where were you when Januarius is presumed to have fallen?'

'I was asleep in the cabin, with Atepaccius and the ship's captain, a man called Frontinus, when it must have happened, *Vir Spectabilis*.' Canio tried to keep the relief he felt from showing on his face. It seemed that even if Atepaccius had seen, or suspected, foul play, he had said nothing to Civilis.

'Asleep? In the middle of a raging storm?' Adventus commented incredulously.

'It was the sleep of utter exhaustion,' Canio protested, 'in the depths of the blackest night I have ever known, when the ship had already been tossed by the sea for half a day or more. I was so tired I could barely stand upright – as we all were. Ask Atepaccius if you don't believe me.'

'And yet Januarius seems to have left the comparative safety of the cabin and gone out onto the deck. Now why would he have done that?' Adventus asked.

Canio was acutely aware that Civilis was watching his face like a hawk about to pounce on its prey. 'I simply don't know, *Ducenarius*. The captain, Frontinus, speculated that he may have gone on deck to relieve himself or to be sick. By the way, did Atepaccius mention that part of the ship's rail was smashed by barrels that broke loose in the storm, although nobody realised it until dawn?'

'Yes, Atepaccius told us that,' Adventus said impatiently, adding, 'You didn't like Januarius, did you?'

'Who told you that?' Canio contrived to look puzzled.

'Januarius himself did.'

'Well, I can't pretend that we were close friends, but I assure you that his death was nothing more than a tragic accident. Surely nobody is suggesting otherwise?'

But Adventus would not be drawn. 'Januarius told me, Caninus, that he was looking forward to seeing you burning at the stake for the crime of sorcery. Surely that would have been an excellent reason for wanting him removed from this earth, would it not?'

'But you're forgetting one vital fact: after reading that dispatch from Treveri on the night before we sailed from Bononia, we – Januarius and myself – both knew that I was a free man again. So, I had absolutely no motive for harming him on the voyage back to Britannia. You do realise that, don't you?'

Make damned sure the bastards grasp that point. 'And another thing, it was only Januarius who seemed to want to get back to Londinium in such a hurry, although he never said why.'

Pretend he never told me about that damned notary with a grudge; they can never prove otherwise. At least, I hope they can't. 'If it had been up to me, we never would have been aboard that ship or run into that terrible storm. I was all for staying in Bononia for a few days until the weather looked more settled.' *Well, what's one more lie among so many?*

170

'So you're claiming that you didn't see Januarius fall, or hear him cry out?' Adventus was going over old ground now.

Perhaps, Canio wondered, *to give himself time to think of some flaw in my story?* 'Nobody saw him. We didn't even know he was missing until dawn.'

Adventus sat silently now, brooding. It was as if he somehow knew everything, but realised that he could prove nothing. Not without torture, and Canio was an *honestior*.

'Well, have you any further questions?' Civilis asked him impatiently.

'No, not for the moment, *Vir Spectabilis*.'

'Very well, then the matter is concluded. You have my permission to withdraw.'

Adventus hesitated, as if he wanted to say more, but then he rose, bowed to Civilis and left, but not without giving Canio a searching stare.

Taking his cue from the *agens*, Canio also bowed and turned to go.

'No, not you, Caninus. You two can go though.' Civilis flicked a hand in the direction of the two soldiers, as a man might shoo away a troublesome fly.

The soldiers left and the door closed behind them.

There was a long silence, during which Civilis appeared to be reading one of several scrolls that littered the desk in front of him. At last he looked up at Canio. 'You are a free man now, Caninus, but before you go there are two things I feel you ought to know. Firstly, I am as near certain as I can be that the reason why Flavius Viventius does not wish this matter to go any further has nothing to do with his opinion of your innocence or otherwise.'

'Then why—?' Canio began.

'Be so good as not to interrupt me. The reason is that the late Caristanius Sabinus was the brother of Viventius's wife. Indeed, wife, brother-in-law and – from what I have recently been told

– Viventius himself, all came from the same city in Pannonia: the city of Siscia, I believe. Furthermore, and this is the crucial point, it is well known that Viventius personally recommended Caristanius Sabinus for the post of *praeses* of the province of Britannia Prima, giving me little say in the matter. Thus, *if* – and I stress the word *if* – it were to be found that Sabinus had been practising black magic, something which our sacred emperor Valentinianus rightly abominates above all other crimes, it would reflect very badly on Viventius. Very badly indeed. This is, of course, only speculation, and is not to be repeated to anyone, ever… Do you understand?'

'Yes, *Vir Spectabilis*, I understand perfectly,' Canio replied. And he reflected how fortunate it was for him that Viventius was not as unflinchingly just and principled as Civilis was rumoured to be. 'And the second thing you wanted me to know?'

'The second is that I, personally, am far from satisfied that, in the matter of Sabinus's death, you are the innocent victim your statement makes you out to be. You did have reason to hate Caristanius Sabinus, did you not?' And before Canio could say a word, Civilis continued, 'No, don't attempt to deny it. Adventus told me about your friend Antoninus and how he came to die at the hands of Julius Castor, the same man who – only a few months later – apparently went mad and murdered his master, Sabinus. Nemesis herself could not have devised a more fitting act of retribution, or so the pagans might say.'

'And what do you say, *Vir Spectabilis*?' Canio asked cautiously.

'I say that, occasionally, the pagans are right,' Civilis replied cryptically. 'Quite apart from my suspicion that you know – or at the very least, think you know – exactly what happened in that triclinium at Villa Censorini, including the identity of that mysterious woman, there is also the matter of the pagan figurine you claim to have found where that man…' He paused momentarily to glance down impatiently at one of the scrolls on his desk. 'That man, Peltrasius, is supposed to have thrown it away, over two years before, in a place that Sabinus had ordered searched – no doubt thoroughly – and yet found nothing. I therefore find your claim to have subsequently discovered it in a nearby patch of brambles somewhat implausible. Indeed, it suggests to me that you were, in fact, in possession of that figurine or figurines – your own statement makes it clear that there were at least two – the whole time. Or, at the very least, you knew all along where one or both could be obtained... Well, what have you to say to that?'

'Only, *Vir Spectabilis*, that I have faithfully recorded only what happened and what I witnessed. If it does not wholly make sense to you, it is because it does not wholly make sense to me either. I was, and still remain, bewildered by what happened on that fateful night. I can only point out that, if it were my intention to kill Caristanius Sabinus, I could have devised a method of doing so that would not have placed me in such danger and left me attempting to explain the inexplicable. Something as simple as, say, a hired assassin's arrow would have done the job and left me unsuspected.'

'Unless, of course,' Civilis pointed out, 'that hired assassin were to be captured and reveal the name of his hirer – as he doubtless would have done under torture. But if, on the other hand, the murderer were to create such dense clouds of smoke that, afterwards, nobody could see through them to determine what had actually happened, then that murderer might well get away with his crime, might he not, Caninus?'

'Smoke, *Vir Spectabilis*?' Canio contrived to look puzzled. 'But there was no smoke in the triclinium that I can recall.'

'Don't act the fool with me, Caninus,' Civilis said irritably. 'You know exactly what I mean. And understand this: if, one day, I or Antistius Adventus, or anyone else under my command, should discover that even the smallest part of your testimony is a lie, then you will be dragged back before me to answer a charge of perjury, which would be a capital crime in these circumstances. Nemesis, Caninus, is a patient goddess and never sleeps. Understood?'

'Perfectly, *Vir Spectabilis*.'

'Good – then you have my permission to leave Londinium. Oh, and before you go, I suppose you'd better have this back.'

Civilis extracted, from where it had been hidden under a litter of scrolls, Canio's belt pouch, which Januarius had confiscated on his first night in Londinium, leaving him with only a dozen or so *siliquae* to buy food. Civilis tossed it carelessly to Canio, who caught it with both hands. For a moment he instinctively contemplated opening it and counting the contents, before realising that the action – and its implication – would not be well received.

But it seemed that Civilis was reading his thoughts. Glancing down and reading from one of the scrolls, the *vicarius* said, 'There were twelve *solidi*, three *miliarensia* and eighteen *siliquae* in that purse when the late Januarius relieved you of it, and I can assure you that they are all still there. Now get out of my sight – and pray to whatever god, or goddess, you believe in that I never discover the true extent of your responsibility for the death of Caristanius Sabinus.'

Amen to that, as the Christians say, Canio thought, but he said, with as much humility as his suppressed anger would allow him to simulate, 'Thank you, *Vir Spectabilis*. However, I can assure you that, if a full explanation of the strange events that happened on the nones of this month should ever come to light, then I shall be shown to be as innocent as a newborn baby.'

Civilis merely grunted with what Canio interpreted as amused contempt.

As Canio opened the doors of the audience chamber, he heard the *vicarius* call out to the two guards standing outside that they should escort "that man" out of the *praetorium*. Canio was tempted to turn and assure Civilis that he did not need an escort, and furthermore, that he had not the slightest desire to linger in that place or in his company for a moment longer than he had to. An inherent survival instinct ensured that he said nothing.

✻

For reasons known only to the guards, reasons into which Canio did not enquire, they let him out via a side door into a street that ran at right angles to the main entrance.

'I recognise this door; it's the notaries' entrance, isn't it?' he remarked casually.

One guard was already turning back into the *praetorium*, but the other looked puzzled. 'No. The notaries, junior *rationales* and other clerks use the door at the back of the building, so they can creep up and down the rear staircase without the *vir spectabilis* seeing them come and go.'

'Idle little bastards that they are,' came the voice of the second guard, already hidden in the gloom of the corridor.

'My memory must be failing,' Canio murmured as the door thudded shut behind him and a heavy bolt was thrown. In the gathering dusk of the late-November afternoon he pulled up the hood of his *cucullus* and made his way round to the north side of the *praetorium*. The far side of the street was largely in darkness, with only one or two windows barely illuminated by the lamps or candles burning behind them, but the room behind the *praetorium's* rear door appeared to be lit by at least one oil lamp, which gave sufficient light for Canio to observe the faces of everyone who came out. He did not have to wait long.

CHAPTER THIRTY-THREE

The third person that Canio saw emerge into the night was Bruscius, the notary who had so kindly authenticated Aunt Peregrina's will two years before. Hidden by the darkness, Canio followed him until, only one *insula* block later, the man slipped into what appeared to be a good-quality *taberna* called, as Canio saw by peering up at the sign when directly underneath it, *The Full Moon*.

He waited long enough for Bruscius to settle, then eased through the door and glanced around. Inside, there were a dozen or more customers, some standing and some seated, but all clutching pottery mugs from which they were drinking – either sipping or gulping, *Depending*, Canio thought, *on how anxious they were to return home*.

There was no heating, not even a small charcoal brazier, and it was almost as cold inside as it was out in the street. Bruscius was sitting at a table on the far side of the room, apparently alone.

Canio walked over to the bar and ordered a mug of the best house wine. Sipping it, he turned and continued to observe the notary, hoping that someone might be joining him, and that someone might be Vepogenus, although he had no idea what the man looked like. *Two birds with one stone*, he hoped. However, after a while it seemed that Bruscius was not expecting company tonight.

After buying another mug of wine, Canio sidled over to the notary's table and sat down on the other side. The man had not changed much over the past two years, but he was now nearer thirty than twenty-five, with the same ink-stained fingers Canio remembered, which the man would probably still have on the day he died. Bruscius looked up briefly, but apparently without recognising Canio.

Canio eased back the hood of his *cucullus* as he slid the new mug of wine across to the notary's side of the table. Bruscius looked up again, and this time he realised the identity of his uninvited companion.

He looked about to speak, but Canio put a forefinger to his lips, then said, 'No names; just listen. Four days ago, a man called Januarius – an *agens in rebus*, no less… Ah, I see the name means something to you. You encountered him when he was making enquiries about a certain will, did you not?'

Bruscius nodded warily.

'Well, this Januarius told me that he had been approached by another notary from your office, a man going by the name of Vepogenus – do you know him?'

Bruscius nodded again.

'Good. Well, this Vepogenus told Januarius that he, Vepogenus, had recently learned that, at about the same time you authenticated a certain old lady's will, you had a slice of financial good fortune yourself. Indeed, inspired by Bacchus's gift here – ' and he dipped the same forefinger into Bruscius's mug, withdrew it, then slowly licked it – 'you were unwise enough to hint, or perhaps more than hint, that your good fortune was linked to your authentication of that will.'

'I swear I never—' Bruscius began

But Canio silenced him again with a raised finger. 'Oh, but I think you did, which is why your friend Vepogenus asked for a share of your good fortune and was said to be most upset when you refused – which brings us back to *agens* Januarius. I believe we need to talk to Master Vepogenus, you and I, so where can we find him?'

'He has lodgings in the Street of the Coopers – that's in the north side of the city. He left the *praetorium* some time before me, so he's probably there by now.'

'Then finish your wine and we'll pay him a little visit.' Canio knocked back the last of his and offered the other mug to Bruscius, who shook his head. Even in the chill of the unheated *taberna*, Canio could see, and his nose could detect, that the man was sweating.

*

With Bruscius leading, one pace ahead, they walked through the dark, damp streets, where the gloom was only relieved by pale lights behind tiny windows and the occasional brighter lamp placed ostentatiously in the window of a *taberna* or brothel. They met few other people on that chill November night, and those were mostly muffled shapes that loomed out of the darkness, a pale blur of a face glimpsed momentarily before he or she disappeared back into the darkness.

The Street of the Coopers must once, Canio assumed, have been home to a guild of barrel-makers. But it seemed that those worthy craftsmen had long since moved elsewhere, and now both sides were lined with small but apparently well-constructed timber-framed houses with tiled roofs.

At one of these, Bruscius halted and rapped on the door. There was no response, so he knocked again.

'Who is it?' came a muffled voice.

'It's Bruscius; we need to talk.'

'About what?'

Bruscius turned and looked at Canio, who nodded his assent. 'About a certain lady's will.'

Canio heard two bolts being drawn back, and the door opened about six inches to reveal a small, heavily bearded man holding a pottery oil lamp that cast an eerie, yellow light onto the faces of both notaries.

'Are you alone?'

'Everyone's alone in this hard world,' said Canio, stepping out of the darkness and into the glow of the lamp. 'And the "certain lady", as I'm sure you know, was called Peregrina. I'm her nephew – and not a happy man.'

Vepogenus attempted to slam the door, but Canio was too quick for him and barged it fully open, forcing the notary to stagger backwards and almost drop the lamp. Canio stepped quickly through the now wide-open doorway, and Bruscius scuttled into the house behind him, then shut and bolted the door.

Vepogenus kept retreating backwards into the house until, at last, he stood in the middle of a room that was illuminated by the sparkling light of three oil lamps and heated by the glowing charcoal in a large brazier on a stand.

The light and warmth seemed to embolden the man. 'Just what is it that you want? I've never even heard of anyone called Peregrina.'

Canio thought the words came out far less assertively than intended. 'This is a nice room,' he remarked, looking around at the painted plaster of the ceiling and walls, and at the geometrically patterned floor mosaic. Then his eyes settled on the other occupant of the room: a young woman in a long, blue dress who was standing in the far corner. She was petite and pretty, with long, black hair, and she looked more curious than scared. He smiled – reassuringly, he hoped – and indicated the doorway with an outstretched palm. She took the hint and sidled towards the door, never for a moment taking her eyes off the three men.

Canio closed the door behind her. Moments later, he pulled it open again, just in case… but the young woman had vanished.

Vepogenus folded his arms and looked indignant, or at least he tried to do so. 'So what do you want?' he asked again. 'I warn you, if you're trying to—'

'Sit down, Vepogenus, and I will tell you exactly what I want,' Canio said, settling himself in one of the room's four wickerwork armchairs and waiting until the notary had reluctantly sat in another on the other side of the table.

'What I want, Vepogenus, is the obliteration of your memory. Only part of your memory, of course – and I'm sure you know which part. Although, if that should prove impossible, then something more drastic will have to be considered.'

'You say you're the nephew of a woman called Peregrina, so you must be…?' The question hung in the air unanswered until, finally, Vepogenus whispered, 'Caninus?'

Canio smiled his best wolfish smile. 'Aulus Claudius Caninus, a name I'm sure you remember from your furtive reading of my dear old aunt's will.'

'I still don't understand; what do—?'

'You don't?' Canio sighed. 'Then let me remind you. Four days ago, when you heard that he had been making enquiries about that will, you went to see an *agens in rebus* called Januarius. You told him that, some two years before, not long after he had proved the will of the late Peregrina (of blessed memory), my friend Bruscius here happened to come into a small legacy of his own. It was, of course, wholly unrelated to my legacy, but from something he said, when you were both under the influence of Bacchus's great gift to mankind, you formed the extraordinary misconception that the two legacies were in some way connected. In short, you believed that I had bribed Bruscius to prove the will – which, seeing as it was absolutely genuine, would have been completely unnecessary.'

'So you want me to forget what Bruscius said that night?'

Canio gave Vepogenus what he hoped was now a benign smile. 'Exactly. Erase it from your memory, as though it had never been there at all.'

'And if I can't?' Vepogenus's bearded chin jutted upwards a fraction.

The benign smile, Canio realised, had been a mistake. 'If you can't, then your memory might have to be eradicated. Wholly. Which could be very painful. Fatal, even. Do you understand what I'm saying?'

But Vepogenus was not to be intimidated so easily. 'You can't frighten me. When Januarius gets to hear of this, he'll see it as confirmation that everything Bruscius said was true – and he has the power to protect me from anything you can threaten.'

For someone who couldn't be frightened, Canio thought Vepogenus looked distinctly nervous. Canio smiled again and stuck the metaphorical knife in: 'But Januarius will never hear of our amicable little chat tonight,' he said silkily. 'Haven't you heard? The poor man fell overboard on our voyage back from Bononia. In the middle of a terrible storm, he simply vanished into the raging sea, never to be seen again – unless what's left of him, after the fishes and gulls have eaten their fill, washes up on a lonely beach somewhere. A tragic accident, of course, with no suspicion of foul play by anyone. But it does makes you think, doesn't it? One moment a man can be alive and well, and the next... And if it could happen to a man of such high status as an *agens in rebus*, then it could happen to anyone. Even to you or I.'

He saw the look of uncertainty on Vepogenus's face, so he added, 'Oh, it's quite true, I assure you. Civilis knows and Antistius Adventus knows; and I'm sure that the news will be all over the *praetorium* tomorrow. Anyway, we must be going now, back out into the night... Oh, Hades, how I hate these endless, dark winter nights. You can never know what might be out there in the darkness, only a step ahead of you... or behind you.'

Canio stood, turned towards the door, then turned back again, contriving to look puzzled. 'You know, I've quite forgotten what I came here for. Can you remember, Bruscius?'

Bruscius understood. 'No, I can't remember either. What about you, Vepogenus?'

'No,' Vepogenus muttered dejectedly. 'I can't remember a thing.'

'Which means we've all forgotten. How strange. And soon we'll have forgotten that we were ever here at all, and that this conversation ever took place. Isn't that right, Vepogenus?'

'That's right,' Vepogenus agreed, his voice now little more than a whisper.

'But perhaps,' Canio said thoughtfully, 'this evening shouldn't be entirely forgotten.' From his belt purse he took a single gold *solidus* and placed it on the table in front of him. 'Your dagger, please, Bruscius.'

'I'm not allowed to carry—' the notary began.

'I know, but lend it to me anyway.'

Bruscius hesitated, then extracted a small dagger from a sheath beneath his *cucullus* and handed it to Canio. 'Londinium can be a dangerous city, especially at night,' he muttered by way of explanation.

'It's a dangerous world.' Canio smiled at the increasingly alarmed-looking Vepogenus, then suddenly raised the dagger to head height and stabbed downwards. The point of the dagger hit the thin gold coin almost dead centre and pinned it to the table. Lifting the dagger, he eased the impaled *solidus* off the tip and squinted at Vepogenus through the oblong perforation it had made.

'Here – accept this with my compliments.' He tossed the coin to the notary, who just managed to catch it by clapping both his hands together. 'Look on it as a sort of lucky charm. Keep it with you always, and it will always protect you – but only for as long as you remember to forget. Understood?'

Vepogenus opened his hands and stared down at the little gold coin. He nodded.

'Good. That's settled then. No, don't get up; we can see ourselves out.'

*

Once back outside in the frigid darkness, Bruscius whispered, 'But what if he decides to try his luck with Adventus?'

'He won't. Your little indiscretion happened, what? Two months ago? He could have gone to Adventus then, but he didn't. It was only when he learned that Januarius was sniffing around Peregrina's will that he decided to try his luck. The man's a chancer. He'll weigh the chances of getting a little gold against the chances of getting badly hurt, and then he'll decide against pushing his luck any further.'

'But if he should?' Bruscius persisted.

Canio sighed, his breath condensing in the bitter air. 'Then I fear friend Vepogenus's lucky charm will cease to protect him. I've heard that daggers are cheap in this city – a little gold buys a lot of them... You do still have some of that gold I gave you, don't you? Or perhaps you could hire one of those magicians I've heard about. You know, the ones who can make a man vanish without a trace, never to be seen again. I'm sure Vepogenus knows the danger of falling foul of those people... as, of course, do you,' he added as an afterthought. And he smiled at Bruscius, although the smile was not intended to convey benevolence.

CHAPTER THIRTY-FOUR

Night 27th – 28th November

After parting with Bruscius (and a couple of *solidi*), Canio took a room in what appeared to be a good-quality *hospitia* that he had noticed when he first entered the city from the Calleva road nearly three weeks before – three weeks that now seemed as long as years. If questioned, he could not have given a convincing explanation as to why he had given Bruscius those two *solidi*. Perhaps it was with a vague idea of keeping him loyal, or perhaps it was simply because he was happy?

And he had good reason to be happy. He was a free man again; Januarius, the man who wanted him dead, was himself dead; Vepogenus had been intimidated into silence; and tomorrow... tomorrow, he would seek out Trifosa and persuade her to return with him to Villa Canini.

But that night, as he slept contentedly in the best bed he had occupied since leaving Villa Canini in mid-October, Tulius stole into his dreams again. And as he spoke, Canio remembered something that his child's mind had long forgotten: that the old man's voice had sounded strangely agitated as he told this part of his story.

＊

'I swear that Allecta was the last person on this earth that any man present on that fateful day would have wanted dead. But when she burst into the room and saw Carausius lifeless and Allectus writhing on the floor, his face a mask of blood, she must have thought that the soldiers had attacked them both. She couldn't have known that Allectus's wound had been caused by the heavy brass inkwell Carausius had thrown at him.

'Did she think that the soldiers were about to kill her brother? Or was she simply determined to avenge her husband's death, even at the cost of her own life? Perhaps it was both of these? Or perhaps all rational thought vanished in those last chaotic moments?

'The only thing I know for certain is that she gave a strange little cry, a sort of choking scream, before crouching down and wrenching Carausius's sword from his dead hand. Springing upright, agile as a cat, and gripping the sword with both hands, she rushed at the nearest of the soldiers. The man parried, and before Allectus – who was still only half-conscious – could call out to stop him, he had struck back.

'There was a frozen moment when time seemed to stop, and she stood there with the sword transfixing her body. Then, blood began to well out of her mouth, and in what was almost certainly a horrified reflex action rather than a deliberate act of brutality, the soldier wrenched his sword out of her body and she crumpled onto the floor.

'Neither Allectus nor anyone else could have foreseen that tragic turn of events. If he had, then I'm certain he would never have gone along with the assassination, even at the risk of his own life. But who can see into the future? Who can know what mean tricks the gods will play on us when we think we are acting for the best? Isn't that the tragedy of so many lives?'

'Afterwards – and there always is an afterwards, no matter who has died or even how many have died – the soldiers acclaimed Allectus as their new emperor. They had to choose somebody, and quickly: if Constantius got to hear that we were leaderless, he might have invaded immediately. And Allectus had been Carausius's de facto deputy – Caesar to his Augustus, as it were – but he had also led the opposition to the plans to reinvade Gaul, so it was logical that they should choose him as emperor. Also, in his role of rationalis, he had controlled Carausius's treasury, so he had skills that the other officers in Carausius's inner circle lacked.

'But I know that the guilt of Allecta's death stayed with him for the rest of his life, and even though he now had complete control over the mints at Londinium, Camulodunum and elsewhere, he never again allowed allusions to Virgil to be put on the coins. That innovation would stay unique to her, so that people would look at them and remember her for as long as the coins survived.

'There were those among the senior officers who said that Carausius's and Allecta's bodies should be buried secretly in an unmarked grave, but Allectus angrily refused to allow that. Instead, he had them both cremated in a formal public ceremony outside the walls of Londinium, on an enormous, fiery pyre that burned for a whole day and a night.

'And afterwards, the urns containing their ashes were placed in a magnificent tomb of polished Purbeck marble, which he ordered to be built beside the Calleva highway, a few hundred paces beyond the city walls, among the tombs of the illustrious dead of centuries past.

'That tomb was an impressive sight: it was like a great chest, gabled on top and decorated with the figures of gods and goddesses and scenes from the Aeneid carved in deep relief on both sides, and with leafy garlands and trailing vines at each end. And it bore an inscription which read:

"To the Spirits of the Dead – the Dis Manibus – and to Marcus Aurelius Mausaeus Carausius, emperor of Britannia and Northern Gallia. And also to his beloved wife, Aelia Allecta, who was faithful unto death."

'I remember that it took four skilled craftsmen several months to make, and when the low morning or evening sun caught it the marble seemed to blaze with a fire as bright and fierce as the funeral pyre itself.'

CHAPTER THIRTY-FIVE

28th November

Canio woke in the grey dawn, his mind still full of the dream and the lingering sense of melancholy that the dream had left behind. But, in a curious way, it reminded him that there was something that he had to do before going looking for Trifosa.

Conscience is a curious thing, he reflected, as he ate breakfast in the *hospitia's* communal dining room surrounded by noisy guests – some chattering in languages he barely recognised and did not begin to understand. Apart from his inability to erase from his memory the image of Januarius's terrified face as he toppled into that raging sea, he was almost as conscienceless as a cat in the matter of the *agens'* death. For had not Januarius – for reasons that, even now, he did not fully understand – been determined to see him executed? So was killing the man not both philosophically logical and morally justifiable? (Not that anyone could have accused him of being a moral philosopher).

Atepaccius, though, was different. Canio was now almost certain that the courier suspected that he had tipped Januarius over the side of the *Capricornus*. He may not have actually seen him do it, but he might well have seen him follow the *agens* out of the cabin and then return alone. Furthermore, who else on board that ship had a motive? Yet, evidently, he had not voiced his suspicions to Civilis, and at the *mansio* in

Durobrivae he had offered friendship, one which seemed to be based on a mutual antipathy towards the corps of *agentes in rebus*. A friendship which Canio had rejected out of a suspicion that he was being lured into making a confession – a suspicion he now realised was unfounded. And he had not even thanked the man.

His breakfast only half-eaten, he wriggled into his *cucullus* and set out to find the courier. But at the stables where the horses used by the couriers were kept, he found he was too late: it seemed that Atepaccius had set off at dawn to carry dispatches back eastwards to the Saxon Shore forts at Regulbium and Rutupiae.

'So soon? – I thought he had a wife here in Londinium?' Canio remarked to an ostler who had apparently seen him go.

'He has, and a good-looking woman she is too,' the man replied. 'But that's the way it is: if you're ordered to go, you have to go.'

'When will he be back?'

The man shrugged. 'Difficult to say. In three days at the very least – probably more like four at this miserable time of year. Who shall I say was looking for him?'

Canio hesitated, then said, 'Oh, I'm just someone he met a few days ago. I'm leaving Londinium myself today and I thought we could share a drink or two before I set off. It's nothing important.' At the last moment, he had decided against leaving his name: the instinct to trust no one was still too strong, although his conscience was jabbing him again.

✳

From the stables, he made his way eastwards, until he neared the great basilica of Saint Paul, the church that Januarius had taken him to ten days before – the same church where he had seen

Trifosa. It stood, vast and sombre in the grey light of that winter morning, the high double doors of its main entrance standing open, as if a congregation was again expected.

In a street below the basilica he found a *taberna*, and in it a seat beside a window with a gap in the shutters through which he could observe those doors. And there he sat, cradling a beaker of filthy wine, waiting and watching.

People – both men and women, singly and in small groups – began arriving and disappearing into the cavernous interior of the basilica. He started counting them, but after a hundred he gave up. Time passed, and the stream of arrivals dwindled to a trickle, and still he had not seen her come. But if she were wearing a *cucullus* with its hood pulled up, as she had been when he last saw her, it was possible that he had missed her. He cursed himself for a fool for not waiting much closer to the basilica.

There was now only one thing to be done. The basilica doors were still open as he hurried up the hill, went cautiously inside and stood at the back of the congregation, his eyes straining in the dim light as he scanned the sea of backs. Suddenly, he realised that there was someone of about Trifosa's height standing near the back of the nave, not far from the place where she had stood before. But the long *cucullus,* with its hood covering the person's head, made it impossible to be sure whether they were man or woman.

Fortunately, although the congregation must have been two hundred or more strong, the size of the basilica meant that the individuals were quite widely spaced, presumably to give each *orans* room to extend their arms in prayer. He eased his way through the open crowd until he stood close beside the woman – he was now sure that it was a woman – in the *cucullus*.

She became aware of his presence and turned her head towards him, at the same time easing sideways to increase the distance between them. Their eyes met, and the mutual recognition was immediate, although not a flicker of surprise showed on her face.

She gave a faint sigh. '*Salve*, Canio,' she whispered. 'I wondered if you would return... although I prayed that you would not.'

'Do you still hate me that much?' he asked.

'Is Antoninus still dead?'

The quiet vehemence of her response disconcerted him, but he said, 'We must talk.'

'About what?'

'About us, of course.'

'There is no "us". To me, there never was.'

'That's not true. You once felt something for me. Not love, perhaps, but at least a sort of affection.'

Their conversation, which had begun in whispers, was growing louder and was beginning to attract the attention of several other members of the congregation. She lowered her voice. 'Go away, Canio. Please, please, just go.'

'I'm not going anywhere until you agree to talk.'

'Not here, Canio; not here.'

'Then where?'

More people were watching them now, and Canio saw a mixture of concern and disapproval on their faces.

'The bridge over the Tamesis,' she whispered hurriedly. 'Be on the middle of the bridge at noon – I'll come to you there.'

The location surprised him. 'Wouldn't you prefer to meet indoors? Somewhere we could sit in the warm and have something to eat while we talked?'

But she gave a quick, emphatic shake of her head. 'No; it's the bridge or nowhere.'

'All right, if that's what you want... Do you promise to be there?'

'Yes, I swear it. Now please go. Please.'

'Then I'll see you there at noon.' He tried to pat her hand in what he thought would be a gesture of affection, but she recoiled as from the touch of a flame.

❖

Well before noon – or as accurately as he or anyone else could guess the time on that chill, sunless day – Canio entered the docks and started walking across the old wooden bridge that spanned the Tamesis some three hundred single paces east of the *praetorium*.

The river at that point was over four hundred single paces wide, the bridge flat, not arched. On glancing casually over the balustrade handrail as he walked, Canio noticed hanks of dead seaweed hanging from the massive time-and-water-blackened baulks of roughly-hewn timbers supporting the bridge decking framework above.

Every hundred paces or so the carriageway was projected out over the water, forming refuges where pedestrians could shelter from the carts, carriages and the like that rumbled across the narrow deck. At the refuge nearest to the midpoint of the bridge, Canio halted and waited for Trifosa, alternately watching the passers-by and looking down at the grey-brown water as it lisped and swirled around the timbers below.

He was expecting her to come from the northern shore, the city side, and that was the direction in which he was looking when some instinct made him turn. As he did so he saw her, not a dozen paces away and approaching from the south.

Does she live over there? he wondered, *Perhaps in one of the houses in the affluent suburbs which lay beyond the low-lying islands at the southern end of the bridge? Or had she crossed the bridge some time before I arrived, simply to conceal the true location of wherever it is that she is living now?*

He looked enquiringly at her, but she ignored the unspoken

192

question and said briskly, 'Well, Canio, here I am. What is it that you wanted to talk to me about?'

Guessing, he asked, 'What name do you go by now – not Trifosa, I assume?'

'No, not Trifosa,' she confirmed.

'Then what?'

But she shook her head, silky strands of hair the colour of fresh oat straw straying from beneath the hood of her *cucullus* as she did so. 'No, Canio, don't ask. What is it that you want?' she asked again.

He decided on a circular approach. 'Sabinus is dead; did you know that?'

'The whole city knows. I also heard that a man called Caninus is suspected of having some involvement in that evil man's death.'

'*Was* suspected,' Canio corrected her, wondering just how much she did know. 'I'm a free man again, and Sabinus is officially the innocent victim who frustrated Julius Castor's wicked plan to become fabulously wealthy by means of black magic and a little figurine of the goddess Hecate. By the way, did you know that Castor's dead too, killed by Sabinus's bodyguard troops? He was the one who stabbed Antoninus.'

'Yes, of course I know: it was you who told me as I was bathing his body – don't you remember?' She hesitated. 'That is, I knew Castor was the beast who actually killed Antoninus, not that he himself was dead... What part did you really play in their deaths?'

For a moment he was tempted to claim that he had engineered the fates of those two men who had murdered the only man she had ever really loved. However, he decided to tell her the truth, or something reasonably close to it: basically, a reiteration of his official statement. She listened, her face expressionless as she stared out over the grey-brown water.

And when he had finished she said nothing, and so to break

the unnerving silence he said, 'Of course, Sabinus was actually the prime mover in their scheme to acquire fabulous wealth by way of the Hecate figurine and a spot of sorcery, but I thought it safest to tell Civilis and the rest of them what I thought they wanted to hear – that Sabinus was the innocent victim of Julius Castor's plot. As was I, of course.' He tried not to make that last statement sound ironic.

Still she stood in silence, gazing downriver, apparently watching two ships approaching slowly as they were drawn up by the incoming tide. Then she asked, 'Don't you really know the identity of the mysterious woman who brought the second Hecate figurine?'

'Apparently, she was a woman called Trifosa – or at least that was what an *agens in rebus* called Januarius suspected. While I was detained here in Londinium, he went back and made enquiries at Villa Canini and elsewhere, and he came to the conclusion that not only was this Trifosa associated with me but, even better, she had an excellent motive for wanting Sabinus dead. By the way, Januarius was the man you saw me with ten days ago, together with those two guards. He'd made up his mind that I – and this Trifosa woman too – were guilty of sorcery and other crimes, and he was determined to see us both executed.'

'But you are free now, aren't you?'

Perhaps it was only his optimistic imagination that made Canio think he detected a note of concern in her voice? Perhaps there was hope for him yet? 'Free as the wind. Viventius, the Praetorian Prefect of Gaul—'

'I do know who Viventius is,' she said quietly.

'But you didn't know that he was Sabinus's brother-in-law, did you? I certainly didn't. And being mindful of Emperor Valentinianus's horror of sorcery and the like, it seems that Viventius realised that it would do his career no good at all to be known as the brother-in-law of a man who might have been practising black magic. It might even be suspected to run in the family. So, it was politically expedient to accept my version of events, which was that both Sabinus and I were as innocent as newborn babes. And whatever Civilis and Januarius may have suspected me of, I was officially blameless. That is why Januarius is no threat to me now – or to you.'

'Why not to me?'

'Because he's dead. There was an accident: he fell overboard in a terrible storm on our way back from Bononia, where we'd been waiting for a messenger from Viventius.'

'I see… Did you…?' She hesitated.

'Did I what?'

'Assist his falling?' she said carefully.

He didn't want to lie, not to her, but truth can be such a dangerous thing in the wrong hands. And whoever and whatever she was now, this woman was not the Trifosa who had once shared his bed.

'No, it was simply an accident… of sorts,' he couldn't help adding, before continuing quickly, 'But don't shed any tears for that bastard. While he was at Villa Canini, trying to discover where you'd gone, he tortured Aniceta to try to make her talk – or so he told me with undisguised pleasure when he got back to Londinium.'

He hadn't known, although he'd tried to guess, how she would take the news. With a little feminine gasp of horror perhaps, or maybe hide her face in both hands and weep? In the event, she stood there, silent and still, her face a mask as she stared out over the unchanging, ever-changing, water of the Tamesis.

At last, she said, 'That poor child. I deliberately told no one where I was going – not that I had any clear idea myself on that July evening. Why is it that, so often, it's the innocent who are made to suffer?'

'I don't know. Perhaps you should ask your God?' The words had slipped out before he could stop them.

'I do,' she said, her voice little more than a whisper.

'And what does he say?'

But she slowly shook her head: it seemed that she wasn't going to be drawn into a futile debate, particularly one which they had been through before. 'How badly was she hurt?'

'I don't know. All that swine Januarius told me was, "I'm sure she'll recover in a few days: I don't think I broke any bones," whatever that means.' Then, impulsively seizing the moment, he said, 'Come back with me to Villa Canini. You could heal Aniceta faster than anyone else in this entire world.'

But she closed her eyes and moved her head slowly from side to side, the look on her face almost one of pain. 'No, Canio; no. Here in Londinium I have a new name and a new life. If I went back with you, I'd be Trifosa again, and for all you know there are *agentes* in the Corinium area still looking for her. And if someone were to betray me, they would think Aniceta lied to that man Januarius – and that she had known where I was. What would they do to her then?'

'Nothing, if I were around.'

'Like you were when she was being tortured?'

There was nothing he could say to that. 'Can't I even tell her that I saw you and—'

'No! Of course you can't, Canio. For her own sake as much as mine.'

'And if that swine Januarius had never taken it into his fool head that you were the mysterious woman who brought the second Hecate figurine to Sabinus, would you then have considered coming back with me to Villa Canini?'

'As what, Canio? Your mistress? Your whore?'

'As my wife – as the chatelaine of Villa Canini.'

He saw the look of surprise on her face. It seemed that the offer was unexpected. But the look faded as quickly as it had come. 'No, Canio. No. I have a new life here, among people who believe as I believe. People who know nothing of what I once was, but only what I am now.'

'Which is?'

'What, for the first time in my life, I choose to be. Goodbye, Canio – and please, please, don't follow me.' She turned and began walking rapidly southwards. Suddenly she stopped, reached into a slit in the side of her *cucullus* and pulled something out. Walking back to Canio, she said, 'Give Aniceta these. It's not much, but it's all I have with me. I didn't think that I'd... But whatever you do, don't tell her that they came from me.' She handed Canio five gold *solidi*, and as she did so their fingers touched. For a long moment it seemed to him that she did not want to end that fragile contact, but then she snatched her hand away, turned again and began hurrying away, almost running, her footsteps echoing on the planking of the bridge deck.

He looked down at the five little gold coins nestling in his palm and his fingers closed around them, feeling the slight warmth that still lingered from her hand. He watched as her figure slowly receded and dwindled, as she continued across the bridge over the low-lying mudflats and islands on the southern shore, before finally vanishing among the buildings beyond.

For a moment he had thought of following her, but the moment had passed; it would have been futile. She would almost certainly be suspecting that he might try to discover where she lived, and even now she might be waiting and watching to see if he was coming after her. Besides, she might not actually live there, with her coming from south of the Tamesis being only a ruse to mislead him. Too late, he realised that he should have kept watch on the city side of the bridge from a time well before noon.

After carefully stowing the five *solidi* in a separate division of his belt pouch, he walked slowly back northwards into the city, turning several times in the hope that he might see her hurrying back to join him. Even as he did so, he knew it was pointless, but sometimes longing triumphs over logic.

CHAPTER THIRTY-SIX

28th – 30th November

Back on the dockside a wind from the north-east was blowing the stenches of the city into his face. With noon now past, there were only a few hours left before sunset. He was well aware that the sensible thing to do now would be to go back to the *hospitia* on the Calleva road and take a room for the night. But Canio was not feeling sensible. Whatever hopes he may have entertained earlier that morning had died with the realisation that Trifosa would never come back to him. Not today; not ever. So now he wanted to be away from this damned city and all the unhappy memories it held – and quickly.

There were three *mansiones* in Londinium, but to his increasing anger, not one would loan him a horse to reach Pontes, the location of the first *mansio* outside Londinium on the Calleva road, not even for a substantial bribe. Each *mansionarius* piously repeated that, without an official diploma, he would incur serious penalties were he to let him have one. He wondered bitterly if Civilis was behind their new-found rectitude; certainly they were among the very few *mansionarii* he had encountered who were unmoved by the sight of little pieces of silver stamped with the emperor's head on one side.

Still angry, he headed back towards the *hospitia* where he had spent the previous night. But then, on a defiant impulse, he walked straight past it; past the houses, shops, *tabernae* and workshops; and on until he passed under the massive archways of the Calleva Gate, through which he had entered the city some twenty days before.

He was well aware that the rational thing to do would be to wait until morning, and then search out somewhere to buy a horse and saddle. But that would mean spending another night in Londinium, and he felt an overpowering, visceral need to get away from the city.

So he strode on, knowing that he had not the slightest chance of reaching Pontes in daylight on that cold and dreary November day, and knowing too that the riding boots he was wearing meant that his feet would probably be blistered well before then – but on he went.

Once out beyond the extramural suburbs, he came to the stretch of road where the remaining funerary monuments lined both sides of the highway: great chest and altar tombs, and massive tombstones, taller than a tall man and a hand's-span thick. Many of the oldest must have long since disappeared, broken up and incorporated into the city walls. Even so, he found himself scanning each one as he trudged past, in the faint hope that, somehow, the monumental tomb that, according to Tulius, had been set up by Allectus over the ashes of Carausius and Allecta, had survived.

It was a foolish hope, as well he knew. The tomb – if it ever existed – had, in all likelihood, been destroyed by Constantius's victorious army when it marched into Londinium some three-quarters of a century earlier. Yet he still continued to peer at each as he passed, driven by what he came to realise was the need to find tangible proof that something – anything – that he remembered Tulius saying in the dreams was verifiably true.

*

Pontes lay some twenty miles to the south-west of Londinium, and it was long hours after sunset before Canio, footsore and chilled, limped into the little unwalled town. The night sky had cleared and the frost came down early, with glittering stars and a waning moon, some two days past its last quarter, giving some light.

For at least the last ten miles he had cursed himself for a fool for not obtaining, legally or illegally (he was indifferent as to which), a sword or some other weapon before quitting Londinium. In the darkness he was conscious that black shapes might suddenly loom out of the night at any moment, and he might find himself fighting for his life.

But it never happened. The only people he encountered on that road were a few pedestrians and two ox-drawn carts, all hurrying to reach Londinium before the gates were closed at sunset. After that, there was no one, and he had the mysterious and dangerous world of night all to himself.

Fortunately, the *mansionarius* at Pontes proved to be less conscientious than his brethren in Londinium, and he provided Canio with a meal and a bed for the night – for a bribe, of course. But in the morning fear triumphed over greed, and he declined to provide him with the hoped-for horse to take him to the next *mansio,* some fifteen miles distant. So, he was forced to find a dealer and spend a further four of his rapidly diminishing stock of *solidi* on a horse and saddle, both of which appeared to have seen better days.

Over the next two days he travelled the remaining eighty miles on the same highway that he and Januarius had journeyed along some three weeks before. Trying to find something to lift his spirits on those sullen days, as he rode along he looked out for the few flowers that had earlier been resisting the onset of winter. In particular, for a remembered patch of a dozen or so knapweeds, their shaggy purple-pink heads a welcome splash of colour in the drabness of early November.

At last he spotted them, but there were now only two flowers left, and those draggled and wan, trying in vain to resist the coming winter and their inevitable death. For flowers, winter was their Atropos; for men, it was time. The melancholy thought occurred to him that men too try to resist the irresistible, but they never succeed. The difference was that, for the flowers, after winter comes spring, and with it a resurrection of sorts – but for men, after death, there was nothing. He had always hated late Novembers, when the last gallant remnants of summer finally died, but never more so than now.

*

Eventually he reached Corinium in the late afternoon of the last day of November. There he discovered that news of his official exoneration, and the sad demise of Januarius, had both reached the city on the previous day. It seemed that Civilis had dispatched a courier early on the morning of his own last day in Londinium. The letter had also informed Flavius Vadomarus, who was apparently still in charge, that a decision on the appointment of a new *praeses* for Britannia Prima had not yet been made by the Praetorian Prefect of Gaul.

Probably, Canio thought cynically, *because Viventius wanted to make absolutely certain that any sins which a prospective appointee might go on to commit could not possibly reflect badly on himself – unlike those of the late Sabinus.*

CHAPTER THIRTY-SEVEN

1st December

Canio stayed the night in Corinium, and early the next morning, while the frost was still white on the grasslands, he began the twenty-mile ride northwards back to his Villa Canini. Some four miles from home, he rode through the little market town of Fonscolnis. With the hood of his *cucullus* pulled well forwards and on an unrecognised horse, he attracted little attention. Nobody but a stranger passing through.

Halting on the trackway on the upper slopes of Coel's Hill, he sat and gazed over the lichen-stained tiled roofs of the villa, which – in the long, dark nights in Londinium – he had wondered if he would ever see again. Spotting a figure in a short *cucullus* walking away from the villa, he urged the horse down the hill, across the wooden bridge over the stream and then, where the track divided on the far side, took the right-hand fork, which led up the slight incline towards the villa courtyard.

Austalis, the blacksmith-cum-ostler, must have heard the horse approaching, because as Canio rode up he saw the man waiting outside his forge, which occupied one end of the great aisled barn. He pushed back the *cucullus's* hood, swung one leg over the horse's back and slid down out of the saddle.

With his hair and beard untrimmed for the last six weeks, and wearing clothes that had not been washed or changed for almost as long, it was little wonder that Austalis stared uncertainly at him for several moments.

'Master? It is you, isn't it?' he asked hesitantly.

'Yes, it's me.'

'We heard you were being held prisoner in Londinium.'

'I was.'

'So how—?'

But Canio raised his right hand, palm outwards. 'Later. Stable this nag, then collect everyone you can find and bring them to the triclinium. When you're all together, I'll tell you the whole story.'

*

It was clammy-cold in the triclinium, almost colder than outside in the open air, the cold seeming to seep out of the walls and floor. Canio sat, without speaking, at the far end of the long, U-shaped table until as many as Austalis could find were assembled.

Crowded around the table were the two bailiffs, Felix and Senuacus; Regina, the cook; her assistant, Diodora; two maidservants, Justina and Quartilla; and old Diovicus, who never ceased to tell anyone who would listen how much better things had been in the old days. And right at the back, largely hidden behind the bulk of Senuacus, was young Aniceta, Diovicus's granddaughter.

Canio then gave them an edited account of where he had been and the things he had done in the five weeks and more since he was last there. He was at pains to emphasise that he was no longer under suspicion of being in any way responsible for Sabinus's death, which no lesser person than Viventius, Praetorian Prefect of Gaul, had confirmed. He was conscious that he was exaggerating slightly.

They of course knew – the whole province knew – of the murder of *Praeses* Sabinus by Julius Castor, and they had heard rumours that Canio was somehow involved, although nobody present could have said exactly how. They also knew, or thought they knew, that Trifosa had played some part in Sabinus's death. They knew it because an evil bastard of an *agens in rebus* called Januarius, accompanied by a squad of soldiers, had come to the villa looking for her. And when everyone had denied knowing where she was, not having seen her since the day she fled back in July, he had tortured Aniceta, just to make sure that neither she nor anyone else there was lying.

'Is that vile man still hunting for Trifosa?' Regina asked anxiously.

'And will he be coming back?' Canio heard the fear in Aniceta's voice.

'No, he's not still searching for Trifosa, and he won't be coming back; you'll never see him again – ever,' Canio assured them.

'Are you sure? I mean, if he came again tomorrow, with soldiers, you wouldn't be able to stop him, would you?' This from Aniceta again.

'He'll never come back. Not tomorrow or any other day, because he's dead. Dead and gone forever.' Seeing the varying degrees of uncertainty on all their faces, Canio added, 'He was aboard a ship returning from Bononia, and on a dark night, in the middle of a raging storm, he fell overboard. Whatever's left of him now is somewhere in the Oceanus Germanicus.'

'Are you absolutely certain of that? I mean, there's no chance that he might have…' Felix's voice trailed away, as if the bailiff hesitated to doubt Canio's word, but…

Which brought home to Canio just how much the bad memories of the *agens'* visitation were still vividly etched on all their minds. 'Yes, I'm utterly certain,' he assured them. 'I was there, on the same ship, when he went over the side.'

'Hades, you didn't throw the swine overboard, did you?' There was excitement in Senuacus's voice and a sudden alertness in all their expressions.

Canio realised that they were actually willing him to admit that he was the one who had sent Januarius on his last, dark journey. They wanted vicarious revenge on the *agens,* and what better than to be in the presence of the person, the hero, who had slain the man who had tortured Aniceta?

And the temptation to play the hero was almost overwhelming. Only a few weeks before he might have succumbed to it, but those weeks of mental and often physical solitude had induced a heightened sense of caution and an inability to trust anyone but himself.

He shrugged. 'No, it was just an accident. I didn't even see him fall, and as far as I know, no one else did either. Perhaps the howling wind or a giant wave caught him and sent him over the side?' he added blandly. Looking at their faces as he spoke, he was not sure that everyone there believed him. Which was both gratifying and slightly worrying.

*

When the little gathering had broken up, he discreetly followed Aniceta until he saw her climb the stairs at the end of the east wing. Intrigued, he waited for a short time, and then crept up the stairs himself. Halting outside the door of the small, windowless room that Trifosa had converted into a Christian shrine, he listened until he heard a faint rustling, as of a *stola* brushing against wall or table, and then he knocked gently. The rustling ceased. Silence.

He opened the door, and as he did so, Aniceta turned quickly to face him, her back now to the little table that served as an altar. The only light in the room had come from a single candle burning on top of the altar, but by the light from the open door he could see something close to fear on the girl's face.

Before he could say a word of reassurance, she said defensively, 'Mistress Trifosa said I could come here whenever I wished, Master.'

'Of course you can – you and anyone else who wants too.' The frightened look had not completely gone away, so he added, 'I only came to ask if you had fully...?' But he knew it was a stupid question. 'What did that bastard Januarius do to you?' he asked quietly.

She didn't answer immediately, but turned back to the altar table, covered with a cloth embroidered with a large chi–rho monogram. 'Is he really dead?'

'Yes, of course he's dead. I swear it. He can never hurt you or anyone else again... and nobody is looking for Trifosa either. You're safe here – completely safe.'

In a voice that barely rose above a whisper, Aniceta said, 'I told them – everybody told them – that nobody had seen Trifosa since she fled away on that evening in July when you buried Antoninus. But they said that if anyone knew where she was, it must be me. So they tied my wrists behind my back with a rope looped over a beam in the great aisled barn and hoisted me off the ground. Only for a few moments at a time they did it, but the pain was terrible – far worse than anything I'd ever felt before. Five times they did that, and the pain was so bad that...'

'That what?'

There was a long silence, before she whispered, 'That if I had known where Trifosa was, I would have told them. I would have betrayed her to end the agony.'

And guilt like that lingers long after the pain has gone, Canio thought, but he said, 'That's nothing to be ashamed of. I would have given in at the first lift, never mind the fifth... Does it still hurt?'

'Yes, a little… For the first week, I could barely lift my arms at all, and Regina had to feed me. Even now, it hurts to lift them any higher than my shoulders. That man, Januarius, wanted to continue with the lifts, but the soldier in charge – I think the other soldiers addressed him as *"Centenarius"* – refused, which made Januarius angry… Do you think that God punishes us for the wicked things that we do?'

It was not a concept that Canio felt comfortable with. By the tilt of her head she seemed to be looking down at the small triptych that stood on the centre of the altar, from which the nimbussed head of Christus in the central panel gazed out at the beholder. He chose to assume she was referring to Januarius's fate. 'It was probably just the wind, the storm and the slippery deck that sent that swine overboard.'

'But who sent the wind and the storm, Master?'

Canio decided to change the subject. 'I've got a little gift for you.'

'A gift? What is it?'

'Turn around and you'll see.'

She turned, and he held out the five *solidi* that Trifosa had given him. She stared at the little gold coins, but seemed reluctant to take them. So he gently seized her right hand and tipped them into her open palm, noticing as he did so that the rope burn scar on her wrist was still an angry red.

'Gold,' she murmured wonderingly, and he realised that she had probably never before possessed a gold coin. 'But I don't deserve them; the only reason I didn't tell that terrible man where he could find Trifosa was that I simply didn't know.'

He wondered whether to tell… and why shouldn't he? Nobody was looking for Trifosa now. 'You do deserve them – and anyway, they're not from me. They're from a friend.'

For a moment she looked puzzled. 'Not from Tri—?'

But Canio quickly put an index finger to his lips. 'I met her quite by chance, a long way from here. She's well and living under another name, although what that name is she wouldn't say. But for her sake you must tell nobody – nobody at all. It's our secret, yours and mine. Understood?'

Aniceta nodded. 'But will she ever come back?' she asked.

Although her face was in shadow, Canio heard the wistfulness in her voice. 'Perhaps.' But then felt compelled to add, 'But not for a long while.'

She nodded and turned back to the altar and the triptych. In the silence that followed, Canio closed the door quietly and crept away, trying to convince himself that he had no reason to feel guilty.

Nevertheless, he told himself that, tomorrow or perhaps the next day, he would take her to Glevum (he had decided that it would be prudent not to go back to Corinium until memories had faded somewhat) and buy her a new *stola*, or a pretty ring or bracelet.

*

That night, lying in his own bed for the first time in many weeks, he suddenly realised that three nights had now passed without hearing Tulius's voice in his dreams.

And as the days, weeks and months slowly passed, it did not return. It had ceased as unexpectedly as it had come, leaving Canio mystified as to what had caused those long-buried memories from his childhood to resurface. It was a question that, he assumed, would never be answered and the old man's voice would never return. But he was wrong.

PART TWO

CHAPTER THIRTY-EIGHT

11ᵗʰ – 12ᵗʰ May AD 371

Canio had been back at Villa Canini for over five months. He had lived there all through the seemingly endless days of rain and frost in the long, dark, cold months of December, January and February. Months when the grasslands, woods and ploughlands seemed to be permanently sodden, and all life in the natural world appeared to be doing nothing except grimly enduring, trying to survive until the arrival of the longed-for spring.

January had seen the first faint signs of returning life, with catkins lengthening and turning yellow on hazel bushes, and small, bright-green leaves appearing on the honeysuckle bines in the woods. In late-February had come the deep-yellow celandines, pale-yellow primroses and the green spears of bluebell leaves beginning to push up through the leaf litter of woodland floors.

By late March the pace of resurrection had quickened, with white flowers on the leafless twigs of the blackthorn bushes, and hawthorn buds bursting to reveal fresh, green leaves. And on the rough grasslands beside the high Salt Way, the gorse bushes were covered with rich, yellow flowers; while overhead, in the increasingly blue skies, skylarks sang.

Early April saw the first bluebells in Guito's Wood; and cowslips and red campion, as well as bumblebees and sulphur-yellow butterflies. In his vineyard the buds were beginning to burst, and by the end of the month the vine leaves were slowly expanding.

And when early May came at last, Canio's spirits had completely revived. Memories of last winter's miseries were fast receding, and the next winter seemed far, far away, banished by anticipation of the long months of summer still to come.

It was the time when late spring shades into summer, when there is magic in the earth and in the things of the earth. That short-lived time when the newly unfurled leaves of beech trees are moist-fresh and light green, with a delicate fuzz of hairs along their edges, while still retaining at their bases the golden-brown remains of their pointed bud sheaths.

The time when the waysides are seas of tall cow parsley, their white flowers dancing in the warm breeze. When on the lowlands and the lower parts of the hills, the hawthorn bushes are already smothered with white blossom, which sometimes hides their leaves completely. And when the banks of the stream that tumbles down on the north side of Villa Canini are carpeted with thousands of the white stars of wild garlic, the oniony smell of their leaves permeating the whole area around the villa.

And still he had not once dreamed of Tulius. That dream of Januarius, though – the one that had first come in the *mansio* at Durobrivae, the one where he saw the *agens'* face superimposed on a huge full moon rising out of a dark sea – that had come perhaps ten or so times. However, as the months had passed, its frequency had declined, until in April it did not come at all.

He was not unaware that a cynic might have said that time had simply dulled his conscience. But that cynic would have been wrong: he had no conscience whatsoever over Januarius's death, only a vague unease lest some previously unknown witness to the murder – one of the sailors on the *Capricornus* perhaps? – should come forwards. An unease that the lengthening and warming days were rapidly dispelling.

✵

It was around noon, as he and Felix were walking in one of the lowland fields near the villa, inspecting the progress of a crop of March-sown Celtic beans, when Aniceta scurried up to say that a stranger – a woman – had arrived at the villa and was demanding to see Canio.

She said that the woman would not give her name, but that Canio would know her when he saw her. The description Aniceta gave – quite attractive, mid-twenties and dark hair – could have fitted several women of Canio's acquaintance.

He found this stranger sitting in the triclinium, with Regina the cook keeping her company (and ensuring that she did not go wandering around the villa).

The woman must have read the uncertainty on his face, because the first thing she said was, '*Salve*, Caninus – do you remember the last time we met, at Villa Censorini? My hair was shorter then and styled differently, not as it is now.'

Now, Canio observed, it was more natural: long and loose and lustrous. She swept it up with both hands and held it behind her head for a few moments – and then Canio recognised her.

'Valeria…?'

'Faustina,' the woman reminded him. 'Valeria Faustina.'

She was, Canio recalled, the late Caristanius Sabinus's mistress. The woman who had tried to stab him on that frosty early morning in November, after Sabinus had been murdered the previous night. And with recognition came unease. *Was she about to…?*

But as if reading his thoughts, she said, 'Don't worry, I haven't come here to harm you. On the contrary, I've come to sell you something that could save your life.'

'Oh,' he said warily. 'And what might that be?'

'Silence. My silence.'

'About what?'

'About the things Sabinus told me concerning you and that little figurine of Hecate.'

'Such as?'

'Such as that he was certain you had used it to acquire the money with which you bought this villa, and that if he could get his hands on it, he would become the richest man in all Britannia.'

'He told you that, did he?'

'He was drunk at the time, and we'd just…' She finished the sentence with an ambiguous gesture of one be-ringed hand.

'So what? Sabinus was a greedy swine. We both knew that.'

'Quite, but I've seen a copy of the sworn statement you made on the night he was killed. In it, you claimed that Sabinus was the innocent victim of Julius Castor's wicked plot, as you yourself were.'

'Really? And how did you get hold of a copy of my statement?'

'Vibius Natalis showed it to me. You see, we've become quite friendly over the last few months. He's a sweet boy, and one day, when his father dies, he's going to become a rich one too.'

You'll eat the poor fool alive, Canio thought, but he said, 'Even if Sabinus did think possession of the Hecate figurine would make him rich, I still don't see how this affects me. All it does is suggest that he deceived me into thinking that he was as innocent as myself.'

Faustina smiled. 'Natalis also told me that *Vicarius* Civilis has given instructions to our new *praeses* that, should anything come to light that throws doubt on the truthfulness of your statement – anything at all – then it must be reported to him. It seems that Civilis does not wish you well. So if he were to learn that what you said about Sabinus being a blameless victim was a lie—'

'No,' Canio interrupted. 'I only said that I was as near certain as I could be that Sabinus was a blameless victim. I didn't swear he was. If challenged, all I'd have to do is look shocked and say that he deceived me, just as he must have deceived everyone else.'

'But from what I've heard, Civilis might not want to believe you, so my testimony could still spell trouble for you.'

'But you won't give that testimony, for at least three very good reasons.'

'Which are?' Valeria Faustina was still smiling, evidently still confident that her dice had thrown Venus.

'Firstly, Praetorian Prefect Viventius, for reasons not unconnected with the fact that Sabinus was his brother-in-law, will most certainly not want the virtuous dead exposed as someone who practised black magic.

'Secondly, after all this time, questions are bound to be asked as to why you didn't come forwards with this information earlier.' He paused to let her ask the inevitable question.

'And the third reason?'

'Can't you guess? No? Well, Civilis and his pet *agens*, Adventus, would need to be certain that you were telling the truth, and there would be only one way to do that.'

It took several moments for her to grasp the implication. 'Torture?' she whispered, and Canio could tell by her astonished look that the thought had never even crossed her mind. 'They wouldn't dare! I was the companion of a *praeses*; had he lived, we would have been married by now.'

Canio decided that there was no point in puncturing that particular delusion. 'Whatever your relationship to the late *praeses* may have been, you're still classed as one of the *humiliores*, so Civilis could have you tortured until no man would ever look at you again.'

She stared at him as the full meaning of the words struck home, and he watched as her smile disappeared and fear crept into her eyes.

It was his turn to smile. 'It's a long ten miles back to Villa Censorini. Do you want something to eat and drink first?' When she didn't answer, he said solicitously, 'Give me a little time and I'll take you back in my carriage.'

'No, don't trouble yourself,' she said angrily. 'I can make my own way back.'

Which made Canio suspect that Vibius Natalis did not know she had come. 'As you wish. Here, buy yourself something to eat and drink at Fonscolnis.' He took five silver *siliquae* from his purse and placed them on the table in front of her.

She snatched them up, and for a moment he thought she was going to throw them back at him. Pragmatism overcame anger, and she thrust them into her own belt purse. They both stood, and she pushed past him on her way to the triclinium door.

But in the doorway, she turned and said with quiet venom, 'By the way, Natalis tells me that your saviour, Viventius, may not be Praetorian Prefect of Gaul for very much longer. He's moving on, and do you know who his replacement is going to be?'

Canio said nothing: she was going to tell him anyway.

'No? A Pannonian called Maximinus, that's who. Natalis says that he's a lawyer of sorts, and when he was in charge of the grain supply in Rome he used his position – with our glorious emperor Valentinianus's enthusiastic blessing – to have dozens of senators and their relatives tried and executed on charges of sorcery. It's his speciality, sorcery and black magic, and it's said he owes his latest appointment as Praetorian Prefect to his performance in Rome. Oh, and he also has no love of Britannia – do you know why?'

Canio again said nothing, simply waited.

'Because Valentinus, the man who had his head chopped off by the *Dux* Dulcitius after his failed rebellion two years ago, was his bother-in-law. Strange world, isn't it? I mean, Sabinus was Viventius's brother-in-law, which worked in your favour, and Maximinus was Valentinus's brother-in-law, which certainly won't, should another of your lies come to light.'

'Sabinus, Viventius, Maximinus and Valentinus – all of them Pannonians. Just like our two esteemed emperors,' Canio observed. 'Do you think there could be something in the water in that part of the world that makes them all a bit peculiar?'

'Oh, you may think it's funny now, but you won't be laughing if Maximinus scents fresh opportunities to accuse rich men of sorcery and black magic, and so decides to investigate you further. From what I was told, he thinks that everyone even suspected of those crimes is guilty until proven innocent – which never, ever happens. Not if he can prevent it,' Faustina added, as a Parthian shot.

With that, she was gone, and Canio stood listening to the receding patter of her feet on the plain mosaic floor of the corridor.

He was left thinking that he had handled the situation rather well, except that, if it were true that this man Maximinus was going to be the next Praetorian Prefect of Gaul, and if it were also true that his activities in Rome included persecuting rich men suspected of involvement in sorcery, then the implications for him were worrying. *But,* he told himself, *Faustina is a bitter woman seeking revenge and money, so she was probably lying. Although if she wasn't...*

✤

So, early next morning, he rode the twenty miles south to Corinium. He took a circuitous route so as to avoid, as far as was reasonably possible, Villa Censorini and its inhabitants, particularly Valeria Faustina.

At Corinium he made discreet enquiries and was annoyed and concerned in equal measure to learn that Faustina had told the truth about a man called Maximinus being the designated successor to Viventius as Praetorian Prefect of Gaul. More worrying was the confirmation that Maximinus had indeed won the favour of Emperor Valentinianus by prosecuting, with fanatical zeal, members of the senatorial aristocracy and their families – women as well as men – for various crimes, including poisoning, adultery and fornication, but principally the practice of sorcery and black magic.

As he rode home, he tried to remember if there was anything in his sworn statement that – with Sabinus, Castor and Peltrasius being safely dead – could be proved to be untrue?

There was, of course, the mysterious woman who had brought the second Hecate figurine, the genuine one, the woman whose identity he had sworn he did not know. However, in the unlikely event that they were ever to find Trifosa, she could surely prove that she had been in Londinium on the nones of November last year. And as for Bodicca, she was hardly likely to come forward and identify herself as the mystery woman, and nobody who mattered knew that she even existed.

He had forgotten the fake Hecate figurine, the replica with which he had tried unsuccessfully to deceive Sabinus. But someone else had not forgotten it, as he was to learn the following day.

CHAPTER THIRTY-NINE

Night of 12th – 13th May

That night, as if to further unsettle him, the voice of Tulius returned briefly in a dream. In the morning, Canio tried to tell himself that, even after an absence of over five months, it was of no particular significance. Even so, he had the faintly uncomfortable memory that, whenever he had chanced to wake in that night of sporadic moonlight, he had kept his eyes tightly closed. The reason, he told himself, was to get back to sleep quicker. It was certainly not to avoid seeing what – or who – might be there in the room with him, half-hidden in the moon shadows. But whether in a dream or otherwise, he was certain that he had heard the old man's distinctive voice again; if anything, it had been clearer and more insistent than ever before.

*

'Now that Allectus was emperor, everyone hoped that, if we stayed in Britannia and made it clear we had no ambitions beyond the shores of that island, then Maximianus and Constantius would accept the status quo and leave us in peace. It was thought that the never-ending warfare against the various Germanic tribes on the Rhenus and Danube frontiers would keep them tied down and make them reluctant to look for further trouble. It

was a foolish hope really: by then we should have known that tyrants do not always think or act rationally.

'However, for the first two years of Allectus's reign it seemed that all would be well. We told ourselves that the memories of Maximianus's disastrous invasion attempt were still so vivid that not even a mad dog like him would have the stomach to try again. And in those years, relieved of the burden of taxes to pay for the huge armies of the empire, Britannia prospered.

'So secure did Allectus come to believe himself to be, and so confident that the gods were smiling upon him, that he commissioned the building of several prestigious civic buildings in Londinium, overlooking the Tamesis. They were constructed of fine worked stone in the old monumental style, the like of which hadn't been built in the island for half a century or more.

'Another thing, minor perhaps, but to show he had been listening to what people needed by way of small change, he introduced a small copper coin he called the quinarius. He minted millions of them, and every single one had his radiate-crowned head on one side and a liburna war galley on the other, so as to remind everyone that he controlled the seas around the island and so could ensure their safety against both the hostile forces of the empire and Saxon pirates.

'So it was that he began to think that his little empire would last forever. My, how the malicious gods must have laughed.'

CHAPTER FORTY

13ᵗʰ May

It was in the early afternoon of the following day that bailiff Senuacus came to report that he had come across another stranger – this one wandering near the villa. A man who, when challenged, had asked if somebody called Claudius Caninus lived there, and, if so, he wanted to see him. 'Said his name was Baculo.'

'Baculo?' For a moment the uncertainty was genuine, but then Canio remembered. 'What does he look like?'

'Not young – forty or more I'd say. Quite short, but strong-looking. Hands like shovels. Do you know him?'

'I might. Where is he now?'

'I left him near the vineyard. Told him to wait there while I tried to find you.'

Canio stood and walked to the door of the kitchen, where he had been talking to Regina the cook. 'Right, I'll go and see what he wants. No need for you to come with me,' he added, guessing Senuacus's intention.

He walked across the walled courtyard, down the stoned track and across the wooden bridge over the stream. The man was still waiting at the edge of the vineyard.

'*Salve*, Baculo,' the man said.

'*Salve*, Ivomandus,' Canio replied. 'You're a long way from Vertis.'

221

'Thirty miles and more,' Ivomandus confirmed. 'Have you still got it?'

'Got what?'

'That little orichalcum figurine I made for you back in October of last year.'

Canio gave him a long, cold stare. 'We had an agreement, Coppersmith: neither that figurine nor Baculo ever existed – remember?'

'Yes, I remember – and I wouldn't be here if I wasn't desperate.'

'How much?' Canio made the obvious assumption.

Ivomandus shook his head. 'I don't want money. I want your help; you are an *honestior*, aren't you?'

'I am,' Canio agreed warily, 'but what of it? And how did you find me?'

'It wasn't hard. The whole province knows what happened at Villa Censorini last November. Even in Vertis I heard about three mosaic workers from Corinium who are still cadging free drinks by telling everyone who'll listen the tale of how they retrieved a figurine of Hecate from a bramble patch for a man they afterwards realised was you, Aulus Claudius Caninus. Have you still got it?' Ivomandus asked again.

'The figurine? No, an *agens in rebus* called Januarius took it, and I haven't seen it since. He probably had it destroyed as soon as he could, pious Christian that he was.'

I was going to throw the damned thing into the Coln, until I realised I needed it to support my sworn statement, Canio didn't say.

'But the man's dead now. He met with a nasty accident,' he added, hoping the implication would not be lost on Ivomandus. 'So, what sort of help do you want?' He noticed that Diovicus and a couple of other men weeding the vineyard appeared to be moving slowly closer, no doubt curious to learn what the master and this stranger were talking about.

222

Ivomandus had evidently noticed them too. 'Can we go somewhere more private?' Without waiting for Canio's reply, he started walking towards the track that led up Coel's Hill.

Canio followed, and the two men walked in silence until they came to a place where the friable, orange-brown soil of the trackside bank had slipped down in the winter rains. Ivomandus sat on the sun-warmed earth, stretched his legs out in front of him and gestured Canio to do the same.

'Do you remember that I told you my son – his name's Ixarnius – was taken for a soldier six years ago and sent to one of the forts on The Wall?'

As it happened, Canio did remember. 'And you said, as I recall, that he was still there some four years ago when the Picts overran it in the *Conspiratio*, and you've never heard from him since.'

'So I thought he must be dead – if he wasn't, he would surely have got word to me somehow. But yesterday morning a man came to my workshop and gave me some news about my son. Actually, "gave" is the wrong word – I had to pay the bastard. Anyway, he said that he had been one of Ixarnius's comrades in that fort on The Wall, which – like all the others – was undermanned, and had been for years.'

'So?'

'So, one day, he and half a dozen others were in one of the small towers between the milecastle forts when the Picts invaded – hundreds and hundreds of the screaming savages, their near-naked bodies covered in blue tattoos. And straightaway he knew – they all knew – that if they were stupid enough to stay and fight, then the ravens would be eating what was left of them by nightfall. So they ran for their lives. Not back to the milecastle, because they'd have stood no chance there either, but south. They ran until night came and The Wall and the Picts were many miles behind them.'

'He deserted?'

Ivomandus shrugged. 'What else could he do? A day or so later he heard that The Wall had been overrun from end to end, *Dux* Fullofaudes was probably dead – to this day, nobody seems to know for sure what happened to him – and all was chaos. Anyway, Ixarnius and his comrades, all conscripts, hated the army and saw the invasion as their chance for freedom. So they kept moving south; at first stealing a little here and there, just to survive.

'But as the weeks passed, and the anarchy around them increased, they grew bolder and greedier until, I suppose, they were nothing more than a gang of brigands. And apparently, that's how they've been living ever since – gradually moving south, always one step ahead of the army. Until now.'

'They've caught him?'

'I don't know… Perhaps. The man – he wouldn't give his name – told me that, when he left them, they were near Ariconium, a place just north of the Great Forest which lies beyond the west bank of the Sabrina—'

'I know where Ariconium is,' Canio interrupted.

'And while they were there,' Ivomandus continued, ignoring the interruption, 'they heard that a squad of cavalry from Glevum had been hunting for them up north, around the town of Magnis, and was now working its way southwards. That was when he – the man who came to see me – decided it was time to quit. He said he had a premonition that their luck was running out. But the rest of them, including my son, were determined to continue on south and hide in the forest. They reckoned the cavalry would never find them there, and they could prey on travellers on the highway that runs along the west bank of the Sabrina from Glevum to Venta Silurum.'

'So, your son isn't dead, but he is a brigand and has been for several years. Wonderful! But you still haven't told me what you want of me?'

'I want you to help me bring Ixarnius back, before the army can catch him. Because if they do catch him, there'll be nothing

I can say or do to save him. But you, *honestior*, can maybe open doors that are locked and bolted shut to me.'

'I doubt if I'd ever get the chance: if the army catches him, they'll probably kill him on the spot. Those lads don't mess around.'

Ivomandus considered this in silence for several moments. 'Perhaps, but since he's recognisable as their leader, they might decide to take him back to Glevum – to show him off to the world before they—'

'Their leader? You didn't mention that – and how is he recognisable?'

'From what I was told, he wears a large gold ring – one he persuaded a cloth merchant to give him when they met on the road some miles south of Eboracum. Apparently, it's inset with a red gemstone engraved with a standing figure of Mercury.'

'The protector of merchants and thieves – how apt,' Canio murmured. 'So what do you expect me to do?'

'Come with me. Help me to find him and bring him home.'

'Why me? You must have friends in Vertis.'

'Not friends who could negotiate with the army like you could, being an ex-soldier as well as an *honestior*.'

Before he could ask, Canio remembered that the coppersmith had guessed that he was ex-army back in his workshop in Vertis, and he had never denied it. 'And if I refuse?'

For several moments Ivomandus did not reply as he gazed towards the north-west, at the blue line of the Malvern Hills on the far horizon. Then he said slowly, 'I've written an account of how and when I came to make that figurine for you, and I've left it with someone – two someones actually – who you never met or even knew existed. And if I don't return to Vertis within the next seven days, those someones have sworn that it will be handed to the new *praeses* in Corinium, even if they have to take it themselves.'

Canio, trying to keep his face expressionless, considered the implications of what Ivomandus had just said. If the coppersmith were to swear that he had made the figurine in late October, then his own claim of having organised its finding on the nones of November would be shown to be false.

Even worse, him giving the coppersmith detailed instructions, including a sketch from memory, would suggest that he had benefited from a much more recent acquaintance with the original than the mere glimpse he had admitted to before Peltrasius had thrown it away, over two years earlier.

And most damning of all, any recent acquaintance with the original would imply that he probably knew the identity of the mysterious woman who had brought it to Sabinus on that fateful November evening.

Could Ivomandus be bluffing? Perhaps, but calling that bluff was too great a risk to take. Later, in a few months' time, after the coppersmith had returned to Vertis, it might become necessary to arrange a disappearance not unlike that of the late Januarius, but Canio really didn't want it to come to that: back in Vertis he had rather liked the man.

'And if I agree, then what?' he asked at last.

'We go to Ariconium and start searching,' Ivomandus replied. 'Somebody there might know where Ixarnius and his comrades are, or at the very least, they could tell us how long ago they left and which way they went. If you were to lend me a horse, we could be there by this time tomorrow.'

'Very well, if that's what you really want. We'll leave as soon as the horses are saddled.'

'How many men will you bring with you?'

'None. It will just be you and me,' Canio replied. On seeing the doubting look on Ivomandus's face, he explained, 'It doesn't matter if there are two or ten of us, we can't take on the army, can we?' His real reason, of course, was that he didn't want Felix, Senuacus or anyone else from Villa Canini learning what the coppersmith knew about the fake Hecate figurine.

Whether or not Ivomandus realised his true motive, he didn't argue. He simply shrugged and said, 'If that's the way you want it.'

'It is. By the way,' said Canio, changing the subject, 'how did you get here?'

'I begged a ride on an empty grain boat sailing down the Sabrina from Vertis to Glevum, hopped off at Confluens, and then walked eastwards the dozen miles or so across country to this place.'

'But how did you know where I lived?' Canio asked, suddenly suspicious.

'It didn't take a genius to find that out, not once I knew your name, Claudius Caninus.'

Canio grunted his acknowledgement. 'You might as well call me Canio; it was my first and only given name. Have you eaten today?'

'No: I haven't eaten since leaving Vertis, and I've drunk nothing but stream water.'

'Then you'd better have something before we leave. Don't worry, I won't poison you – not here, anyway. There are too many witnesses.' He gave Ivomandus a tight smile, confident that he would find it less than reassuring.

*

They set off in the mid-afternoon to ride the more than twenty miles to Glevum; Canio on Antares, Ivomandus sitting awkwardly astride Protus. For the coppersmith's sake, to avoid steep ascents and descents, Canio chose a route that skirted the edge of the hills. However, this meant they had to travel by a circuitous route, first north, then west and, finally, south. Which is why it was not until the long evening of that early summer's day that they rode under the North Gate and into the little walled city of Glevum.

CHAPTER FORTY-ONE

From the North Gate they trotted along the streets, looking for somewhere to stable the horses and spend the night, but found nowhere that wasn't full. The only exception was the *mansio*, where the *mansionarius* – a man of high principles, but little commercial sense – refused to accommodate them without an official *diploma*. Remembering his experiences back in November, Canio concluded sourly that there must be an outbreak of virtue among the ranks of the *mansionarii*. He hoped it wouldn't spread among the general population.

Obliged to leave the walled city to find beds for the night, they went into the extensive extramural settlement on the west side of Glevum. There, they took rooms at *The Caduceus*, the *stabulum* where he, Bodicca and the boy, Nectovelius, had spent a night back in the previous October. He wondered if the locals were still looking for Vario, sometime owner of *The Brindled Hound popina*, the man who he had a strong suspicion Bodicca had murdered and thrown into the nearby docks on that dark autumn night.

After seeing Antares and Protus properly fed and watered, Canio ordered a couple of bowls of lamb stew with beans and a flagon of wine for himself and Ivomandus. Halfway through the meal, the coppersmith – who had seemed increasingly preoccupied, only answering Canio in monosyllables – suddenly stood up and announced that there was somewhere he had to go.

'Where?' Canio asked.

'Back into the city,' Ivomandus explained.

Canio did not ask why, for the simple reason that he suspected Ivomandus would not tell him. The man appeared to be wrestling with some inner conflict that Canio had no wish to share. 'Well, you'd better be quick then. They close the gates half a summer hour after sunset.'

The coppersmith did not reply. Canio gave a dismissive shrug and poured himself another beaker of wine.

✣

By the time that Ivomandus returned it was already twilight in the streets, and in *The Caduceus's* dining room a couple of lamps had been lit. But the coppersmith was not alone: striding behind him was a youngish woman wearing a *stola* of plain, undyed wool, with a shawl of the same cloth wrapped around her shoulders. She had a strong, hard face, which might once have been quite beautiful, but on which years of hard living had taken their toll. Canio judged her age to be somewhere in the mid-twenties, although he was to learn later that she was only twenty-two.

Ignoring Canio, she stood defiantly in front of Ivomandus. 'Well, we're here. So now you can tell me – what have you heard about Ixarnius that you couldn't tell me back in the city?' She paused, then said quietly, 'Has his body been found?'

'No – he's alive, girl. He's alive! That's what I couldn't tell you back there,' Ivomandus almost whispered.

Canio saw astonishment, elation and then scepticism flit in quick succession across the young woman's face.

'Are you sure? Have you seen him?' she queried.

'No, I haven't seen him, but—'

'So how can you know he's alive? Have you been drinking again?'

'I'll tell you how I know in a moment,' Ivomandus said impatiently. 'First, this is…' The coppersmith hesitated and looked questioningly at Canio.

Canio understood, but saw no point in deception. 'My name,' he said to the young woman, 'is Aulus Claudius Caninus, but you can call me Canio.'

'And this,' said Ivomandus, 'is my daughter, Sulicena.'

'Which puzzled Canio, but before he could ask, Ivomandus explained, 'When I told you last October that Ixarnius was my only child, it was because—'

'It was because he was ashamed, that's why. Ashamed because when the soldiers came to kidnap Ixarnius and drag him off into the army, he was so drunk that he didn't even think to warn his only son that the bastards were looking for him.'

'I was mourning your mother; that's why I was drinking – as well you know!' Ivomandus protested.

'I was mourning Mother too. We all were – so don't you dare use her as an excuse!' Sulicena's voice then softened slightly, and she said, 'Anyway, that's all in the past. Tell me about Ixarnius; where is he, and is he well?'

So Ivomandus told her the same tale he had told Canio. Sulicena listened in silence, although Canio could tell by her increasingly unhappy expression that the news her brother had become a robber (and probably worse) was corroding the exhilaration she had felt on learning that he was still alive.

When Ivomandus had finished, Sulicena asked, 'This man, Canio, isn't the one who told you about Ixarnius, so why…?'

The real reason was potentially embarrassing to both men, so before Ivomandus could reply, Canio said quickly, 'I'm a friend of your father from years ago. I was a soldier once, so he asked me to help him find your brother before the army does.'

Sulicena appeared to accept this, but then said, 'I'm coming with you – to Ariconium and beyond – until we find him.'

The two men exchanged sceptical glances, and Ivomandus said flatly, 'You can't. We've got horses, so you'd slow us down.'

'You've got a horse?' she said incredulously. 'You've never even sat on a horse in your entire life.'

'I lent it to him,' said Canio, adding, 'but he's right – you would slow us down. And if we do find your brother, things might get dangerous.' He did not elaborate on what he meant by that, mainly because he wasn't sure himself.

'I'm coming anyway,' she said defiantly. 'I've got to go back inside the walls now, before they close the gates, but I'll be back here first thing in the morning, well before you leave.'

Don't count on that, Canio thought, glancing towards Ivomandus. And, judging by the expression on the coppersmith's face, he guessed that the man was thinking much the same.

'How did you know she was in Glevum?' Canio asked, when Sulicena had gone.

'I've been back here several times over the years,' Ivomandus replied, 'trying to make things right between us. But all she'd ever say was, "I won't come back until Ixarnius returns," by which, of course, she meant never.'

CHAPTER FORTY-TWO

Night of 13th – 14th May

That night, as Canio slept beneath a musty blanket in a less-than-fragrant bed, his bedroom door bolted and his scabbarded *spatha* hidden under the blanket beside him, he dreamed he heard Tulius again, telling of the beginning of the end of Allectus's little empire.

✻

'With the hindsight of years, I can see that Maximianus never had any intention of letting us live in peace. The reason he gave to his soldiers for needing Britannia back in the imperial fold – not that the cur ever felt it necessary to give reasons to anyone, except to his master, Diocles – was that the army needed the hundreds of shiploads of wheat and barley that, before Carausius seized the island, had been exported to Gaul every year. I say, "exported," although "extorted" is the more accurate word.

'We didn't have the network of spies in Northern Gaul that existed in Carausius's heyday, but we did receive some news from merchants who traded across the Oceanus Britannicus. Although due to them having interests on both sides of that sea, they were never fully trusted, not even when they told of rumours that Constantius was building a great fleet at Rotomagus on the banks of the Seine.

'What we did know for sure was that Constantius was waging war against our Frankish and Frisian allies on the Rhenus frontier, in the north-east of Gallia Belgica. This was why some Frankish warriors, after having been driven out of their homelands, crossed over to Britannia and were recruited by us to increase the size of the garrisons of the Saxon Shore forts – just in case those rumours that Constantius was assembling an invasion fleet should turn out to be true.

'But time passed, life in Britannia went on smoothly, and in his second year as emperor Allectus conferred on himself a consulship, just as Carausius had done before him. "Vanity of vanities; all is vanity," as the Christians are so fond of saying.

'It was in mid-May, some three years after the death of Carausius, that Allectus received a report from the captain of one of our liburnae, saying that a fleet of enemy warships was sailing eastwards along the coast of Gaul, keeping close to the shoreline. In that captain's opinion, those liburnae were heading for Gesoriacum – quite possibly to launch an attack on Dubris from across the Fretum Gallicum. Or perhaps even to attack Londinium via the Tamesis Estuary, as Maximianus had attempted to do some seven years before. That fleet, as we learned later, was commanded by Constantius himself.

'What we didn't know was that Julius Asclepiodotus, Constantius's Praetorian Prefect, was in command of another fleet, which was sailing out of the mouth of the Seine at that very moment and heading towards the island of Vectis and the south coast of Britannia.'

CHAPTER FORTY-THREE

14th May

Determined to make an early (and Sulicena-free) start, both men rose in the spectral predawn light. As they led Antares and Protus out of the stables, Canio heard the creaking of the city's West Gate being dragged open on its rusty hinges. Out in the street, to Ivomandus's evident dismay, the very first person they saw was Sulicena, walking quickly towards them wearing a short *cucullus* and carrying a bulging small sack.

'*Salve* Father. Anyone might think you were planning to leave without me,' she said coldly.

Ivomandus was not best pleased. 'That's just what we are doing. Like I said last evening, you'll slow us down – you know you will.'

'Not if your good friend Canio here hires me a horse, I won't. And you can afford to, can't you, Canio? You being an *honestior* and all.'

'*Honestior*? What makes you think that?' Canio asked disingenuously.

'I'm not stupid. That is the tip of a sword scabbard I can see beneath your *cucullus*, isn't it? And aren't *honestiores* the only people, besides serving soldiers and the like, allowed to carry them?'

Canio looked at Ivomandus, who shrugged. 'She's got her mother's sharp eyes... And her mother's sharp tongue as well,' he added in a murmured aside, which Canio suspected only he was supposed to hear. But by the abrupt way she turned and stared at her father, Canio suspected that Sulicena had heard it too.

'I suppose she could be useful in persuading Ixarnius to come home,' Ivomandus admitted, perhaps embarrassed by her hearing his remark about her late mother.

'So does she come or not?' Canio asked.

Ivomandus hesitated, then said, 'She comes.'

Canio grunted his exasperation.

'Just outside the North Gate there's a horse dealer called —' Sulicena began.

'Proxsimus,' Canio interrupted. 'Yes, I know: I've been here before.' And he had, of course – back in October, when he had bought a pony for Bodicca and Nectovelius. It occurred to him that there was something faintly disconcerting about the way fragments of his recent past seemed to be repeating themselves. 'Wait here. I'll go and see what nags he's got.'

*

Unfortunately, Proxsimus had sold two horses on the previous day, and now had only mules to offer. Canio tried to hire one, but the dealer refused, saying that he had been cheated too many times by hirers who never came back, so it was a sale or nothing. Canio hadn't the time to argue, so with a certain ill-grace, he bought the sturdiest-looking mule, together with a cheap saddle and halter.

He met up with father and daughter again outside the West Gate, Sulicena carrying another sack containing the bread, cheese and wine she had just bought with money he had given her before he went to see Proxsimus. He relieved her of the wine and promptly stowed it in one of Antares' saddlebags.

After helping Sulicena up onto the mule's saddle, and instructing her in the basics of controlling the animal, Canio led the little party across the massive old timber bridge that spanned the Sabrina, their mounts clopping on the planking, the low morning sun sparkling on the sheets of grey-brown water below.

Once past the bridge, they continued on the stone-paved highway that led westwards. After a couple of miles, they came to a point where it forked: west for Ariconium and south for Venta Silurum, which was the road that, some miles further on, ran alongside the west bank of the Sabrina. They took the west fork, the less well maintained of the two, only occasionally meeting other travellers, and those mostly trudging wearily along on foot.

As they rode along the highway, Canio leading, the enforced proximity of the trailing pair nudged Ivomandus and his estranged daughter into a halting conversation.

'What have you been doing this past year? Are you still working at the weaver's place near the North Gate?' Ivomandus asked.

'There and a few other places. Anywhere where they'll pay me.' There was a long pause, then she asked, 'What else did that man in Vertis say about Ixarnius?'

'Nothing, really – nothing that I haven't already told you.'

But she must have detected something evasive in his voice. 'Surely you asked him what Ixarinus looks like now, after six long years away?'

'He's got much more of a beard, of course, and a few scars.'

'Scars? On his face?'

'One on his forehead, or so the man said.'

'How did he get that?'

'At a small farm, somewhere north of Eboracum. Near a town called Isurium Brigantum, I think he said, and… Do you really want to know?'

'Yes, of course I do.'

Ivomandus sighed. 'Apparently, they were starving and all they wanted was to get a little food —'

'To steal a little food?'

'Perhaps – if they had to. But the farmer came at them with one of those long-handled hedging sickles and... there was a fight.'

'What happened to the farmer?'

'Does it matter?'

'What happened to him?' Sulicena persisted.

'He died. Are you satisfied now?'

✢

Some five miles on from the fork in the road – five miles of fields, pastures and small woods – they came to the hilly north-eastern spur of the Great Forest, where the ground rose sharply and the road twisted and turned as it attempted to follow the lower ground of the valleys and the shallower gradients. Aware that time was not on their side, and abandoning caution, neither Ivomandus and Sulicena dismounted, but clung on grimly to their mounts, no matter how challenging the ascents or descents they encountered were to their embryonic riding skills.

Even so, crossing this spur of the forest took time, despite the frustrated impatience of father and daughter, and it was near noon when they at last broke clear of the trees and hilly ground and emerged into an area of undulating, unkempt grasslands and scattered small fields. Two miles further on, they came in sight of the low hill on which stood what was left of the little town of Ariconium.

Canio had heard that the place had been attacked in the *Conspiratio* four years before, when a war-band of Hibernians had come rowing up the Sabrina in a fleet of seagoing currachs. They had first tried, and failed, to capture Glevum, before turning westwards in search of easier prey. But until that moment, Canio had not realised just how badly Ariconium had suffered.

In the town itself, the few buildings left intact were mostly those with stone walls and tiled roofs. Greatly outnumbering the stone buildings were the remains of timber structures, now mostly nothing but heaps of fire-blackened timbers, which the rains of four winters had made even more desolate. Aggressively thriving brambles and beds of rank nettles had already invaded the ruins and the areas around them.

Twisting in the saddle, Canio scanned southwards, seeing the vast, undulating sea of fresh, green leaves that was the Great Forest stretching to the horizon. Over to the west, on the shallow downslope of the hill, he saw dozens of small, waist-high, cylindrical clay and stone shaft furnaces, most seemingly abandoned and in various stages of dereliction. A few, perhaps still in use, were sheltered beneath open-sided timber structures with roofs of roughly split sandstone tiles.

Dotted around the surrounding countryside were innumerable heaps of what Ivomandus called *scoria* – the slag separated from the molten metal during centuries of iron smelting. The very soil under their feet, where exposed, was black from the ash of the charcoal used to fire the furnaces, in marked contrast to the rich, reddish-brown earth of the surrounding countryside. He realised that, at some time in the not-so-distant past, the town must have been an anthill of activity, but now...

A track, metalled with *scoria* and partially overgrown with weeds, led up to the largest of the stone buildings. Standing on high ground, on the north-east side of the ruined town, it had walls of pale-reddish-brown sandstone and rows of lozenge-shaped roof tiles of the same material, which – from a distance – looked like the scales of a giant lizard.

As they dismounted to rest the horses and the mule, an old man emerged from the building and eyed them warily.

'*Salve*,' said Canio, and smiled – encouragingly, he hoped. 'Do you live here?' he asked, by way of opening the conversation. 'By the way, my name's Baculo, and you are…?'

'You can call me Litugenus,' the old man replied cautiously. 'It's as good a name as any. And this is where I live now, seeing as how poor old Eberesto the *mansionarius* is dead and gone, slaughtered by those Hibernian bastards, and the powers that be aren't intending to replace him.'

'So this used to be the *mansio* then?'

'It was. That, and the local headquarters for the tax collectors who used to come around every few months – in the days when there was anything worth taxing. It was them who said I could live here,' Litugenus added. 'Just to keep the place tidy, like.'

'So there's no *mansio* here anymore?'

Litugenus shook his head. 'There's no call for one now, not with so few rich travellers using this road.'

'Really?' Ivomandus contrived to look puzzled. 'I'm sure I heard someone in Glevum say he'd seen a man with a big gold finger ring near here, only a few days ago.'

It was Litugenus's turn to look momentarily puzzled. Then he said, 'Him! He wasn't no rich man – he was the leader of a gang of thieves that had come down from the north, from Magnis way. A nasty lot they were too. They didn't stay long, not when they realised there was nothing here worth stealing, especially when I told them some soldiers had been here looking for them not a day before.'

'How long ago was this?' Sulicena asked anxiously.

'Oh, maybe three days ago. Four at the most.'

'Which way did they go?' she asked. 'Not north towards Magnis, I hope,' she quickly added.

'No, eastwards; back along the same road you came on – back towards Glevum. From what someone overheard, we reckoned they were heading for the highway that leads south alongside the Sabrina. There's many a traveller, rich as well as

poor, who uses that road on their way to and from Glevum.'
The old man paused, then asked anxiously, 'They're not friends
of yours, are they?'

'No, not friends,' Canio reassured him, 'Definitely not
friends, but we think that among that pack of brigands is this
lady's brother. They kidnapped him a month or so ago, and
from what we've heard they treat him like a slave. Little more
than a boy he is, so we want to rescue him before he comes to
worse harm. You know what the army's like: if they catch them,
they'll kill them all – the lad as well, no questions asked.' *Which
is,* Canio, told himself, *near enough to the truth.*

'Oh, like that is it? Well, I can't tell you more than I have
done already. All I know is that they went off eastwards, and
I've never seen them since, the gods be thanked.'

'So, it looks like we've got to go all the way back to that
place where the road forked southwards,' Ivomandus observed
angrily. '*Merda*! If only we'd known, we could have saved the
best part of a day.'

'If it's the Venta road you're wanting, there's a quicker way
to get to it. Over there' – Litugenus said, pointing to the south –
'is a track that leads through the Great Forest for eight miles or
so to the Temple of Sabrina at Ten Springs, and from there, it's
only a mile or so downhill to the Venta road.'

'Are you sure?' Canio asked.

'I've never been surer; it's one of the tracks they used to bring
iron ore and charcoal up from the forest to this place, though it's
not used much nowadays. Four years ago I was on it, coming
back from where I'd been bargaining for a cartload of charcoal,
when those Hibernian savages attacked the town. If the forest
hadn't hidden me, I'd be as dead as most of the people I once
knew here.'

The old man looked down at the ground, closed his eyes and
slowly shook his head: and Canio guessed that in his mind's eye
he was seeing some of those dead people.

But Ivomandus was hardly listening. 'If that way's quicker, then let's go through the forest – we can't afford to waste any more damned time,' he muttered, scrambling inexpertly up onto Protus's back and making the horse whinny.

Canio looked towards Sulicena, but she was already vaulting nimbly onto the back of her mule. 'So, it seems that's the way we're going,' he murmured. 'The track's over that way, then?' he asked Litugenus, peering southwards.

The old man simply nodded, and Canio realised that his thoughts were still not with the living. 'It's not far... not far. Just follow this track you're on now for a bit, then turn south at the crossroads.'

'So why can't I see it from here?' Canio asked.

The old man sighed. 'It's a bit overgrown these days. Time buries everything in the end – both the tracks and the men who made them. But I know the track into the forest is still there, because I walked half a mile along it only a few days ago, gathering firewood.'

The coppersmith and his daughter were already fifty yards away. Canio shrugged, grasped one of the horns of Antares' military saddle, swung himself up onto the horse's back and prepared to follow them. But before he did so he tossed the old man a *siliqua*; he wasn't entirely sure why. If someone had suggested that it was an offering to one who had walked with the local forest gods, into whose territory he was about to trespass, he would have laughed and denied it. Even less likely would be an admission that, ever since an incident over ten years before while soldiering in Germania, he had been irrationally wary of forests – and of the things that might be lying in wait, hidden in their depths.

CHAPTER FORTY-FOUR

Three hundred yards to the east they came to a crossroads, turned right and headed southwards on a *scoria*-metalled but overgrown track. After a mile it crossed the road along which they had travelled from Glevum, and then continued on into the Great Forest itself.

The scattered trees on the forest margin soon gave way to a tract of hazel bushes, which Ivomandus said had probably once been coppiced for charcoal, but now looked as if they had not felt an axe for the last ten years at least.

The track continued deeper and deeper into the forest, following narrow valleys where the hazel thickets gave way to densely planted oak and ash trees, which towered above them, straight and tall and unbranched, on the steep slopes on both sides.

For the first mile or more they made good progress, but after that the track grew narrower and the metalling less and less distinct, before ending altogether. Further on, the track branched several times, forcing them to guess which route would take them to the temple. Twice, they guessed wrongly and found themselves heading south-westwards, before the track petered out completely, deep in the heart of a wilderness of ancient woodland.

Then, they had to dismount and lead the horses and mule south-eastwards through dense undergrowth, in places where nobody seemed to have passed for years and where they could frequently see no more than a dozen yards ahead.

Forests, Canio remembered, *are deceptive things. A man may think he knows one well and is familiar with all its paths and landmarks. But let him return after only a few years away and he will find himself in an unknown land. For the forest is itself a living creature and ever-changing, though the pace of change is often so gradual that a man who frequently visits it might deceive himself into thinking that, in any given season, it has hardly changed at all.*

Ivomandus took these setbacks stoically, but Sulicena became increasingly agitated, and Canio had imagination enough to guess what was going through her mind.

'Don't worry,' he assured her. 'If your brother is hiding somewhere in this forest, the army will never catch him. In fact, he's more likely to find us.' Tactfully, he did not speculate what might happen in that eventuality.

The forest was not all impenetrable wilderness. Sometimes they stumbled upon glades where shafts of sunlight slanted down between the trees and where the ground was covered with dense carpets of bluebells. In one glade, they came across a hawthorn tree that was fully twenty-five feet high, its branches so smothered with dazzlingly white blossom that the green leaves were almost completely hidden.

In another small clearing, they disturbed a family of wild boar – a sow and half a dozen small piglets; the sow grey-black, the piglets striped front to back in alternate bands of dark brown and tawny. The old sow stared balefully at the intruders for a few moments, then turned and trotted silently off into the undergrowth, the piglets tumbling and squealing behind her.

From time to time they heard the sound of unseen creatures moving nearby in the depths of the forest. Occasionally, Canio caught a glimpse between the leaves of a fallow deer which, on realising it was being observed, leapt crashing away through the undergrowth.

With increasing frequency they came across irregular-shaped pits of varying sizes and depths, almost all colonised by vegetation – mostly mosses and ferns growing on their rough and creviced stone walls.

'Scowles they're called,' Ivomandus informed Canio. 'They're where the miners hacked out the iron ore, following the seams until they petered out.'

'But how did they know where to dig?' Sulicena asked.

'From what I've been told, the pits have always been there since the beginning of time. The miners just made them bigger as they followed the ore seams. These ones don't appear to have been worked for decades, maybe even centuries.'

Estimating the distance covered was impossible as they forged their tortuous way southwards, guided by occasional glimpses of the sun. Canio reckoned they had covered at least four miles without meeting or even glimpsing a fellow creature until, as they were passing yet another scowle, Canio heard a slight scuffling and realised that there was somebody inside it. He halted and listened, but that somebody was now keeping very still, very silent.

After dismounting and handing Antares' reins to Ivomandus, he went and peered over the edge of the scowle, and saw a heavily bearded man in a dirty tunic crouching at the bottom. The man stared up at him like a startled animal, but did not speak.

So Canio said, '*Salve.* We're trying to get to the Temple of Sabrina at Ten Springs. Can you tell us if we're going in the right direction?'

'How many of you are there?' the man asked, in a voice that sounded rusty from infrequent use.

'Three – just the three of us,' Canio replied. 'Is there still any iron ore to be got out of this pit?'

The man hesitated before answering, 'A little, only a very little; nothing worth stealing.'

Canio ignored the implication. 'So are we going the right way for the temple?' he asked again.

'Yes… yes, I think so. Just bear slightly that way' – the man pointed to the left – 'and it's some three miles, or maybe four.'

Canio thanked the man and threw him a *siliqua*, for much the same superstitious reason that he had given one to Litugenus. When they were a hundred yards further on, he remarked to Ivomandus that he had not seen any piles of iron ore in the scowle.

'He wasn't looking for iron,' the coppersmith replied. 'Didn't you notice his hands?'

And then Canio recalled that the man's fingers were blotched yellow, with something he had assumed was plant juice. 'They had some sort of yellowish stain; what of it?'

'Ochre – I'll lay long odds that's what he was after. It was often found in small quantities mixed in with the iron ore seams. My guess is that man has found a pocket of it, one that the early miners missed. Sometimes it's yellow, and sometimes it's red or brown or even purple, but whatever its colour it fetches a good price.'

'Who from?'

'Painters – wall painters. For fancy murals and the like. They reckon it doesn't fade over time like some colours do.'

'How come you know so much about it?'

'When I was a boy, my father brought me here once. He worked on a boat that brought iron ore and charcoal up the Sabrina to Vertis, so he thought he'd show me where they mined the ore. Thirty years ago that was. Thirty years, all gone,' he sighed.

※

They pressed on, up and down the wooded slopes, trying to head slightly east of south, but sometimes having to divert around areas where the sheer density of the trees and the understorey of hazel and holly forced them to go back and find another way.

Judging by the occasional glimpses of the sun, now low in the north-western sky behind them, Canio realised that it was well into the evening when they came at last to a place of steep valleys and hillsides, but where the trees thinned and the ground began rising towards the east.

Thinking to getter a better view of the land ahead, they laboured up the next hillside, at the top of which was a grove of young ash trees. After pushing impatiently through it, Canio emerged into a wide clearing, in the centre of which stood a large and magnificent stone building. Other than a few timber huts in various states of dereliction, it was the first man-made structure of any sort that he had seen since leaving Ariconium.

To come across it so abruptly after long hours of struggling through the seemingly endless tangle of wild woodland was astonishing. At first sight, he had thought it was a villa, but as he approached from the north-west, still leading Antares by the reins, it soon became apparent that this must indeed be the Temple of Sabrina.

At the western end was a tall, stone-walled structure with a complicated arrangement of tiled roofs, and at the eastern end was what he assumed was a large courtyard, surrounded as it was by a high wall.

Beyond this walled courtyard was a raised platform – large, flat and paved with stone slabs – and beyond the platform the ground fell away, down to the Sabrina Plain some mile and a half distant. A well-worn track led downhill towards what must be the Glevum to Venta Silurum highway running alongside the Sabrina.

As he was completing a slow circuit of the place, during which he noticed a large, projecting apse on the western side of the temple, Canio saw a man in long, flowing robes appear from a doorway in the courtyard wall. For several moments they stared curiously at each other, before Canio said, '*Salve.* This, I assume, is the famous temple of the goddess Sabrina?'

'It is indeed,' the man replied, still eyeing Canio uncertainly. 'And I am Aurelius Feliculus, its head priest. Are you seeking a cure? The temple is the spiritual home of the healing goddess herself and her attendant nymphs.'

'No, just beds for the night for myself and my two companions.'

By then Ivomandus and Sulicena had caught up with Canio, both leading their mounts. Feliculus looked at the pair in their rough clothes and appeared not to like what he saw. 'I regret that we can only offer accommodation to those seeking a cure through the intercession of the goddess.' He did not sound very regretful.

'So how much does the goddess charge for a cure – and three beds?' As he was speaking, Canio was fingering through his belt pouch and bringing out four little silver *siliquae*, which he displayed on his open palm.

Feliculus moved closer, as if to confirm that they really were *siliquae*. He smiled. 'The goddess is always ready to assist those who require her help,' he said smoothly. He smiled again and, with a wave of his hand, indicated a door into the temple.

Canio smiled back, with equal insincerity, and explained that they must see to their mounts first.

*

There was no proper stabling, but there was a small, fenced paddock with a rough shelter and water in a trough served by one of the numerous springs in the area. After the horses and mule had drunk and been unsaddled, they were turned loose to crop the lush grass of early summer. Carrying the saddles, plus the bags containing their food and wine, all three then walked back to the temple.

As Feliculus escorted them into the temple, through a door that led to the pilgrims' accommodation, Canio heard Sulicena whisper to Ivomandus, 'Shouldn't we keep going, at least down to the highway?'

'No. It's best we stay here for the night.'

'But on the road we might find Ixarnius,' she persisted.

'Or his bunch of cut-throats might find us – in the dark, where nobody would recognise us. So, no, we wait here. At this time of year the dawn will come soon enough.'

Canio caught the drift of their *sotto voce* conversation. 'I heard a rumour,' he said casually to Feliculus, 'that there's a gang of brigands preying on travellers on the highway that runs beside the Sabrina. That's why we came through the forest. I assume they haven't troubled you?'

'No, mercifully not, although I too have heard that rumour. However, the man who told me also said they were last heard of some way to the south of here, not far from the Temple of Nodens. It's nearer the highway than our temple and somewhat larger, so it's possible the brigands would find it a more tempting target.'

Canio got the distinct impression that, if Nodens' temple were to be attacked by Ixarnius and his gang, Feliculus would be somewhat less than heartbroken. Business is business.

After showing them to their rooms – which were more like cells, both in terms of their sizes and spartan furnishings – Feliculus insisted on showing Canio all around the temple complex. *Perhaps,* Canio wondered cynically, *in the hope of extracting more silver coins by reciting the menu of services that the goddess could offer?*

The walled courtyard turned out to contain a large, rectangular, spring-fed pool, the walkway around it being sheltered on all four sides by a tiled lean-to roof, the inner edges of which were supported by a row of stone columns built off the pool surround.

'Persons tormented by ailments of the eyes, or persistent skin sores, come to bathe in these waters, and often leave completely cured,' Feliculus informed Canio.

Canio nodded in apparent acceptance of this statement, but said nothing. He knew of at least a dozen temples and shrines where such claims were regularly made by priests and quack doctors. Made to the chronically ill, who so desperately longed to believe that they could be cured by those sellers of hope – and almost invariably were not.

Perhaps sensing that Canio was less than impressed by the sacred pool, Feliculus led him into the cella: the heart of the temple. There, set into the apse at the western end, was a large, open-fronted shrine with a pedimented roof supported by columns.

Inside the shrine – seated on a high, throne-like chair – was the larger-than-life-sized stone figure of a woman, whose sculptor had somehow captured the essence of a goddess who was both youthful and as old as time. Her abundant hair flowed down almost to her waist, but neither her hair nor the folds of her elaborate *stola* altogether concealed the sensuous contours of the body beneath.

Both woman and throne appeared to have been carved from the same huge block of stone, but the large torc she wore around her neck was made of plaited ropes of thick silver wire, terminating in two intricately decorated globular finials. In the dim evening light of the cella the polished silver gleamed, almost as though it were generating its own light.

'Behold the goddess Sabrina,' murmured Feliculus, with practised reverence. 'Guardian goddess of the Great River, and mistress of all the nymphs who live in its waters and on and around its banks.'

Canio made what he thought were the correct appreciative noises.

Both he and Feliculus had entered the cella through one of two doors in the east wall. Above these doors were three semicircular windows: one large central one and a smaller one each side.

It suddenly occurred to Canio that these windows gave the goddess, seated on her high throne, a view over the pool courtyard. Conversely, they also allowed people in the courtyard and pool to see the face of the goddess watching over them as they bathed. Even more importantly, the goddess could look beyond the courtyard, out over the wide Sabrina River as it wound its way through the distant plain below.

Hearing movement behind him, Canio turned to see that Ivomandus and his daughter had come into the cella. Sulicena was staring up at the goddess, whispering something that he was too far away to hear properly, although he thought he heard her say the name Ixarnius several times.

Another priest, whose name Canio later learned was Albanus, now approached from where he had been standing, unseen, in a shadowed corner of the cella. Easing between Sulicena and the statue, he murmured, 'The goddess is always more moved to give favourable answers to those who show their faith in her by way of an appropriate gift.'

Sulicena stared at him, and by the almost savage expression on her face Canio feared that she was about to say, or quite possibly do, something undiplomatic. 'Two *siliquae?*' he asked quickly, before she could speak. 'Or is it three? Someone once told me, but I've quite forgotten.'

'Three *siliquae* is a very handsome gift,' Feliculus said smoothly, waving Albanus away with a tiny movement of one hand.

'I thought it might be,' Canio replied, not letting the sarcasm show as he handed over the three little silver coins.

Sulicena still looked as though she wanted to do violence to Albanus for interrupting her prayer to Sabrina, so Ivomandus took her arm and gently led her away. 'The sooner we sleep, the sooner the dawn will come and we can be away,' he whispered.

'Have you eaten?' Feliculus asked, as if the thought had only that moment occurred to him. 'I only ask because our guests usually—'

'We brought our own provisions, thank you,' Canio assured him, and thought, *Which, it would seem, was just as well.*

'Then I will leave you to commune with the goddess,' the priest replied, and he moved almost soundlessly away in the gathering twilight.

Canio had not the slightest wish to commune with the goddess, and was about to leave the cella himself when he noticed that there was a smaller apse on each side of the main one in which Sabrina sat.

Walking closer in the dying light, he saw that each contained the figure of a naked water nymph reclining on a water lily leaf, her long, luxuriant hair preserving her modesty. (*Although,* Canio reflected, *I've yet to meet a nymph unduly inconvenienced by that particular virtue.*) Each nymph held a large pitcher, from which an abundant stream of petrified water flowed. Their faces, he noticed, were distinctly prettier than the somewhat stern expression on Sabrina's stone face. He saluted all three ladies.

After going outside to check that both horses and the mule were still securely tethered, he made his way back to the austere pilgrim's cell in which he was to spend the night.

CHAPTER FORTY-FIVE

Night of 14th – 15th May

It had been a long, tiring day, and despite the hardness of the bed, Canio soon fell asleep. And as he slept he heard again the voice of Tulius, a voice tinged with an air of fatalistic sadness as the old man neared what Canio realised was the end of his story.

*

'By the time news of the sighting of Asclepiodotus's fleet reached us, the enemy host had already made landfall on the south coast of Britannia, somewhere a few miles to the east of Noviomagus Regnorum. A number of our liburnae were supposed to have been stationed off the island of Vectis, but it seemed that Asclepiodotus took advantage of a large patch of sea mist to slip past them unseen.

'Why the garrison of the fort at Portus Ardaoni did nothing to oppose the landing, I never knew, unless the same mist left them as sightless as the crews of the liburnae. Or perhaps none of them felt like playing the hero on that particular day. How wise they all were.

'Once ashore, Asclepiodotus ordered his ships to be burned, so that there was no way back: "triumph here or die here" was the message he was sending to his soldiers. As the hours passed, Allectus received a steady stream of reports from his dispatch riders, telling him that Asclepiodotus's men had started marching along the highway that ran north-eastwards from Noviomagus Regnorum all the way to Londinium, some sixty or seventy miles distant.

'Allectus was now faced with a terrible dilemma. He still expected the main invasion force to be led by Constantius, whose fleet surely had already set out from Gesoriacum. But what if it wasn't heading towards Dubris or some other landing place on the south-east coast? What if its destination was actually the Tamesis Estuary, the sea route into Londinium?

'If that were so, then waiting on the coast somewhere close to Dubris, ready to repel an invasion by Constantius, would leave Asclepiodotus's forces free to advance unchecked. And that would risk Londinium, his capital, being caught in a pincer movement between the twin armies of Constantius and Asclepiodotus.

'His tribunes were unanimous: the wisest course of action would therefore be to confront and destroy Asclepiodotus's forces before they could join up with those of Constantius. Given the number of ships thought to have been in Asclepiodotus's fleet, it was reckoned that he could only have taken, at most, some four hundred men with him. Although, worryingly, the reports Allectus was receiving from his scouts were inconsistent, with one saying there were considerably more than four hundred men.

'But time was flying, and Allectus knew he had to act quickly. He selected about six hundred men, mostly Frankish mercenaries, from the garrisons of the south-eastern Saxon Shore forts, and then marched westwards. From dawn to dusk they marched, travelling some fifty miles or more along the coast roads, until he reached the fort of Anderitum. There, he rested his exhausted soldiers for the night, and then, early the next morning, headed inland, planning to intercept Asclepiodotus on the Noviomagus Regnorum to Londinium highway.

'It was in the early evening of that long day, when Allectus's soldiers had already marched another forty miles, that they reached the highway. And at almost the same moment they sighted Asclepiodotus's invasion force, little more than a mile ahead. Until then, it had been hidden by trees and the folds of the land.

'The plan had been that, once our scouts had located the enemy, we would rest for the night, so we would be fresh to attack in the morning. But it seemed that the gods were impatient for blood, because Asclepiodotus's men spotted us at the very same moment we saw them. Worse still, the scouts had been wrong, and there were far more of them than we had anticipated; they outnumbered us by something like three to two, as near as anyone could tell. And they were fresh and unwearied; not hurrying towards Londinium as we had feared. With hindsight, it was almost as if they had been waiting for us.

'There was no time to form up into a regular order of battle. The two armies simply rushed at each other and the result was chaotic, like hundreds of savage tavern brawls all happening at once. In a battle like that, skill and knowledge of military strategy and tactics are of little use. The only things that matter are brute strength, stamina and sheer numbers – and they outnumbered us.

'It was all over in little more than half a summer hour. Faced with Asclepiodotus's troops, men hardened by years of fighting the Alemanni on the Rhenus frontier, our Frankish mercenaries began to be driven back like startled sheep. First they wavered, then they panicked, and then they fled. After that, the battle degenerated into a massacre as Asclepiodotus's men pursued them, howling like wolves that have tasted blood. And when the killing was at last over, all across the low hillsides of that smiling summer countryside, for a mile and more around, there lay the hacked and mutilated bodies of the slain'.

*

Canio woke, sweating profusely. The dream had been so vivid that, even awake and staring into the dimness, in his mind's eye he could see the bloodied and twisted bodies of those Frankish mercenaries, lying stiffening in their death agonies where Asclepiodotus's men had cut them down as they tried to flee.

He waited. Time passed, but sleep would not come again. Becoming aware of a faint light seeping in between door and frame he thought that the dawn must be coming. Rolling off the narrow bed he dressed hurriedly, groped his way to the cell door and went out into the corridor. Opening the outer door he found himself gazing at a world illuminated only by the pale, bluish light of the moon. A mysterious world, alien to all creatures who lived by the light of the sun.

Feeling a strange compulsion to do so, he went out into the night where, looking up, he saw a huge, nearly-full moon high up in the southern sky. Beguiled by the moonlight, he turned and began walking slowly eastwards, keeping close beside the wall of the nymphaeum pool courtyard. At the north-east corner he halted, suddenly aware of a figure standing at the far end of the raised platform, which he vaguely remembered Feliculus calling the "viewing court".

The figure was that of a slim young woman. Her face was turned away from him, but he could see that she was completely naked, standing absolutely still, her arms held vertically, as though stretching up towards the full moon, bathing in its light. Easing back into the moon shadow cast by the nymphaeum wall, Canio watched, fascinated and curious.

It took him only moments to realise that the woman must be Sulicena, although she was no longer the plain, work-stained creature of the day. The soft moonlight had removed all blemishes and imperfections from her skin, which seemed almost to glow in its caress.

Beyond the spot where she stood, the ground fell away in a long, uneven slope that led down to the plain of the south-flowing Sabrina. There, the moonlight, reflecting off the surface of the water, made the river stand out like polished silver against the twilight plain through which it flowed. And far beyond the Sabrina, on the eastern horizon, Canio could just make out the line of his own Long Limestone Hills, silhouetted black against the lighter sky.

At the point directly opposite the temple, the river was several hundred yards wide. It twisted first westwards, then southwards, then eastwards and, finally, back southwards again, forming a huge, noose-like loop. As Canio watched it shimmering softly in the moonlight, it came to him that it resembled a giant silver torc. A torc of which the one worn by the stone goddess seated inside the temple behind him was only a pale imitation.

He assumed that Sulicena was praying, asking the goddess to keep Ixarnius safe and to assist her in her search for him. From where he stood he could hear nothing, and if she was praying aloud, then the words must have been whispered, so that only the goddess herself could hear.

Still hidden in the moon shadow, Canio saw her lower her arms to her sides. He waited in unchaste anticipation for her to turn and face him, becoming conscious of his heart beginning to thump in his chest. Hearing a slight sound behind him, he spun around, only to see Sulicena standing there, no more than two yards away.

He stared at her, thunderstruck, then whispered, 'What in the name of sweet Venus? – How long have you been there?'

She did not reply, apparently gazing past him towards the naked woman, but when Canio turned again, the woman had vanished. He stared at the place where she had been, wondering where she could possibly have gone in so short a time. He strode rapidly over to the far end of the viewing court and looked around, but there was no sign of her. She seemed to have dissolved into the moonlight.

Hurrying back, he caught up with Sulicena just before she reached the temple door. 'That woman – did you see her?'

'In a way – yes, I suppose I saw her,' she replied.

'What do you mean, "In a way"? Who was she?'

'As I lay asleep in bed,' Sulicena answered obliquely, 'I dreamed that I was praying to the goddess, standing where that woman stood in the moonlight. And when I woke, I was here behind you, and she was gone.' In the moon shadows her face was a pale, unreadable blur.

Canio shook his head. 'I don't understand – what are you saying?'

'I don't even begin to understand it myself,' she replied quietly, 'but it doesn't matter; what does matter is this: that I now believe that the goddess has promised to protect Ixarnius and keep him safe from harm.' And before he could question her further, she had unlatched the temple door and slipped inside, quickly disappearing in the darkened corridor.

He waited, uncertain whether or not to question her further, torn between wanting, and not wanting, to understand what he had just witnessed. Eventually he gave up, opened the temple door, walked slowly back to his cell, undressed and tried to sleep.

CHAPTER FORTY-SIX

15th May

It seemed only moments after he had at last fallen asleep when he was woken by the sound of someone rapping loudly on his cell door. Swearing under his breath as he opened it, he was confronted by the sight of Ivomandus and his daughter, both fully dressed and apparently ready to leave, although it was barely light. There was no sign of either Feliculus or Albanus.

'Sulicena thinks she spotted half a dozen horsemen travelling south along the highway near the Sabrina, just as dawn was breaking,' Ivomandus explained.

'Soldiers?' Canio queried.

'Yes, of course they were soldiers,' Sulicena broke in impatiently. 'Who else would be travelling at this time of the morning?'

'You don't know that, not for sure; you said yourself they were too far way,' Ivomandus reminded her.

'But I just know they were soldiers. Please, please – we've got to hurry!' she begged.

'All right, so they might have been soldiers – but even if they were, they were probably just on a routine patrol, not hunting your brother,' Canio said, trying to calm the increasingly agitated young woman. Nevertheless, he finished dressing and followed them out to where the horses and the mule were tethered, surprised to find their two mounts already saddled and with saddlebags attached. He checked the tightness of their girths, then hurriedly saddled Antares.

*

Led by Sulicena on her mule, which slipped and slithered at first, they descended the grassy track that led down the hillside and at last reached the highway, which there ran right alongside the wide Sabrina. The road was in reasonable condition, with patches of compacted stone rubble in places, indicating recent repairs after the ravages of winter.

There were no other travellers in sight as they set off southwards. Sulicena kicked her heels into the mule's flanks in a futile attempt to make it go faster, but only succeeded in provoking indignant brays from the poor beast.

One mile passed, and then another, as the sun rose slowly higher in the north-eastern sky behind them. They overtook a solitary pedestrian, weighed down by the large pack he was carrying, and who – to Sulicena's evident distress – confirmed that the six horsemen she had seen in the crepuscular dawn light were indeed soldiers.

They continued on their way, and another mile passed, the highway now edging further away from the Sabrina shore.

Far out on the ever-widening estuary, Canio noticed four or five coracles bobbing on the misty water, with nets slung between them as the fishermen hunted the salmon coming upriver with the incoming tide.

When, by his reckoning, they had gone at least six miles south along the highway, they came upon two men and a woman sitting on the grass beside a carriage drawn by two horses. The carriage appeared to have been travelling northwards. The woman seemed distraught, with the older of the two men attempting to comfort her.

Canio dismounted to speak to them, and only then noticed the body lying in the roadside vegetation on the far side of the carriage. 'What's happened here?' Canio asked, rapidly scanning around the immediate landscape, but seeing no one else.

'Brigands,' the younger man replied angrily, 'that's what happened. The bastards came out of the woods up there, shot an arrow into our coachman and took everything we had: money, jewellery – everything.'

'Is he dead?'

'The coachman? Yes, I think so – I'm not sure. They even took my mother's gold betrothal ring.' He did not seem overly concerned about the coachman's fate.

Saying nothing, Canio crouched beside the body, which was lying prone among the tall stems of cow parsley, the white flower heads waving gently in the soft breeze. There was no obvious sign of a wound on his back, but when Canio heaved the body over he saw that the arrow had hit him under the armpit, entering obliquely and snapping off as he hit the ground. By the amount of blood pooling on the flattened grasses and feathery cow parsley leaves, he reckoned it must have penetrated his heart.

He sighed. 'Yes, he's dead all right. So, which way did the brigands go?'

'That way, I think… I'm not sure.' The older man pointed southwards, and then stooped again to comfort his near-hysterical wife.

'Would you recognise any of them if you saw them again?' Canio asked.

'I'd recognise their leader,' the younger man replied. 'He was a tall man in a dirty tunic, and he wore a big gold ring on the forefinger of his left hand. And there was something else: the little finger of that same hand looked as if it had been chopped off, the stump still red and angry-looking.'

Ivomandus glanced quickly at Sulicena, then asked Canio, 'I wonder where the soldiers were when all this was happening?'

Hearing him, the younger man exclaimed bitterly, 'Soldiers! A mounted squad of half a dozen of the useless bloodsuckers passed us not long before the brigands ambushed us. Those murdering swine must have been waiting until the soldiers had gone before they pounced.'

'But where's Ixarnius now ? Surely he wouldn't have gone the same way as the soldiers, would he?' Sulicena whispered to her father.

'Why shouldn't he? With him on foot and the soldiers on horseback, there would be no danger of catching them up,' Ivomandus pointed out.

'Then what are we waiting for? – he can't be far ahead.'

Sulicena was already some thirty yards past the carriage, with Ivomandus close behind her, when Canio – ignoring an angry shouted question from the younger man – remounted and urged Antares into a trot to catch them up.

❖

They had gone no more than another mile when Canio heard shouts and screams from somewhere in front, somewhere hidden by a slight curve in the highway as it shadowed the course of the Sabrina, and also by the trees of the Great Forest, which just there came down to within a hundred yards of the highway.

Kicking his heels into Antares' flanks and urging the horse into a canter, he rounded the curve in moments, but saw nothing on the road ahead. Glancing westwards, up towards the rising ground, he saw several horses at the edge of the trees. A solitary soldier stood holding their reins. More yelling came from that direction. It seemed that the other soldiers were inside the forest.

As he watched, two soldiers emerged from beneath the trees, dragging what could only have been a body – and then Canio realised what was happening.

It seemed that both father and daughter had guessed too, because Sulicena gave an anguished cry and began urging her mule up the slope, closely followed by Ivomandus.

Canio quickly overtook them both, cut in front and waved them to a halt. 'Sweet Venus, will you let me deal with this?' he hissed.

He trotted up to the two soldiers who had been dragging the body. 'Is that one of those damned brigands?' he asked in his best officer's voice of command, making sure that the scabbarded *spatha* dangling from his hip was clearly visible.

'It is… sir,' one of the soldiers replied. 'Junius Rufus – our *ducenarius* – and our mates are back there finishing the rest of them off.'

'Are they now?' said Canio with feigned enthusiasm. 'How many of the bastards were there?'

'Don't know exactly, sir. They'd almost reached the trees when we spotted them.'

'There were at least five – maybe more,' the other soldier added.

Meanwhile, Ivomandus – who, with Sulicena, had quietly ridden up beside Canio – peered at the dead brigand, whose blood was still dripping from the gaping slash wound to his throat. Catching Canio's eye, he very slowly shook his head. It was not Ixarnius.

Sulicena too must have already realised it was not her brother's body, because she was already scrambling down off her mule.

Realising that she was about to run into the forest, Ivomandus reached down and grabbed her arm. 'No!' he whispered. 'There's nothing you can do, not now.'

Seeing the uncertainty forming on the face of the soldier who had spoken last, Canio explained quickly, 'The swine robbed her and her father of all the money they possessed. They would have taken their horse and mule too, if they'd had any use for them.

But how did you come to catch them? From what I was told, I thought you would have been miles away to the south by now?'

'We should have been, but when we were almost opposite the Temple of Nodens, we met a man who told us that he'd seen the vermin creeping into this part of the forest last night, so the *ducenarius* decided to turn around and come back here to check. Lucky really, or we'd be halfway to Venta by now,' the man added, exaggerating somewhat.

Sulicena was still trying to struggle free from Ivomandus's grip when, from the forest, an officer appeared carrying a *spatha*, its bright-steel blade bloodied, although his eyes seemed fixed on something small he held in his other hand. Seeing Canio and the other two, he halted and looked suspiciously at them.

'Junius Rufus, I assume?' Canio enquired, with well-feigned joviality. 'I hear you've caught the swine who robbed this poor couple on the road yesterday evening.'

'Caught and slaughtered,' the *ducenarius* replied.

'What, all of them?'

'All five of them,' Junius Rufus confirmed. 'And you are...?'

Canio ignored the anguished gasp that came from Sulicena. 'Baculo – Aulus Claudius Baculo. Former *primicerius*,' he replied, awarding himself a rank two rungs above *ducenarius*. 'Left the army when I inherited my late uncle's estate,' he added, realising that he had to explain the lack of insignias of status – *clavi* and *orbiculi* – on his tunic and other clothing.

Junius Rufus grunted in acknowledgement, and then went back to admiring the object in his left hand, which Canio was now close enough to see was a gold ring. Without looking up, the *ducenarius* barked, 'You two – Veldicca and Bitucus – go and help the others drag the carcasses out. I've got better things to do than hang around here all day.'

Canio risked a glance at Sulicena. She was standing beside her mule now, her face set in an impassive mask, as if fatalistically resigned to what was coming.

So he asked the inevitable question: 'I was told that the leader of those criminals wore a big gold ring – something he must have stolen from one of his victims. Is that it?'

'It is indeed,' Junius Rufus said proudly. 'Solid gold, set with a red stone engraved with a standing man – Mercury, I think it is.' He held the ring about four inches from his right eye. 'And now it's mine – the spoils of war.'

'Unless its original owner can be found,' Canio objected mildly.

The *ducenarius* appeared to find this amusing. 'Oh, I think there's very little chance of that happening. Very little chance indeed,' he sniggered.

By now, four soldiers (including Veldicca and Bitucus) had emerged from the trees, each ducking awkwardly under the low boughs as he dragged the lifeless body of a man by the feet.

'Do you recognise them as the bastards who robbed you?' Canio asked Ivomandus.

The coppersmith understood. 'I'm not sure,' he replied, his voice a flat monotone. 'It was late in the evening and already quite dark. The one I got the best look at was their leader, the one with the big gold ring. Which was the one wearing it?' This to Junius Rufus.

The *ducenarius* glanced casually at the bodies, which were now lined up in a bedraggled row, like so many dead animals slaughtered by hunters. 'That one there,' he said, pointing to the second in the row.

From where Canio sat astride Antares, there seemed little to tell them apart, all of them being heavily bearded, and the long grass hid the gold ring man's left hand. From unlooked-for experience he knew that all dead men tended to look much the same. But it was strange, he reflected, how much less the dead body of a stranger affected him, compared with that of someone he had known, even briefly, when alive.

For the stranger had always been dead: to Canio, he had never lived. But, if he had seen that same man walking, talking and perhaps even laughing, then the transformation into the irreversible finality of death was so much more stark and unsettling. *Memento mori – was it Trifosa who had said that?*

Ivomandus dismounted stiffly, walked through the trampled long grass, crouched beside the body that Junius Rufus had indicated and looked carefully at the dead man's face. After several long moments, he stood up, and as he did so, Canio noticed, he let his eyes roam over the faces of the other dead brigands. Then, looking directly at Canio, he gave a barely perceptible shake of his head. But to Junius Rufus he said, 'Yes, it's him all right. I'd recognise that face anywhere... Can I take back the money he robbed me of?'

'Only if you can prove it's yours.'

'But how can I do that?'

'You can't,' Junius Rufus replied smoothly. 'That's why we have to take it all back to Venta, along with their heads.'

'Their heads?' Ivomandus queried.

'Of course – how else can we prove we killed the swine?'

And claim whatever reward that might be going, as well as all the money they have on them, Canio thought.

'You, Bitucus – you're always boasting that you've got the sharpest *spatha*, so now's your chance to prove it. See if you can take that one's head off with one blow.' And the *ducenarius* pointed to the body that Ivomandus had examined most closely, the one from whose hand the ring had been taken.

On hearing that, Sulicena's iron self-control finally cracked. With a smothered scream of anguish, she began racing back down the grassy slope towards the highway. Ivomandus hurriedly scooped up her mule's and Protus's reins and began hurrying after her.

Junius Rufus frowned and looked questioningly at Canio, who forced himself to shrug and grin apologetically. 'That's women for you – weak stomachs. Too squeamish for men's work. Anyway, I'd best be away myself now.' Glancing towards the five bodies, he added, 'You've done this part of the country a great service today, ridding it of those parasites. A splendid service.' And with that he gave the *ducenarius* a cheery wave and started Antares ambling back down to where he could see Ivomandus, now dismounted and with an arm around his daughter's shoulders.

Remembering the coppersmith's reaction as he had looked at the faces of the dead brigands, a suspicion was already forming in Canio's mind. And as he drew closer to Sulicena and saw that, if not smiling, she did not appear distressed, the suspicion crystallised. He looked from father to daughter, then said, 'It wasn't Ixarnius, was it?'

'No. None of them were,' Ivomandus confirmed. 'And all the little fingers of their left hands were intact.'

'Did you know about that missing finger?'

'Yes, the man who came to see me at Vertis told me; didn't I tell you?'

'No, not that I recall. So, he's got away.'

'Of course he has,' said Sulicena. 'The goddess is protecting him.' It was the first time that Canio could recall seeing her smile, and it transformed her face for the better.

'He must have slipped his ring onto the finger of one of his dead comrades while the soldiers were still searching for him, then escaped into the depths of the forest,' Ivomandus suggested.

Yes, but was it really the soldiers who killed the man they found that ring on? Canio couldn't help wondering. On reflection, though, he thought it better to let the question remained unasked.

'When the soldiers have all gone, we're going back into the forest to search for Ixarnius. And when we find him, we'll bring him back to Vertis with us,' Sulicena added, still smiling.

Canio was doubtful. 'Do you really think he'll want to be found?' he asked Ivomandus. 'He's probably a mile deep into the forest already, and still running.'

The coppersmith shrugged. 'Perhaps. But it's possible that he could be lying wounded not far from where the others were killed. In any case, we can't just ride away. Not now – not when we've come so close to finding him.'

CHAPTER FORTY-SEVEN

So they rode a few yards back along the highway, to a place where, through a screen of leafy hazel bushes, they could keep watch on the hillside beyond. They did not have too long to wait.

Six soldiers, led by Junius Rufus, came riding down the grassy slope. Hanging from the saddle horns of three of the soldiers were lumpy sacks with dark blotches on their bottom halves, sacks which bounced slightly as the horses jogged along. Turning south, they trotted briskly down the highway, soon dwindling into the distance.

The soldiers were barely out of sight before Sulicena had urged her mule onto the road and back up the slope to the edge of the forest. Ivomandus followed, and after him trailed an unenthusiastic Canio. Once there, he found his eyes unwillingly drawn to the five decapitated bodies, which were sprawled obscenely among the lengthening grasses and yellow cowslips of that smiling late-spring countryside.

Life had taught him to appear unmoved by such sights, and in that – as in so many other things – he was an accomplished dissembler. Swarms of black flies had already begun to cluster on the raggedly severed necks, and the all-pervasive smell of curdling blood was beginning to make the spot reek like a butcher's yard.

*

Leading their mounts by their reins, all three spread out and began walking into the forest.

'Ixarnius!' Sulicena began shouting. 'Ixarnius – it's me, Sulicena! The soldiers have all gone, and it's safe to come out now.'

Silence. The only sounds, other than those made by the horses and the mule, were the faint singing of the wind in the treetops high above and the calls of unseen birds.

'Ixarnius – our father's here with me! It really is safe to come out.'

Some bird, probably a jay, took off and flew between the trees, squawking raucously and startling them all. But if Ixarnius really was somewhere near, then he clearly had no intention of making his presence known. The thought occurred to Canio that perhaps he was waiting for one of the searchers to stray too close to his hiding place. Instinctively, his right hand moved to the hilt of the *spatha* hanging from his left hip, easing it in its scabbard.

For hour after wearying hour they searched, spreading out further and penetrating deeper and deeper into the forest, but meeting nobody, except for the occasional miner down in a scowle, hacking his way along a thin seam of iron ore.

Several times Canio tensed as he heard scuffling and rustling deep in the undergrowth, but when he cautiously investigated he found nothing and realised that it must only have been some woodland creature going about its furtive affairs.

Once a cock blackbird flew shrieking out of a bush, not a yard in front of him, and before conscious thought took over he had drawn his spatha and swiped at it, missing it, but only by inches. He realised that it was a measure of how tautly stretched his nerves had become, in a place where an armed and desperate man could be crouching unseen only two rapid paces away.

At noon, they regrouped at the edge of the forest, and by then, even Sulicena had to concede that Ixarnius could not be anywhere within the mile-deep semicircle of forest they had searched.

'It seems you were right,' Ivomandus admitted to Canio. 'He's probably miles away by now, and still moving westwards.'

'So back to Glevum then?' Canio asked, hoping the answer would be, 'Yes.'

Both men looked at Sulicena, who was staring at her father, as if willing him to—

'No. We – Sulicena and me – have got to keep searching,' Ivomandus replied. He must have seen the sceptical look on Canio's face, because he added, 'Look, if we went back now, I'd always be tormented by the thought of what might have been. And who knows – if we go far enough west we might find him waiting for us, sitting on the banks of the River Guoy?'

Being pleasured by half a dozen nubile water nymphs, no doubt, Canio thought, but he said, 'Only if he wants to be found.'

'Perhaps – but we've got to try.' The coppersmith hesitated, then said, 'I wouldn't expect you to come with us, of course. You've done all you could, and we – both of us – thank you for that.'

'How long do you intend to keep searching?' Canio asked.

Ivomandus shrugged. 'As long as it takes, I suppose.' Then, as if realising what was behind the question, he added, 'I never actually left an account with anyone back in Vertis about how I came to make that Hecate figurine of yours, if that's what you're worried about?'

It was, but... 'Is that the truth?'

'Yes, it's the truth.'

'Well, that's good to know.'

So kill them both, here and now. No one will ever know, and then he'll never be able to blackmail you again – because he will; you know he will, the old, hard voice of self-preservation whispered inside Canio's head.

For a moment, and only for a moment, his felt his right hand moving as if by a will of its own, across his stomach and on towards the hilt of the *spatha* hanging at his left hip. The temptation shamed even him, and to drive it away, he said quickly, 'I'll take Protus back with me, but you can keep the mule if you like?'

Ivomandus looked to Sulicena, who paused, and then shook her head. 'Thank you, but no,' she replied. 'If we were trying to move quickly and quietly through the dense forest, and it started braying... No.'

She untied the sack containing bread and cheese from the mule's saddle and slung it over her shoulder. Ivomandus did the same with the other sack which Protus had been carrying.

After a brief struggle with conscience, Canio took the wineskin from Antares' saddlebag and handed it to Ivomandus. It was already half-empty, but he told himself that they could top it up with water from the forest streams, several of which they had crossed on the previous day. 'How much money have you got?' he asked.

'Three or four *siliquae* and a handful of *nummi*,' the coppersmith replied.

Canio wondered what had happened to the five *solidi* he had paid him for the fake Hecate figurine back in October? He decided that it was best not to ask, particularly in his daughter's presence.

'And I've got a few *nummi* too,' Sulicena added.

'Then you'd better take these,' Canio said, unbuckling the flap of his belt pouch and counting out a dozen *siliquae*. He felt the need to be generous, although it was a generosity prompted by guilt; an attempt to disown the evil little voice that had tempted him to murder them both. Seeing Ivomandus hesitate, he added, 'It's best you take them; it may be quite some time before you catch up with your son.' *If you ever do.*

He dropped the little silver coins into the coppersmith's palm. Ivomandus thanked him gruffly, perhaps slightly embarrassed, then turned, and he and his daughter walked back into the forest. Sulicena, smiling, looked back and waved at Canio before the trees hid her. It was the second time he had seen her happy, and the gamine smile quite transformed her face.

*

He waited until the last sounds of their going had died away, then rummaged in Protus's saddlebags for the length of rope that he remembered bailiff Felix usually kept there. With a grunt of satisfaction he found it, tugged it out, and used it to fashion halters for both Protus and the mule.

With Protus on one side of Antares and the mule on the other, he rode down the grassy slope, heading away from the forest and back onto the highway, where he set off northwards to begin the long ride of twenty miles and more back to Glevum.

It was a beautiful day, the sky blue and almost cloudless, the warm air full of the scents of early summer and the buzz and whirr of bees and other flying insects. But Canio's mood was sombre: he doubted that Ivomandus and Sulicena's search would have a happy ending. Also, despite never having seen those men alive, the sight of their five decapitated bodies had troubled him more than he would have cared to admit. He told himself that time would soon erode the memory, if not obliterate it altogether; he had seen far worse in his soldiering days.

At the place where they had come across the ambushed coach and its occupants, there was nothing. Even the body of the dead coachman had gone.

As he was passing the track that led up the hillside towards the Temple of Sabrina, he came across a young man and two women. One of them could have been the young man's mother, the other his sister or wife. As he trotted past, the sound of the twelve hooves caused the young man to turn, startled, towards him, and Canio saw that the lenses of both eyes were cloudy with cataracts. He did not stop, or even look back: all men have secret fears, and one of his was a terror of going blind.

The miles passed slowly. Protus and the mule were often fractious, neither being accustomed to being led that way, and the temporary halters were far from ideal. From time to time he stopped to let them graze the sweet, juicy grasses or drink from a wayside pool. Not fancying the muddy water himself, or wanting to try his luck on the banks of the Sabrina, he became increasingly thirsty and regretted giving Ivomandus his wineskin.

Sunset was no more than an hour away by the time he at last reached *The Caduceus*, the *stabulum* in Glevum from which he had set out at dawn on the previous day. By then, he was tired, parched and depressed. After seeing Antares, Protus and the mule safely bedded down for the night, he settled himself in a quiet corner of the *stabulum* for a meal of venison stew and a large flagon of wine. When he had finished the stew, he retired to one of the bedrooms on the first floor, taking with him a cup and the flagon, now refilled with the hostelry's best Rhenish wine. By the time he at last fell asleep, the flagon was again empty.

CHAPTER FORTY-EIGHT

16th May

At around noon on the following day Canio woke to the sound of somebody tapping cautiously at his bedroom door. He sat up hurriedly and immediately wished he hadn't. After lying down again and clamping his eyes shut to exclude the painful daylight, he called out, 'Yes, what is it?' – all the while trying to keep his head absolutely still.

'Are you all right, sir?' came a voice – a female voice – from the other side of the door.

'Yes, of course I am. Go away; I'll be down shortly.'

'Only the Master says—'

'Go away!' he roared, and after a slight pause there came the faint sounds of retreating footsteps on the floorboards outside.

He lay, eyes closed, for a little while longer, then gently sat up and swung his legs onto the floor. As he opened his eyes a fraction, the room started to spin. He closed them again and groped his way over to the table and the bowl of water he remembered from the previous night. Cupping his slightly trembling hands, he held the cold water against his face, hearing it drip back into the bowl. He slowly repeated this operation several times, and when at last he opened his eyes the walls of the room were no longer rotating.

Less than half a summer hour later he was downstairs settling his bill, refusing the offer of a midday meal (and almost vomiting at the thought of food), and shouting for the ostler to get the horses and mule ready.

*

To his annoyance he found that Proxsimus, the horse dealer on the Vertis road, just outside the North Gate of Glevum, the man he had bought the mule from two days before, was away on a buying trip. Worse still, his wife declared that she could not possibly buy the animal back without her husband's permission.

He should have left it with her anyway; it was clearly what she was hoping he would do. But her unhelpful attitude had irritated him, and so, still leading both the mule and Protus, he set off northwards on the Vertis road, heading towards the small town of Confluens, where the Sabrina and Avon rivers merged. Some four miles south of Confluens he branched off eastwards, onto the same track that he and Ivomandus had ridden down on their journey from Villa Canini three days before.

It was a warm, dry afternoon. High above in the still air skylarks were hovering on rapidly fluttering wings, rising and falling, their liquid songs drifting down to where he jogged along astride Antares. As the slow miles passed, and the last vestiges of his hangover evaporated, so memories of the dream that had come in the previous night began to return.

He remembered that Tulius's thoughts had still not left that terrible battle that he must have witnessed, fighting against Asclepiodotus's army on the undulating grasslands beside the Noviomagus Regnorum to Londinium road.

Had skylarks also sung then? he wondered, *high in the blue sky, oblivious to the savage battle raging below them on that other afternoon in late spring some three-quarters of a century before?*

Tulius had said that the air had been filled with hoarse shouts and screams and the nerve-shredding clash and clang of steel on steel, as men pushed forwards or were driven back across the trampled and increasingly blood-splashed grasses.

Canio recalled him saying bitterly that they would surely have won, if only they had had with them the regular soldiers from one or more of Allectus's legions. As it was, at a critical stage in the battle, when two of their senior officers had been killed in quick succession, the Frankish mercenaries, who had made up the bulk of Allectus's hastily assembled forces on that fateful day, did what barbarians often do when the tide of battle turns against them: they turned tail and ran for their lives.

After that, Tulius said, the battle had turned into butchery, with Asclepiodotus's triumphant soldiers pursuing the Franks like starving wolves maddened with bloodlust, scything them down without mercy. He told again of the fields and gentle hillsides for a mile or more around being strewn with the hacked and dismembered bodies of the dead. It was only the merciful descent of night that allowed a few to escape.

Canio remembered asking what became of Allectus, and Tulius had hesitated before replying, *'Ah, what indeed? They say his mutilated body was found a few hundred yards from the battlefield, although most of his armour and his richly embroidered tunic were gone, stolen by Asclepiodotus's men.'*

'Then how did they know that the body was his?' Canio had heard himself asking the same question he must have asked as a child.

'On account of the big, gold seal ring that he wore on the index finger of his left hand. Very distinctive it was, made by one of the craftsmen who fashioned the dies for his coins. Engraved on the bezel was the image of a liburna *warship, with the figure of the goddess Victoria standing on its prow. He used it to seal all his important documents. I suppose Asclepiodotus would have*

ordered the dead man's head cut off, to prove to Constantius that Allectus really was dead, but it was so badly disfigured by sword slashes as to be unrecognisable.'

'So why hadn't Asclepiodotus's soldiers stolen the ring as well?' the child Canio had asked.

'Who knows? Perhaps it was hidden by blood and dirt, or perhaps an officer came upon them trying to pull it off his finger? Anyway, that body, like all the other dead from Allectus's army, was left to rot where it fell. Whatever armour, clothes and money Asclepiodotus's soldiers didn't loot, the local countryfolk stole in the night.

'I don't know where Constantius was while all this was happening: it seems that something – I never heard exactly what – delayed his fleet sailing from Gesoriacum. Maybe it was the same sea fog that had allowed Asclepiodotus to slip past Vectis unseen, or maybe it was adverse winds? Or maybe he and Asclepiodotus simply failed to properly coordinate their times of landing, setting out as they did from places so far apart? Whatever it was, by the time Constantius reached Britannia the battle was already over and Allectus was no more, although he couldn't have known that at the time.

'As it was, he sailed up the Tamesis Estuary and reached Londinium just in time to save the city from being sacked and looted by some of Allectus's Frankish mercenaries – or so he claimed. Myself, I don't think there was ever more than a handful of Franks left in Londinium, and Constantius exaggerated whatever threat they posed, just to excuse himself for bungling what should have been simultaneous landings.

'But I heard that it didn't stop him from ordering the Treveri mint to strike some big gold medallions to celebrate what he trumpeted as his magnificent victory. Apparently, they showed him on horseback in front of the city walls of Londinium, liberating the kneeling genius of the city, and describing himself as, and I quote, "Restorer of the Eternal Light". But, for those of us who survived that terrible battle, the future seemed to offer nothing but eternal darkness.

'And how did I survive the battle? By crawling away like a wounded animal and lying hidden in a small wood until nightfall. It was around the time of the new moon, and in the darkness I crept away, expecting at any moment to hear a harsh shout as one of Asclepiodotus's soldiers spotted me. But by the whim of the gods, none ever did. So I made my way westwards, always westwards, sleeping during the day and travelling only at night. A strange, lonely journey it was, but eventually I reached the wild lands far beyond Isca Dumnoniorum.

'Like many another soldier, I had taken the precaution of carrying a small purse of gold and silver coins suspended from a cord around my neck, and several weeks later I was able to buy passage on a boat sailing across the Oceanus Britannicus to Armorica, in north-western Gaul.

'And then, for the first five or so years, I became a wanderer, always looking over my shoulder to see if anyone had recognised me, never stopping more than a few weeks in any one place. I could read and write, and I had other useful skills, so I never starved. But I never went back to Britannia: too many ghosts there.'

Now other memories came trickling back, and Canio recalled that, when he had first heard him speak those words, back in Marcia's room all those years ago, Tulius's eyes had already closed, his voice trailing away as he murmured, 'Tired – so, so tired. I must sleep now, but be sure to be here in the morning, because there's something I must tell you, something that you must know. But it's something that you should never, ever repeat to a living soul.'

'Not even Marcia?' the child had asked, mystified.

But the old man, eyes still closed, had moved his head wearily from side to side. 'No, not even her.'

'But whatever it was, you never did tell me,' Canio sighed. 'You died in the night.'

Leading Protus and the mule, he continued jogging slowly homewards, along tracks that led eventually to a broad valley that ran south-eastwards up into the Long Limestone Hills. And branching off that broad valley, and becoming separated from it by the bulk of Coel's Hill, was the little valley that led gently uphill to the place he now called home.

By the time he came to ride the last half mile up the track that led to Villa Canini it was late evening. For some reason, afterwards unremembered, he glanced behind him. And as he squinted into the glare of the sun setting in the north-west, he saw the dark shape of what appeared to be an old man walking some thirty yards behind him. Thinking it was Diovicus, he raised his right arm in greeting, but did not stop.

Halting at the great aisled barn below the villa, he turned the two horses and the mule over to Austalis the ostler, assuring him that all was well. Although the ostler was clearly puzzled by the presence of the mule, Canio did not explain his unexpected acquisition: that could wait until the morning.

He looked for Diovicus, expecting that by then the old man would have caught up, but he seemed to have vanished. He was unsurprised: Diovicus had a knack of mysteriously appearing and disappearing, the latter when the prospect of work was threatening.

As he walked through the archway in the courtyard wall, he saw that the huge, fiery, orange-red sun behind him was lighting up the centre of the courtyard and sending his elongated shadow, black and sharp, across the gravel. As he crossed the courtyard he watched the shadow go before him until, as he reached the villa's large double doors, man and shadow merged and became one.

He spent the last dregs of evening and the long twilight eating, drinking and giving Felix and Senuacus, his two bailiffs, a heavily edited version of where he had been and what he had done in the last three and a half days. He sensed that he was not wholly believed, which did not unduly trouble him.

An hour after sunset, just as a huge full moon was rising in the south-eastern sky, he retired to what had been his and Trifosa's bedroom on the first floor. He carried with him a flagon of wine and his favourite silver cup, the one engraved with a hunting scene in which a mounted huntsman, warmly clad against the winter chill and accompanied by a pair of long, lean hounds, endlessly pursued a vast wild boar around its circumference.

CHAPTER FORTY-NINE

Night of 16th – 17th May

Musing on the events of the last few days he eventually fell asleep, and as he slept he dreamed that he was back on the track leading up to Villa Canini. But now he was sitting on a tree stump at the side of the track and drinking wine from the silver cup as he watched the sun setting in the north-western sky. Half-blinded by gazing into its great glowing disc, he did not notice the tall youth walking rapidly up the track towards him – not until the stranger was almost level with the place where he sat.

'*Salve*, Canio – it's been a long time,' the young man said. 'A long, long time.'

Still with the image of the fiery sun in his eyes, Canio turned and stared uncertainly at the young man.

But before he could speak, the youth – who did not appear to be more than seventeen or eighteen at most – said, 'Don't you recognise me, Canio... Tulcelas? Don't you recognise Tulcelas? No, of course you don't; how could you? But you do remember the name, don't you? Surely you can't have forgotten that?' He paused for a moment and looked quizzically at Canio before carrying on walking up towards the villa, soon vanishing from sight around a curve in the track.

Tulcelas? Tulcelas? Where...? And then, like the lightning flash that illuminates a darkened landscape, Canio did remember: it was the name – the real name – of the old man who had died in Marcia's room in that cold city beside the Rhenus twenty-five years before. The old man whose name he had for so long misremembered as being Tulius. The old man who Marcia had said was his grandfather.

Intrigued now, Canio scrambled to his feet, set the silver cup down on the stump and began hurrying after the young man. But just outside the villa courtyard he halted, suddenly aware that something was wrong. Easing cautiously through the archway he saw that the villa and courtyard – both brilliantly illuminated by the golden light of the setting sun – had been transformed.

The courtyard walls – like the stone walls and the *tegulae* and *imbrices* roof tiles of the villa itself – had lost much of their hoary, time-worn appearance. The limestone was still yellowish-cream, not yet weathered to grey, and the red fired-clay tiles were barely stained by the mosses and lichens he remembered. And gone too was the uniform grey limestone gravel that had covered the entire courtyard.

Now, freshly-crushed, creamy limestone gravel covered the central carriage drive and all the smaller paths which neatly divided up the rest of the courtyard. Planting beds, bordered by manicured hedges of dwarf box and bright with summer flowers, scented herbs and flowering shrubs, filled the rectangular spaces between the paths.

There were people in the courtyard, a dozen or more richly dressed men and women, only one of whom he had ever seen before. They were standing talking and laughing in twos and threes, or sitting on the elaborately-carved stone seats placed on semicircles of gravel cut into the planting beds. On one of the seats a young woman and an older man were engaged in animated conversation. Canio gazed at them all in stunned bewilderment.

And walking towards him was the youth who had passed him on the track – the tall young man who said his name was Tulcelas. He was smiling, carrying two wine goblets and proffering one to him, as if in welcome.

*

Canio woke – perhaps hours, or perhaps only moments later – in the half-light of an early summer's dawn. In his mind's eye he could still see the youth's face quite clearly. It was a face that seemed vaguely familiar, and suddenly he realised why: it was because, years ago, he had seen that same face, or one very much like it. Then, it had been a reflection in the still waters of a lake one hot summer's day as he and a young woman, both naked, lay on their stomachs among the long, flowering grasses, peering over the bank into the greenish-brown translucent water. He had been about seventeen then.

An epiphany: he swung his legs out of bed and walked quickly across the bedroom to his desk. Grabbing a stylus and a wax tablet, he hurriedly incised the name "TULCELAS" in the soft wax, then carefully struck through every letter in the correct sequence, murmuring each one as he did so, until he had spelled out the new name.

The rising sun was beginning to flood into the room. Standing absolutely still, in the centre of a pool of golden light, he thought back – first to the events of the last six months, then to those of earliest remembered childhood.

And at last understood.

GAZETTEER AND GLOSSARY

Gazetteer

Names marked * are my fictional names for real places, the Roman names of which are now lost.

(Flumen) Abus: The Humber Estuary.

(Flumen) Albis: River Elbe, Germany.

Anderitum: Pevensey, East Sussex. A Saxon Shore fort.

Ariconium: An iron smelting settlement near Weston-under-Penyard, Herefordshire. Some 15 (Roman) miles north-west of Glevum.

Armorica: North-Western Gaul, including Brittany.

(Flumen) Avon: The Warwickshire Avon, flowing through Vertis (Worcester) and joining the Sabrina (Severn) at Confluens (Tewkesbury).

Bononia / Gesoriacum: Boulogne-sur-Mer. Apparently called Gesoriacum until some time after the siege of AD 293, when it was renamed Bononia.

Britannia Prima: One of the five (?) provinces into which the *diocese* of Britannia was divided by the later 4th century. Its capital was Corinium Dobunnorum (Cirencester).

Burdigala: Bordeaux

Calleva Atrebatum: Silchester, Hampshire.

Cambria: Wales

Camulodunum: Colchester, Essex.

Castra Vetera: Xanten, on the Lower Rhine. Base of Legio XXX Ulpia Victrix.

Classis Britannica: the fleet of Roman Warships guarding the English Channel etc. against seaborne pirates. Had disappeared from the records by the middle of the third century. Revived by Carausius in the 280s.

Coel's Hill*: Cole's Hill, which separates the narrow coomb containing Spoonley Wood villa from the main valley running first south-east, then south, from Winchcombe up into the Cotswold Hills.

Confluens*: Tewkesbury, Gloucestershire. A small town on the road south from Vertis to Glevum, where the Warwickshire Avon joins the Flumen Sabrina.

Corinium (Dobunnorum): Cirencester, Gloucestershire. Capital of the fourth century Roman province of Britannia Prima.

Cunetio: Mildenhall, Wiltshire.

Deva: Chester, base of Legio XX Valeria Victrix.

Dubris: Dover, Kent. A Saxon Shore fort.

Durocornovium: Wanborough, Wiltshire. A small town on the highway between Corinium and Calleva.

Durobrivae (1): Water Newton, Cambridgeshire.

Durobrivae (2): Rochester, Kent.

Durovernum Cantiacorum: Canterbury, Kent.

Eboracum: York

Fonscolnis*: Wycomb, near Andoversford, Gloucestershire. The large number of small denomination coins found scattered over the area suggest it was a thriving market and temple settlement in the later third and fourth centuries, although its origins go back into Neolithic times.

Fosse Way: Roman road running from Exeter to Lincoln. It passed through Corinium from the Aquae Sulis Gate to the Verulamium Gate as the *Decumanus Maximus* of that city.

Fretum Gallicum: Strait of Dover.

Gariannonum: Saxon Shore fort at Caistor-on-Sea, Norfolk.

Gesoriacum: see Bononia.

Glevum: Gloucester.

Grannona: Saxon Shore fort at the mouth of the Seine.

The Great Forest*: The Forest of Dean, an extensive area of ancient woodland in western Gloucestershire between the rivers Severn and Wye.

Guoy: The River Wye (Nennius, early 9th century. Afon Gwy in Welsh).

Isca: Caerleon, Gwent. Base of Legio II Augusta.

Isca Dumnoniorum: Exeter, Devon.

Long Limestone Hills*: The Cotswold Hills.

Londinium (Augusta?): London. The title Augusta *may* have been bestowed on it by Emperor Valentinianus in 368, following the crushing of the *Barbarica Conspiratio.*

Magnis: Kenchester, Herefordshire.

(Flumen) Margus: The Great Morava river in modern Serbia.

Maxima Caesariensis: One of the 5 (?) provinces into which Britain was divided by the later 4th century. Its capital was Londinium.

Menapia: The coastal regions of modern Belgium, plus East and West Flanders. It also extended into neighbouring France and the river deltas of the South Netherlands.

Menapii: A Belgic tribe living in Menapia.

Moguntiacum: Mainz, Germany.

Niger Hills*: The Blackdown Hills in West Somerset & East Devon.

Noviomagus Cantiacorum: A settlement on Watling Street, just south of the Thames ford at Westminster.

Noviomagus Reg(i)norum: Chichester, West Sussex.

Oceanus Britannicus: the English Channel.

Oceanus Germanicus: the North Sea.

Petuaria: Brough, East Yorkshire. A town and port on the north bank of the Humber Estuary.

Pontes: Staines, Middlesex.

Portus Ardaoni: Saxon Shore fort at Portchester, Hampshire.

Portus Lemanis: Saxon Shore fort at Lympne, Kent.

Promunturium Itium: Cap Gris-Nez, north of Boulogne. The closest point of France to England.

Regulbium: Saxon Shore fort at Reculver, Kent.

(Flumen) Rhenus: River Rhine.

Rotomagus: Rouen, on the River Seine.

Rutupiae: Saxon Shore fort at Richborough, Kent.

(Flumen) Sabrina: River Severn and the tutelary goddess of that river.

Saxon Shore: In respect of Britannia this mainly relates to the system of coastal forts stretching from Portchester (Portus Ardaoni) in Hampshire to Brancaster (Branodunum) in North Norfolk. Its ostensible purpose was to act as a deterrent against raids by Frankish and Saxon pirates from across the North Sea, but the building programme may have received a sharp impetus under Carausius and Allectus to facilitate rapid response to invasion by the forces of the Continental Empire under Maximianus in the late 280s and 290s.

(Flumen) Scaldis: River Scheldt, flowing out into the North Sea.

(Flumen) Tamesis: River Thames.

Temple of Sabrina*: Littledean Roman Temple at Dean Hill, near Cinderford, in the Forest of Dean. Overlooks the great Horseshoe Bend in the River Severn.

Treveri: Trier, Germany, on River Moselle. In the 4th century was one of the largest cities of the empire, a residence of the western emperors and the Praetorian Prefect of Gaul.

Vectis Insula: Isle of Wight.

Venta Silurum: Caerwent, Monmouthshire.

Vertis: Worcester. Town on a ford of the Flumen Sabrina, whose main industry was the smelting of iron ore and blooms brought up the Sabrina from the Forest of Dean.

Via Erminus: Roman road running from Silchester to Gloucester, via Cirencester.

Villa Canini / Arcadia*: Spoonley Wood Roman villa, two miles south-east of Winchcombe, Gloucestershire. Some ten Roman miles by road north of Villa Censorini and twenty miles north of Corinium.

Villa Censorini*: Chedworth Roman villa, Gloucestershire.

Wallacra: An island on the coast of Zeeland at the mouth of the Scheldt Estuary. Its modern name is Walcheren and it is now connected to the mainland by a man-made causeway.

Glossary

Agassian hunting dogs: Small, but with sharp claws and teeth, and a keen sense of smell which made them superb trackers. Said to be exported from Britain to other parts of the empire.

Agens in rebus (pl. agentes in rebus): 'Those who are active in matters' - a suitably vague and sinister term for a corps of men with multiple functions, including intelligence-gathering and acting as a sort of secret police.

Augustus and Caesar: Under the Tetrarchy originated by Diocletian in the late 3rd century, an Augustus was a senior emperor and a Caesar a junior emperor, destined to succeed the Augustus after 20 years. The titles survived after the breakdown of the Tetrarchy in the first decade of the 4th century.

Bagaudae: Marauding bands of impoverished peasants, dispossessed small landowners, runaway slaves, etc. born in the chaos of the late third century, particularly in Gaul and Hispania. Their periodic revolts, fuelled by crushing taxation and levies, persisted until the end of the Western Empire. The rebellion in Gaul in c. 284 was supposed to have been led by two men called Amandus and Aelianus.

Barbarica Conspiratio: (the *Conspiratio*): Circa AD 367/68. The invasion of Britain by seemingly co-ordinated waves of barbarian tribes, principally Picts and Attacotti from north of Hadrian's Wall and Scotti from Ireland.

Bracae (or *braccae*): Woollen trousers, closed at the waist by a drawstring. Originally worn by the Gallic tribes of Northern Europe and later adopted by the Romans.

Cella: The inner heart of a Romano-Celtic temple.

Clavi: Decorative woven or embroidered strips added to the bottom edges of cloaks and tunics (see also *Orbiculi*).

Conspiratio: See *Barbarica Conspiratio*.

Consularis: see *Praeses*. The governor of the province of Maxima Caesariensis ranked as a *consularis*.

Cucullus: Hooded cape or cloak. The shortest were waist-length, the longest were ankle-length.

Cursus publicus: The state-run service by which officials and documents were transported across the empire. The use of this service was supposed to be restricted to persons who possessed the appropriate *diploma*.

Diocese (pl. dioceses): By the early fourth century the large provinces of the early empire had been subdivided, in order to avoid concentrating too much power in the hands of any one provincial governor. These small provinces were aggregated into *dioceses*, each under the control of a *vicarius*. By 370 the *diocese* of Britannia was divided into five (?) provinces. Its *vicarius* was stationed in Londinium and reported to the Praetorian Prefect of Gaul, who in turn reported directly to the emperor.

Genius Cucullatus (pl. Genii Cucullati): Little hooded godlings. Their worship seems to have been particularly prevalent in the Cotswolds (although this may only be due to the availability of easily-worked stone resulting in the survival of their images).

Honestiores and Humiliores: In law, the inhabitants of the later Roman Empire (free, not slave) were divided into either high caste *honestiores* or low caste *humiliores*. *Humiliores*, the bulk of the civilian population, could be tortured as witnesses, flogged and executed by the cruellest means. For the same crimes, *honestiores* could usually escape with banishment. In time, *humiliores* working for the great landowning magnates, either directly or as tenant farmers, came to be legally bound to the land, much like medieval serfs.

Hospitia: Hotel and guest house.

Juthungi: A Germanic tribe living in what is now Bavaria.

Kalends: The first day of every month.

Liquamen: A sauce made of fermented fish, much used in Roman cuisine. Also known as *garum*.

Maenads: Ecstatic, immortal female followers of Bacchus.

Mansio (pl. mansiones): Local government maintained hostels with changes of horses for the use of persons travelling on state business on the *cursus publicus*. Usually sited some fifteen to eighteen miles apart along the major roads.

Mansionarius (pl. mansionarii): The person in charge of a *mansio*.

Miliarense (pl. miliarensia): A 4th century Roman silver coin. When first introduced by Constantine 1st the heavy and light miliarensia weighed 5.4 and 4.5 grams respectively. A *siliqua* of this early period weighed 3.4 grams.

Nemesis: Goddess of retributive justice.

Nones of November: the fifth day of that month.

Nummus (pl. nummi): In the novel the term denotes the small copper coins current in the 360s and later decades. Their relationship (if any) to the gold and silver coins of the period is not now known.

Orbiculi: Decorative woven or embroidered roundels bearing geometrical patterns, stylised plants, animals, etc, attached to cloaks and tunics. Military men sometimes incorporated the insignia of their units in their orbiculi.

Orichalcum: The Roman name for a type of brass.

Parcae: The Roman name for the three Fates. Clotho, who spun the tread of a man's life; Lachesis, who determined its length; and Atropos, who cut the thread, so ending that life.

Praeses (pl. praesides): By the fourth century this term had come to mean a specific class of provincial governor, ranking below *consulares* and *correctores*. In the late 4th/early 5th century document known as the *Notitia Dignitatum*, the governor of Britannia Prima is listed as a *praeses*.

Praetorian Prefects of Gaul: were directly responsible to the emperor and oversaw the dioceses of Britannia, Gaul, Hispania and Mauretania Tingitana. **Viventius** was prefect from 368 to 371, and **Maximinus** from 13 July 371 until 16 April 376.

Praetorium: By the fourth century this term had come to mean the residence of a provincial governor.

Satyrs: Immortal male companions of Bacchus. In late Roman art they are usually depicted as wholly humanoid in appearance, except that sometimes they have goat-like ears. With their female companions, the *maenads*, they form Bacchus's *thiasos*. Sometimes depicted as carefree youths, as on the Mildenhall treasure; sometimes as more mysterious, sinister creatures, as on the mosaic in the west wing triclinium at Chedworth villa.

Siliqua (pl. siliquae): The standard small silver coin of the late Roman Empire, tariffed at twenty-four to the solidus. After AD 356 it was struck at 144 to the (Roman) pound of pure silver and weighed approx. 2.25 grams.

Solidus (pl. solidi): The standard gold coin of the late Roman Empire. Struck at seventy-two to the (Roman) pound of pure gold, it was introduced by Constantine the Great in 312 and replaced the aureus of the earlier empire, which was struck at sixty to the pound.

Spatha: The long sword used principally by Roman cavalry.

Stabulum: An inn for the use of the general public, providing stabling for horses (cf. *mansio*).

Statio (pl. stationes): Wayside stations established along routes used by the *cursus publicus*, mainly for changing relays of horses.

Stola: A long, pleated dress, the traditional garment worn by Roman women. Originally sleeveless, but sometimes with short or long sleeves.

Taberna: Tavern selling food and drink.

Trajan Decius: Emperor AD 249-251.

Triclinium: The dining room of a Roman villa, so called because the couches or chairs were arranged around three sides of the central table.

Valentinus's Conspiracy: In AD 369, in the chaotic aftermath of the *Barbarica Conspiratio*, a Pannonian exile called Valentinus (brother-in-law of the Maximinus who was later to become Praetorian Prefect of Gaul) tried to foment a rebellion. The rebellion was swiftly suppressed and Valentinus executed.

Vicarius: A high-ranking civilian official of the later Roman Empire in charge of a *diocese.* The holder of the post was entitled to the title V*ir Spectabilis.* Ammianus Marcellinus records that in c. 368, at the request of *Comes* Theodosius (the man who had suppressed the *Barbarica Conspiratio* invasions of 367-8) a man called **Civilis**, "of fiery temper but uncompromising integrity," was appointed *vicarius* of Britannia.

Vir Perfectissimus: The lowest ranking of a series of honorific titles bestowed on the holders of high office. The *praeses* of Britannia Prima was a *Vir Perfectissimus.*

THE CARAUSIAN REBELLION: A TIMELINE

AD	
283/4	Emperor **Carinus** campaigns in Britain (possibly against the Picts) and awards himself the title Britannicus Maximus. **Carausius** *may* have taken part in this campaign. Uprising of the Bagaudae begins in Gaul.
285	Carinus is killed at the battle of the Margus River in Moesia fighting against **Diocletian**, one of his generals who has been proclaimed emperor by his troops in Nicomedia. In Gaul, Carausius distinguishes himself against the Bagaudae. Diocletian, now sole emperor, appoints **Maximianus** as his deputy (Caesar) to take charge of the western half of the empire. Due to his seafaring background, Carausius is put in charge of the fleet (Classis Britannica) with orders to clear the seas between Britannia and Gaul of Saxon and Frankish pirates.
286	In April, Diocletian raises Maximianus to the rank of Augustus, possibly as a reward to suppressing the Bagaudae. Later this year Carausius, accused by Maximianus of keeping for himself the loot recovered from the pirates, rebels and seizes power in northern Gaul.
287	Carausius consolidates his position in northern Gaul and Britannia. Maximianus is too busy fighting the Germanic tribes on the Rhine and Danube frontiers to challenge him immediately.
288	Maximianus appoints **Constantius Chlorus** as his Praetorian Prefect, allowing himself to concentrate on defeating Carausius.

289	An April 289 panegyric in praise of Maximianus states that by that date he has built a new fleet and is ready to invade Britain, implying that Carausius has already been driven out of northern Gaul.
290/1	But a panegyric of July 291 makes no mention of this invasion attempt, implying that it had been a failure. The cause of this failure is unknown: possibly a violent storm, or a crushing naval defeat by Carausius. But whatever the cause, the loss of manpower incurred by Maximianus seems to have been so substantial as to leave northern Gaul open to re-conquest by Carausius in late 290 or early 291.
292	In March the campaign against Carausius is taken out of Maximianus's hands by an irate Diocletian and given to Constantius Chlorus. Constantius then makes steady progress in recapturing Carausius's territory in northern Gaul.
293	In March Constantius Chlorus is raised to the rank of Caesar and appoints Julius **Asclepiodotus** as his praetorian prefect. Boulogne (Gesoriacum), Carausius's last continental possession, is besieged and captured. Carausius is assassinated by **Allectus**, who is described in the surviving literature as his finance minister.
294/5	Allectus now rules Britain and issues coins in his own name. Confident in his ability to resist invasion he orders the construction of a complex of large administrative buildings near the banks of the Thames in London. However, Constantius is slowly building two fleets in preparation for another invasion, learning from Maximianus's mistakes.

296	Constantius's fleets set out, one from Boulogne commanded by himself, the other, under Asclepiodotus, from the mouth of the Seine.
	Spies have probably warned Allectus to expect an invasion from Boulogne across the Strait of Dover and so he concentrates his troops in south-east England.
	For reasons unknown, Constantius is delayed. But, in fog off the Isle of Wight, Asclepiodotus evades one of Allectus's fleets, lands on the south coast and marches inland.
	Somewhere in central southern England he encounters Allectus's hastily assembled army and defeats it.
	Allectus is believed killed in the battle.

This book is printed on paper from sustainable sources managed under the Forest Stewardship Council (FSC) scheme.

It has been printed in the UK to reduce transportation miles and their impact upon the environment.

For every new title that Matador publishes, we plant a tree to offset CO_2, partnering with the More Trees scheme.

For more about how Matador offsets its environmental impact, see www.troubador.co.uk/about/